filed under

COUGAR

Cocktales

MAR 2018

Dear Reader:

Buckle up and prepare for five authors who take you on an erotica journey with tales compiled by N'Tyse, whose name represents "**N**ever **T**ell **Y**our **S**ecrets."

Some spin stories of "cougar" women who fantasize about seeking sexual pleasure from younger men while others find that it's spontaneity that leads to these tantalizing escapades. And yes, these ladies are definitely satisfied with their adventures.

If you haven't checked out her novels, you will be excited to read N'Tyse's *Twisted* series filled with deception and drama.

As always, thanks for supporting myself and the Strebor Books family. We strive to bring you the most cutting-edge, out-of-the-box material on the market. You can find me on Facebook @AuthorZane or you can email me at zane@eroticanoir.com.

Blessings,

Zane

Publisher
Strebor Books
www.simonandschuster.com

ZANE PRESENTS

COUGAR
Cocktales

EDITED BY
N'TYSE

**ANNA BLACK, SHAKIR RASHAAN,
MICHELLE CUTTINO AND JADA PEARL**

SBI

STREBOR BOOKS

NEW YORK LONDON TORONTO SYDNEY

Strebor Books
P.O. Box 6505
Largo, MD 20792
http://www.streborbooks.com

ISBN 978-1-59309-616-8
ISBN 978-1-4767-8298-0 (ebook)
LCCN 2015957689

First Strebor Books trade paperback edition March 2016

Cover design: www.mariondesigns.com
Cover photograph: © Keith Saunders/Keith Saunders Photos

10 9 8 7 6 5 4 3 2 1

Manufactured in the United States of America

For information regarding special discounts for bulk purchases, please contact Simon & Schuster Special Sales at 1-866-506-1949

The Simon & Schuster Speakers Bureau can bring authors to your live event. For more information or to book an event, contact the Simon & Schuster Speakers Bureau at 1-866-248-3049 or visit our website at www.simonspeakers.com.

Dedicated to the dynamic, fabulous woman over forty—
the financially independent, and the sexually liberated.
You are the quintessential embodiment of feminine power.
I salute you.

—N'TYSE

TABLE OF CONTENTS

FOREWORD

The title *Cougar Cocktales* caught my attention. Maybe because I've been known to be a Cougar myself. I'm from Louisiana so we like our stuff spicy and *Cougar Cocktales* doesn't disappoint. It's a hot and spicy read. Regardless of the weather outside, it will surely have you fanning as you flip the pages. Hopefully, you've read some novels by these five authors before. If you haven't, *Cougar Cocktales* is a great introduction to each one of the authors' writing styles. At some point in our lives, we all have fantasies. Let the authors of this book take you on an erotic journey. You might see some of your fantasies displayed on the pages. If you're looking for ways to spice up your love life, then be prepared to take notes from the authors Michelle Cuttino, Shakir Rashaan, Anna Black, Jada Pearl, and N'Tyse. *Cougar Cocktales* is more than a simple appetizer; it's a full sensual thrill.

—SHELIA M. GOSS, AUTHOR OF *The Joneses* AND *The Aftermath*

CATCHIN' *Feelings*

MICHELLE CUTTINO

THE TRUTH ABOUT MIMI

Most women will never admit to what I'm about to tell you, but I'm different from most. Surrounded by men my whole life, I guess their ways and thinking rubbed off on me. Why else would I find so much comfort in admitting I'm a freak? I love sex. No, not making love—SEX! Emotionless…raw, but protected, uninhibited fucking. The kind that makes weave tracks slip, inner walls chafe and spoken-for men wander.

It also has a lot to do with my upbringing. Growing up, I was on the heavier side and a tomboy. Hanging with the guys was second nature; I became their BFF (Best Friend I Fuck). It wasn't exactly by choice, but if that was the only way I was going to get these brothers to claim me, so be it. I was game.

By day, I was a loyal friend to their girls. By night, I was fucking their men. I was that shoulder their girls cried on when they discovered their man was cheating. I was always overly attentive when they explained how they were going to beat the bitch down as soon as they figured out whom she was. All the while I looked at their dumb asses and shook my head, because that bitch was me. There was no way in hell any of them would or could kick my ass.

I always kept a journal and recorded my exploits in great detail—down to the color of the condom wrapper. After looking back on one journal in particular, I noticed a pattern. Not only was I a fan of fucking, but I was also a lover of alcohol. Each night the lucky guy and I would get toasted and then get busy. Don't get me wrong; I'm not Jamie Foxx, and I won't blame it on the alcohol. I was always aware of what I was doing, and it was all by choice. If I didn't want to fuck a guy, I never drank with him. Period. I was thick, not desperate. I did have my standards. No matter how limited they were…

I'm no Zane, and this is by no means Fifty Shades of anything. It's simply my sex life—unadulterated, uncensored and usually unspoken. By the way, my name is Mimi Jackson. I'm a forty-two-year-old, childless, never-married account executive at an upscale media-training firm. I'm saying this just to let you know I'm not some young, clueless chick. I'm an intelligent, grown-ass woman with grown-ass desires.

I'm so tired of being misunderstood and misrepresented. I'm neither a slut nor a cougar. I'm sexually liberated. If you can't handle that fact, I suggest you stay the fuck from around me because my temper is just as short as my list of virtues. Besides, after several of my long-term relationships ended in heartbreak and mental collapse, I promised myself I would never get close enough for anyone to hurt me again. I realize now it was actually one of my random *drucking* (drinking and fucking) experiences that led me back to this unwelcome realm called love—a place I said I'd never revisit, but through no choice of my own has now become home once again.

KICKIN' IT

Keith and I have been friends forever, or at least that's how it seems. He came sauntering into my office five years ago, fresh out of high school, looking to gain access to the intern program I was promoting. I liked him right away. He was self-assured, cocky and just the right amount of sexy to be some nice eye candy, but the wrong amount of life span for me to act upon my sexual cravings. He's been in a very committed relationship since then. Whereas his girlfriend is fully committed to him, and Keith is fully committed to getting as much ass as he can on the side. We kick it, but we never "kicked" it because he's not my type. He's just too fucking young, and too fucking pretty. You know the type—spending more time in the mirror than any woman I know, and way too conscious of how he looks. He calls himself a metrosexual; I call his ass borderline bitch, and that's why he's only good for dinner on those rare no-one-else-to-do evenings. He's very intelligent, and I love conversing with him about any and everything. That's where we match—nowhere else.

Here we were at our favorite Harlem lounge, sitting in the back booth next to the DJ. I was enjoying the atmosphere and the music when I decided to mess with Keith because I was feeling horny and my usual booty call canceled to take wifey to the ER. Really the bitch only had the sniffles, but this was a test and he passed it. Well, in all honesty, he had to. How are you going to be a thirty-five-year-old pothead with a $40 a day habit and no job? Easy! You find a "wifey" to foot the bill. But who was I to judge? In the beginning, his wifey was actually my good friend, and he was just her man. Somehow, over time, he and I became best friends, and she was pushed to the sidelines. She's still trying to hang onto our friendship 'til this day.

Anyway, Keith and I were drinking Jack and Coke and my lips became too loose.

"So Keith, are you planning to settle down anytime soon?"

"Nah," he said, chewing with his mouth open and getting on my damn nerves.

"Well, that's not what Phyllis told me," I teased. "She said she has you so sprung that you'll be buying that ring any day now."

"Yeah, whatever. You already know how I puts it down," he countered.

"As a matter of fact, I don't," I said, hitting him with my sex-me smile. "Never had that inclination."

"Fuck outta here with that dumb shit, Mimi." He laughed and sloppily licked his fingers. "You know damn well you've always been feenin' for this dick."

All I could do was laugh. I looked at Keith sitting there looking all smug, smacking on his ribs like it was the last meal he'd ever be treated to. I had to admit, his hands were turning me on. They were huge with nice, long, thick fingers.

"Yeah, I must be drunk," I slurred.

"Why you say that," he asked.

"'Cause I'm over here looking at those crusty shits you call fingers wondering how they would feel inside me. So you know..."

"Oh really now," he asked with a smirk. "Told you you was feelin' the kid. You ain't gotta front for me, ma. Just spread them legs and let me show you what I can do."

He licked his lips seductively and started wiping his hands with the cloth napkin he had balled up beside his plate. I took another gulp of my drink and stared him dead in the eyes.

"Are you serious?"

"Serious as cancer," he said, wiping the last of the sauce from his juicy lips.

He placed the napkin back on the table next to his plate, and then scooted over in the booth until we were shoulder to shoulder. He smelled good and his scent was more intoxicating than the five cocktails I had already consumed. I turned to see him looking at me like I was one of the ribs he was just molesting.

"Keith, if you don't get your husky ass back across that table, I'm..."

He slipped his tongue in my mouth before I could complete my sentence. His kiss was better than I thought it would be, and I found myself kissing him back with a hunger I usually suppress for real conquests. His right hand moved past my breasts, and he began caressing my muffin top, trying unsuccessfully to unbutton my jean skirt. Turned on and pissed off at the same time, I grabbed his hand roughly, spread my legs and pushed his hand between them.

"Negro, if you don't stop playing and lift this shit up," I blurted out. "I'm wearing a fucking skirt. This isn't brain surgery. You..."

"Shut the fuck up," he said, as his fingers slid inside my panties and got lost in my moisture.

I did as I was told. I had no choice. His thumb was caressing my clitoris and his other four digits were fucking me into a frenzy. Something about the way he was twirling his fingers inside me, and thumping his thumb against me while sucking on my neck with a vengeance, had me moaning his name like he was the best shit since sliced bread.

"Damn, ma," he whispered in my ear as he sucked on my lobe. "You're so fucking wet. Wish I was beating that shit up right now."

"I wish you were, too," I cooed. "Your fingers are like magic, so I can only imagine what the rest of you feels like."

"Oh, you like this, huh?" he asked, while intensifying his gyrations.

I couldn't answer. I was on the verge of climax; my legs were partially numb from the sensation. I stared him in the face and blinked three times like the deaf-mute his finger popping was turning me into. He hit me with that first-day, cocky, self-assured smile. Any other time it would have warranted a good cursing out, but his thick fingers were inside me, and his thumb was making small circles in my dampness. I placed my hand on top of his and forced his fingers deeper. I guided his thumb to my spot and helped him massage my core the way I'd taught myself back when I first figured out that masturbation was a great alternative to the real thing. We played in my moisture until I couldn't hold on any longer. I helped him bring me to a satisfying climax. My body pulsed and writhed under his touch and our fingers were soon drenched from my release.

"That's what I'm saying. I want to taste you, ma." He pulled his hand from between my legs and slowly licked his fingers from the palm up.

We didn't take our eyes off of each other as I followed his lead and did the same to my own. I then grabbed his hand and placed each of his fingers in my mouth one by one. I licked my juices from them and gave his fingers a blow job that surely made his dick jealous. I used my jaws to pull his pointer in from the tip to the base and wrapped my tongue around it, sucking my stickiness from his skin.

"Damn, ma, I'm so hard right now," he said, massaging his crotch with his free hand. I placed my hand over his and felt a very impressive bulge.

"Mmmmmmm, Mama may have to do something about that, Boo."

I started repositioning myself in the booth, trying to figure out how I could get my plus-sized frame in a position to jerk him off and then be able to receive his elixir as he peaked. I finally nestled my head onto his chest, placed one arm behind his back and laid the other in his lap. While he stroked my hair, I undid his zipper and maneuvered his shaft through the opening. The bulge I felt didn't do Keith justice. He wasn't only long, but thick as well. He was so thick my hand could only close a little more than halfway around his girth.

"Damn, baby," I murmured. "I wish I was riding this shit right now."

"Me too, ma," he said, resting his head back on the booth and closing his eyes.

My up-and-down motion was starting to make him relax. The low moans escaping his lips let me know he was definitely pleased. I spat into my palm, then stroked the length of his shaft. I moved up in the booth and stuck my tongue in his ear as my hand continued to massage him. His veins began to pulsate, as his moans grew louder.

"Quiet down, baby," I whispered while palming the tip of his shaft and adding pressure.

He began to buck slowly against my hand under the table. I moved my hand down to the base and cupped his balls. I massaged his sack with my fingers while palming him. The double sensation was driving him crazy. He dug his fingers into my neck.

"Damn, Mimi, you gonna make me cum."

"Really, baby?" I prodded. "You want me to speed it up a little?" I asked, already increasing my momentum.

My knuckles bumped the table rhythmically and his hips began to thrust to the beat. I felt him tensing; he was almost there. I quickly ducked my head in his lap and took him into my mouth.

"Oh God," he shrieked as the warmth and wetness enveloped him. I continued jerking him off while sucking him dry. I spat on his tip and deep-throated him until my gag reflex kicked in. I slurped his skin and swallowed his milky secretion, making sure to catch every drop before placing him back inside his boxers.

I straightened myself up and pushed him back over to his side of the booth. He looked deep into my eyes and called my name softly. I didn't answer because the sound of his voice, coupled with the reality of wiping a twenty-three-year-old's cum off the sides of my mouth in the middle of a crowded lounge, undoubtedly had a sobering effect.

"Yo, Mimi, did you hear me?" Keith asked, bringing me out of my reverie.

"No, I didn't. What did you say?"

"Let me find out this good dick and hand game got your ass over there stuck," he said with a laugh. "Imagine when I spread those legs. You're going to be ready to marry a brother."

"See that right there is the reason your young ass should have never experienced any part of a real woman. You just aren't ready."

"What you mean I ain't ready? I just proved I was ready."

"No, you just proved that if I direct you, you could make me cum. You also proved you're so used to handjobs that a two-minute rub-down will surely get your juices flowing…and I mean that literally," I said with venom.

"Wow, ma. It's like that? Why you attacking the kid?"

"Because…" I trailed off. Why was I attacking the kid? That's just it—because he was a kid, too damned arrogant and he was right. I was stuck and oddly intrigued. But what I wasn't going to be was some Sugar Mama, stroking his overblown ego after blowing his inflated dick. "Let's just call it an evening, Keith."

"Yo, Mimi, why you trippin'? It's still early," he said in a sing-songy child's voice. All he needed was the puppy dog eyes and the pouty lips to make the mini-tantrum complete.

"I'm not tripping, Boo. I'm tired. I'm drunk. I'm moist and slimy. I just want to go home, take a shower and dive into my nice, warm bed."

"Well, then let me dive into that bed with you. Why do we have to end the night like this? I want to finish what we started."

"And I want to pretend it never happened. We can't do this, Keith. We are colleagues and great friends. I don't want to confuse anything."

"I'm not confused," he said loudly. "You know I've been wanting you since day one. You've been wanting me, too, but you always got those Similac jokes coming strong. You ain't spending all this extra time with me outside of work just because we're friends. You know you want me just as much as I want you."

"Keith, no one wants you more than *you* want you," I said, standing and throwing four crisp fifty-dollar bills on the table. "Thank you for a lovely evening, but I'm out."

"Yo, Mimi," he said to my back as I made a mad dash for the exit.

ROUGH RIDER

T hank goodness for weekends. I don't think I could have faced Keith without a couple of days to pull myself together. I was dressed to thrill in my red, two-piece skirt set with a black sequined tank and red stilettos to cap off the look when I stepped off the elevator and right into Keith's open arms.

"Good morning, Miss Jackson," he said, taking his hands off my waist and straightening his tie. "Hope you had a good weekend."

"As a matter of fact, I…"

He was already walking down the hall before I could get the "did" out. I tried to pretend that his cold shoulder didn't bother me, but I couldn't. I regained my composure long enough to sashay down to my corner office, close the door and walk over to the floor-to-ceiling window to brood. I was suddenly overcome by the scent of vanilla and jasmine. I looked over and an exotic candle arrangement was in the middle of my mahogany desk. I rushed over to read the card.

This is how us young men do when we find an older woman worth sharing our time with. Sorry if I didn't live up to your expectations, but I'm hoping you will give us a second chance. I also hope you know that us young ones do know all about discretion, and I'm willing to play this game any way you want to play it as long as I win you over in the end. Love, Keith

I was grinning like a Cheshire cat when I heard a faint knock on my door. I stashed the note in my top drawer and walked over to open it when in burst Keith. He was all business, all stiff and sexy as ever. I had to admit, he was wearing the hell out of that gray pin-stripe suit with his pink shirt, matching pocket kerchief, and gray-and-pink-striped tie.

"Okay, Miss Jackson, I'm glad you finally dragged your behind in here because we've got work to do. Your meeting with Max is at one o'clock. A new account for you means a bonus for me, so let's get you ready to make me some money." He said all this while brushing past me, moving the gift onto the corner desk and spreading papers on top of mine.

"Aren't we all business this morning?" I asked with a laugh.

He merely cut his eyes at me and continued. "This report is the only issue I'm having with your presentation," he said while holding up the pie chart I'd created to show the client his marketing visibility predictions. "Max is a devout Muslim who has spoken out against homosexuality, same-sex-marriage and anything gay since day one. I doubt he is going to gain a seven percent following when he is the Antichrist as far as the LGBT community is concerned. You need to tweak that number or remove it altogether. It's not only a turn-off to him, but an insult to homosexuals everywhere."

Well, if all business is what he wanted, two could play that game, I thought. "You're absolutely right, Mr. Myers. Thank you for pointing that out. I will adjust the figure and reprint…"

"I already took the liberty," he interrupted, pulling a new, more impressive pie chart from under the stack on the desk. "I just wanted to make sure we were on the same page." He stacked the papers neatly onto the corner of my desk. He stood, walked over to the door and reached for the doorknob, or so I thought.

"Very impressive," I blurted out, trying to stop him from leaving so quickly. I wanted to apologize for the other night and tell him he was right. I definitely wanted him, too, but my mouth couldn't form the words. I settled on what I did best—talking the talk. "I'm happy to see you taking more initiative when it comes to these projects, Keith. Keep it up and we just may have to plug you in here permanently as a junior executive."

He twisted the lock on the door and turned around with a smile I found irresistible. "How about I plug myself in permanently somewhere else instead?" He rushed over, grabbed me gently, but firmly, and bent me over the side of my desk.

I should have resisted, fought back or cried rape. Anything not to feel him slide his pants and boxers down, slip on a condom, lift my skirt and move my thong to the side with a precision not many young men possessed. He entered me so quickly my breath got caught in my throat. I wanted to protest and ask him what kind of woman did he take me for, but all I could think about was spreading my cheeks wider, hiking my hips higher and fingering my core as he pumped vigorously behind me.

"Damn, ma, you feel so fucking good," he moaned.

I tried to tell him he felt good, too. That I loved the way he was thrusting inside me. That my walls fit his shaft perfectly and the friction was making me lose it, but all I could muster was a soft whimper as I bit into my arm trying to stifle my moans. He grabbed my ponytail roughly and I finally found my voice. "Negro, if you pull my ponytail off, I will…Mmmmmmmmmm." He let go of the ponytail, smacked my ass and started a slower, steadier grind that had me up on my tiptoes trying to take in every single inch of him.

"Mimi, I'm going to make you mine, baby. Watch…I ain't letting this good shit go for nothing or no one. You hear me," he asked, almost pleading.

Instead of answering, I began to bounce my ass against his waist. Taking his length in and out, and countering it with my round and round until I felt that intense tingling building in my center signaling I was about to flood him. I started a low groan and grabbed on to the desk's edge. He pounded harder and faster and we moved in unison like a tandem bike team. His moves matched my own as we raced toward our destination. He tried hard to let me win and reach the finish line first, while I was holding on trying to prove he couldn't satisfy an older woman like me. We were both failing miserably. Keith's knees gave way as he collapsed atop my body. We nearly hydroplaned as we bucked violently from the force of our simultaneous orgasms.

Getting clothed again wasn't as erotic as the undressing. He fumbled with his slacks, and I tried to discreetly wipe the excessive wetness from between my thighs and ass cheeks so I could slide my thong back into its rightful place. Once my skirt was back down around my knees, and not up around my waist, I cleared my throat and began picking up the items we carelessly knocked over while in the throes of lust, because it certainly wasn't passion. He turned away.

"So, can I see you tonight?" he asked, pausing at the locked door.

"Keith, I don't think that's a good idea. We…"

"We just got finished fucking on top of your desk and you don't think us spending an evening together is a good idea?" He walked back over to me and held my face between his hands. "Mimi, come off it. Why won't you give me a real chance?"

"For one, I don't mix business with pleasure; and B, you do have a girlfriend at home in case you forgot." I removed his hands from my face and took a seat behind my desk. "Besides, how far can this possibly go beyond booty call status? And we both know I don't need another BFF in my life."

"Who says I want to be a BFF?" Keith asked while lowering himself onto the edge of my desk. "Who says I don't want more than that?"

"Keith, let's not start this…not here…not now. We are at work, and too much has already happened. That was a definite mistake," I said, gesturing toward my desk. "That can't happen again. I hope you can understand why."

"Mimi," Keith said, sighing and rising. "I don't understand why you keep pushing me away, but I'll let it go for the moment." I watched as he walked to the door and unlocked it. He turned back around and hit me with that 100-watt smile. "You know you got a brother wanting you real bad, Mimi."

"I know, Keith, but let's get back to the basics. I can't do this with you."

"Too late," he said while opening the door. "I'm already all in."

With that, he exited and closed the door behind him, making my heart melt and taking my common sense with him. I didn't even realize I was still in the same position—daydreaming about how good I was just sexed on my desk—until the phone rang and interrupted my dirty thoughts.

"Mimi Jackson, how may I help you?" I sang into the receiver.

"I'm glad to hear you're in good spirits. Perhaps you can come out to play a little after work today."

"I take it wifey is much better now after her triple bypass."

"Ha, ha, ha…very funny," Parish said. "I'm sorry about Friday night, but you know how it goes. Taylor can be a handful sometimes. She…"

"No need to explain. I wound up having a great weekend and an even better Monday morning."

"Well, why don't you complete the day with an even sexier evening? Taylor will be at her mom's and I have some time to kill."

"While the offer sounds tempting, I think I'll pass. Have a good night, Parish."

With that, I hung up. It's one thing to come at me while we are enjoying an evening out and then segue into sex. It's a whole other thing to call me bright and early in the morning with the bullshit because I brushed you off all weekend after you brushed me off Friday night. Who the fuck does he think I am? Oh yeah, I'm the good old always-there girl. But now things have changed. I want more. I think I deserve more, or am I bugging? I think Keith has me bugging.

I hurriedly dialed Parish back and took him up on his offer. I've always been the get-it-in-when-I-could girl. *Why the fuck should I stop my flow? Just because some young buck has my nose a little open? It's time to come back down to earth, Mimi. Make Parish forget about Taylor like you always do, and hopefully Parish will help you forget about Keith.*

AS WE LAY

I jumped and snatched my phone up as soon as I heard Kelly Price screeching something about she was a friend of mine. I peered over at the clock, which read 4:08. "Hello," I mumbled groggily.

"Mimi, it's Taylor. I think something has happened to Parish. We had words this morning and I haven't heard from him since. I've been dialing his cell phone all night, but it's just ringing and then going straight to voice mail. I don't know…"

I rubbed the sleep from my eyes as Taylor continued her rant and made my way to the bathroom. I "uh-huh'd" when necessary and "wow'd" when appropriate while relieving myself. I then swished some Scope around in my mouth and returned to snuggle with the warm lump beside me.

"I know there's someone else, Mimi," she said through tears. "I've known for some time now, but I love him and I just can't let him go."

"Taylor, take a Valium, lie down and get some rest. I'm sure by this time tomorrow you will be back in Parish's loving arms and all will be right with the world."

"You think so, Mimi," she asked hopefully.

"Don't worry, Tay. Even if there is someone else, Parish will never let you go. Trust me. Now go do as I said, and let me get this last hour in before I have to get up for work."

"Okay, Mimi, and thank you for listening. I know you're right and I'm overreacting, but I hate it when we argue and then he's MIA. I just start thinking all kinds of crazy things."

"Well, no need to worry, Tay. Wherever he is, I'm sure he's just fine. Good morning, Love. I will hit you later."

"Good morning, Mimi, and thanks ag…"

I disconnected before she could start on another tear and placed my hands beneath the covers. I found what I was looking for and started stroking it gently.

"Mmmmmmmmmmmm," he moaned. "What you doing?"

"Trying to get something started before we have to get up and face the real world. You got another one in you?" I teased.

He didn't answer. Parish just flipped me onto my back and entered me expertly. With my legs dangling over his shoulders, he thrust with a knowing that Keith lacked. His experience mirrored his years and he had me shuddering beneath him in no time. I forced my legs down and rolled Parish onto his back. I mounted his waist and started bouncing on top of him.

"Yeah, Mimi. Ride that shit. Make me cum, baby. Mmmmmmmmmmm."

"Whose is it?" I purred, knowing damn well it wasn't mine. But as long as it was in me, he had better not call out any other name but Mimi.

"It's yours, baby."

"Whose is it? Say it, baby. Say it," I prodded, hearing Beyoncé singing, "*Say my name, say my name,*" somewhere in my subconscious.

"It's yours, Mimi. It's yours, baby. Yes, bounce it just like that, Mimi."

He said the magic word. I placed my feet flat on the bed parallel to his waist and started to drop it like I was one of those hot bitches in every rapper's music video. I amazed myself at my dexterity and was starting to feel my sex throb as he reached down and massaged my bulb back to life. As I descended on his shaft, his fingers went to work on my clit. My titties started clapping against my belly, and my belly started slapping against his waist. His legs started shaking, my knees started giving out, and we did a slow bump and grind until we exploded together.

"Damn, Mimi," he whispered as I collapsed beside him and he snatched me up to spoon. The condom was still around his sex and was now overflowing onto my sheets. Neither of us seemed to mind. "You sure do know how to spoil a brother. You trying to make me fall in love, I see."

"Just the opposite," I said. "I'm trying to make you fall out of love. By the way, Taylor called." He stiffened a little when I mentioned her name and removed his arm from around my body.

"What did she say?"

"What does she always say? I guess she'll have half an ounce waiting for you when you get home," I said this to his back as he was already standing and making his way to the bathroom.

Thirty minutes later, I was in the shower with tears streaming down my face. I wasn't sure why I was crying. I just knew I felt hurt. Parish left after brushing his lips against my forehead and muttering something about me always being his bottom bitch. If he meant it as a compliment, the flattery went completely over my head. One thing about the sentiment was correct, though—I was definitely at the bottom. I was last to everything important in his life. I know it's my own fault. People will only do to you what you allow them to do, and I allowed myself to be everybody's other woman. Before it seemed like it was enough, but something about my last two encounters with Keith had me wanting more. Something meaningful. Something real. Not this playschool bull-shit I've become so accustomed to.

I spent the day and the rest of the week avoiding Parish, Keith and all my other BFFs at all costs. I declined lunch dates, dinner invitations, after-work happy hours, and any and every idea they could come up with to get me to spread my legs and satisfy their sexual cravings.

By the time Friday rolled around, I was exhausted, so I made a beeline to my truck and burned rubber 'til I hit my driveway. I stepped out and stopped dead in my tracks.

"So I have to play stalker to get you to talk to me, Mimi? Is that it?" He walked over to me and placed his hands on my shoulders. "What's wrong with you? Why have you been avoiding me?"

"Keith, you're crazy. I haven't been avoiding you," I replied, removing his hands from my shoulders and walking toward my door.

"Well, if you haven't been avoiding me, I guess you won't mind if I come in and rap a taste."

"Rap a taste about what, Keith?" I asked with a bit more attitude than I would've liked. "It's Friday. I'm tired, and all I want to do is sit on my ass and eat something."

"Funny, that's exactly how I wanted to spend my Friday night." He smiled that delectable smile of his and I opened my door and my legs with no further argument.

Keith was down on his knees in front of my sofa with his head in my lap and his tongue buried in my wetness. He licked the full length of my inner lips and flicked the tip of his tongue heartily against my clit. He had three fingers inside me while balancing my thick thigh on his shoulder. With his free hand, he massaged my hulking nipples until they were rock-hard and as erect as I'd imagined his manhood to be. He gave my ass oral pleasure as his tongue went in and out of that tight hole with accuracy. I moaned all kinds of filthy things because it felt too good for him to stop. I needed him as hot as he had me so he would fuck me like the bad girl I was.

He must have read my mind. He kissed my muffin top while pulling me down to the edge of the sofa. He leaned up off his knees just enough to insert that thick joystick into my warmth and make my body quiver from the impact. My right leg was wrapped around his waist, my left leg was draped over his shoulder, and he was on top pounding me out like a porn star. I had to kick him off of me after a while because I couldn't take it anymore. My breasts were smothering me, and the added pressure of him on all of this had me straining to catch my breath. I don't know about you, but passing out from a loss of oxygen does not make a sexy scene. I quickly regained my composure and took a seat atop his lap. I loved how I seemed to fit him like a glove; his frame was husky enough to complement my own. Unlike Parish, I didn't feel like a fat girl when I was with Keith. He made me feel sexy, unreserved and comfortable enough to let the thick freaky chick that lives inside of me out. And right now Sheba was working him, too. She was holding onto the sofa's back and making good use of the springs as she rode him into a toe-curling, nipple-biting, ass-smacking, you-are-fucking-the-shit-out-of-me outburst. Followed by a you-thick-sexy-bitch climax.

I collapsed beside him, but Keith was no fool. He knew he had reached his destination, but I was still on the highway. Without a second wasted, he placed his face in the place once again and brought me to a satisfying orgasm of my own.

"Damn, ma. They need to bottle this shit up. You taste so good," he said, licking his lips and slurping up every drop as it escaped my center.

I wanted to respond, but I was still in my ugly-face, don't-touch-me mode.

"Why you pushing me away, Mimi? You know I'm addicted to that shit now. Come here," he said, trying to pry my legs open again.

"Addicted, huh," I asked mockingly. "That's what your mouth says."

"Nah, baby, that's what my heart says," he said, as he rose and walked into the kitchen. "You want something out of here, baby?"

"Ummmmm-hmmmm," I moaned throatily.

"Yeah? What you want, ma," he asked, standing in the doorway looking like a plate of macaroni and cheese, fried chicken, collard greens, mashed potatoes, gravy and Martin's not-my-mama's-biscuits.

"If you have to ask, then I've been doing something wrong."

He gulped down the glass of water he was holding and walked back over to the couch. "Nah, Mimi. That's the problem. You doing everything right."

With that, he pulled me up for one of the most passionate, dizzying kisses I had experienced in quite some time. His lips left mine and I felt dazed, confused and hornier than ever. I did a deep knee bend and took all of him in my mouth. His moaning was in sync with my movements as his fingers became entangled in my weave. As long as he didn't pull one out, he could massage my tracks all he wanted. Besides, I love crowd participation, and the feel of his hips thrusting against my face while his hands were pulling me into him had me wet all over again. I placed my fingers between my legs and brought us back to the brink. He finished us off when he snatched me up and threw me over the arm of the sofa. He hit it doggy-style and I did everything but bark as he hit every spot he was supposed to. We both came in a matter of minutes.

"Got-damn," I mumbled into the cushions, happy to have the chair supporting our dead weight. My face was plastered to the cushion; his face was fused with my sweaty back. We panted like we had just run a marathon. When we finally caught our breath, we made our way to the shower and then to the bed.

I don't even remember us falling asleep, but once again, I awoke when I heard Kelly belting out, *"She was a friend of mine, she left with my man…"* I used to think that shit was cute, but listening to it tonight lying next to what should be the man in my life—but in reality was the man in *her* life—made me feel like a fool.

"Hey, Phyl," I said without even checking the caller ID. "What time is it?"

"Sorry to wake you," she said in a tone that let me know we were not besties tonight. Tonight she was the pissed-off girlfriend, and I was the fucked-up friend who always got her man into trouble. "Where the fuck is Keith?"

"I'm fine," I said unsympathetically. "How are you?"

She exhaled loudly. "Mimi, I don't…"

"Then don't," I said, stopping that bitch in her tracks. *I may be wrong. Matter of fact, I am wrong, but no one is going to call my house at…* "What time is it?" I asked to no one in particular. I finally found the clock down by the bed where I kicked it when Keith had me in a full nelson while hitting it from the back earlier.

"Mimi, can you please put Keith on the phone?" she asked a little nicer this time. "He's not picking up his phone, or I never would have called you." I could tell she was biting her tongue and was going to unleash on him as soon as I put him on the line, but that had nothing to do with me. She and I had an understanding—don't overstep your boundaries and I won't have to kick your ass. I thought that was easy enough to remember and abide by.

"It's no problem, Phyl. He probably fell asleep on the floor or the couch watching videos. Let me put on a robe and get him for you." I rustled some shit around and picked up the remote. I walked over and pushed the door past the point where I knew it would squeak before hitting the wall and simultaneously turned on the TV pretending I was walking out into the living room. I padded back into my bedroom and shook Keith as he slept on my favorite side of the bed. I knew he was going to wake thinking I wanted some more loving, so I smashed the pillow over his mouth before he could utter a sound.

"What the fuck you doing, Mimi?" he asked, sitting up and looking like he was about to hurt something. I was instantly turned on.

"Phyllis is on the phone looking for your dumb ass. I wish you'd stop passing out on my couch so she would stop blaming me for you fucking up all the time," I screeched for effect.

He shook his head, snatched the phone and sighed deeply. "Yo, why you calling Mimi at all hours of the night?... Maybe because I was sleep... Yo, who the fuck you talking to? Yeah, I'll do that... Phyllis, I'll see your ass tomorrow after you've had a moment to cool off because I'm not about to drive home half drunk just to argue with you...Hello? Hello? Hello?"

I snatched my phone and placed it on the nightstand.

"What you smiling about?" he asked, nudging me.

"Why the fuck you screaming hello when you know she already hung up on your silly behind?" I couldn't stop laughing.

"Yeah, I bet I wasn't silly a few hours ago when I had your ass in here screaming my name. You know what time it is. By the time I get home tomorrow, this shit will be squashed. But first, I need to finish what we started."

Keith began kissing on my neck. I pushed him away just as the light started trickling through the blinds. "I can't do this."

"You can't do what?" he asked exasperated. I knew it was his hard-on talking—not his brain or heart—so I ignored him.

I turned over on my side facing the opposite wall. He tried to turn me to face him, but I wouldn't budge. He walked around the bed and knelt in front of me. I tried to hide my face, but his hand caught the first tear as it fell.

"What's wrong, Baby Girl? What did I do?" He sounded genuinely concerned and so sincere it made me cry even harder. "Mimi, talk to me," he said, grabbing me up into his strong arms and rocking me gently. I still couldn't speak. I was just too overwhelmed. "I don't know what's up with you," he continued in the softest voice I ever heard from him, "but you don't ever have to shed a tear over me, baby. I ain't going nowhere. Yeah, I know that Phyllis is there, but she ain't what I want. I knew that the first time I laid eyes on you. Now that you're finally letting me in, Mimi, I ain't letting go. Believe that. I'm in this to stay. I promise you that, on everything I love."

I wanted to explain to him I'd heard those same words so many times before, and in the end, on everything *I* love, boy stays with girl and Mimi gets to eat her way back to happiness. I needed him to know I liked being the other woman because I knew how to play my position. At least, I used to know how to play it. Now I was confused. Now I was lost. Now I was falling in love with a man who was young enough to be my son, but mature enough to bring me out of my shell and break down my defensive walls. Now I was weak, and I made the worst possible decisions when I became this Mimi. I wanted to say all that and more, but once again, I couldn't find my voice. All I could do was weep for the pain I already knew was forthcoming and prepare myself for battle.

HOUSE ARREST

Keith finally left about an hour after my waterworks stopped. He held me, soothed me and made me Christopher Williams promises—promises I knew he wouldn't keep. Hell, he couldn't keep them. No matter how much I wanted his sentiments to be true, I knew they were just words, and his actions would be the things I needed to heed. I lay in silence contemplating my next move.

I wasn't surprised when I heard the *Law & Order* "bong-bong" tone reverberate off my walls. The room was quiet, and the sound was refreshing. I peeked over at my phone and saw that the text message was from Keith.

"I meant what I said earlier, Mimi. I ain't playing no games. It's just a matter of time before you are mine."

I smiled at the display and contemplated how I would respond. Then the tone resounded once again.

"BTW… What you wearing right now?"

I was grinning like a naughty schoolgirl as I tried to think of a witty and nasty response. The "bong-bong" came through once more. This time it was Parish.

"Want some company?"

I wasn't interested in his ass at the moment. All my attention was on my little Yum-Yum who was asking about my attire. I quickly stripped naked and keyed in a response.

"*The skin I was born in. How about you?*"

"*About the same. I'm 'bout to go take a shower so I can lie back and relax.*"

"*Mmmmmmmmmm, wish I were there to join you, baby,*" I typed, beginning to feel that telltale moisture between my legs.

"*You just made my dick hard, Mimi. Want some company?*"

Although I had ignored Parish when he'd asked me the same thing just a few moments ago, there was no way in the world I was about to turn down Keith's delectable offer.

"*Yes.*" Simple. Straight to the point. And desperate, Mimi. Very desperate, but I didn't give a damn. Keith had me sprung on his young ass, and every chance I had to ride that chocolate stallion, was an opportunity I was going to take full advantage of.

"*See you in a few, baby. Get it wet for me…*"

He didn't have to ask me twice. I was in and out of the shower in record time. Applying lotion and spraying body mist on the parts that counted. I reclined on the bed, put on some slow jams and fantasized about my soon-to-be climax as Usher sang about one of a totally different nature.

Just as I looked up at the clock, the "bong-bong" came through loud and clear. I reached for my phone and read the screen.

"Sorry, Ma. Phyllis is feelin' some type of way cuz I'm tryna leave out for the 2nd nite in a row. I gotta take a rain check, Baby."

"Are you serious?" I screamed to no one in particular. I was just about to hit him back and give him a piece of my horny and pissed-off mind, when the "bong-bong" stopped me in my tracks.

"*Yo Mimi. I'm sorry if I came off the wrong way earlier. I'm in your hood. Wanted to pick up some dinner and a bottle and stop by to see you. Is that all right, Baby?*"

Any other time I would've ignored his text and pretended not to have received it. With Keith's ass on house arrest tonight, there was no reason for me not to put out this fire he'd started. Besides, I was heated and a heated Mimi led to a ruthless Sheba. She snatched up my phone and typed in some scandalous shit that I'm even too embarrassed to repeat. Within an hour of her pressing "SEND," Parish walked through the door with two steak and potato dinners and a few bottles of Rose Santero Moscato.

"I hope you know how incredibly sexy you look right now," he said, taking me all in.

"Yes I do," I replied, sashaying by him in a red, crotchless body stocking and matching fishnet thong. My thigh-high stilettos were click-clacking against the parquet floors in tune with the thrust of my hips as I led him to the dining room table.

Halfway through the meal and two bottles of Moscato later, Parish leaned back and stared at me. I batted my eyelashes and went into my shy-girl mode.

"Mimi, why are you still single?"

"The same reason why you're engaged to Taylor, but sneaking to see me every chance you get. It's all about damage control. I'm not a threat to your relationship and my being single is not a threat to my sanity."

"You sure that's the only reason? I think you're scared."

"You're right. I'm scared that I will become Taylor, and that is a position I don't know how to play too well. I'm one of those dish-it-out but can't-take-it females. I prefer to know I'm sharing you, instead of thinking you're all mine and you're not. It's my way of keeping my feelings in check."

"And that's what you're doing with us," he slurred. "Keeping your feelings in check? I mean, would you want more from me if I was able to give it to you?"

"Why you doing this tonight, Parish?" I asked. "Does it look like I'm dressed for a job interview?"

We laughed, but his was half-hearted.

"Nah, Mimi, I'm just saying. You make me second-guess my whole relationship. Like I placed a ring on the wrong finger. You're a great woman, and I think you keep selling yourself short."

"Parish…" I started, and then I fell silent. What was there to say? He was right, but this was not the conversation nor mood I'd anticipated this evening so I switched it up a little. "How about we take this bottle to the bedroom and finish our conversation in there?"

"Why you always running, Mimi? You know once I get your thick, sexy ass in that bedroom, there ain't going to be no more talking."

"Exactly," I countered, jumping up unsteadily from my chair and grabbing him up out of his. "Follow me," I said, feeling the heat on my ass cheeks from the holes his eyes were boring into them.

Once in the room, Parish grabbed and kissed me like he loved me. Deep and passionate—all tongue and soft caresses. Folding my body into his. Lying me back onto the bed gently. Maneuvering a condom on and my thong to the side with ease. Filling me up slowly and purposefully. Uttering words and emotions I never heard fall from his lips until now. Bringing my body to the brink and then joining me in several well-deserved orgasms that had the both of us panting and sweating profusely. Had we not fallen into a coma-like sleep soon after, I would have heard the "bong-bong" and read the message from Keith.

"I have to see you tonight…OMW over, baby."

COMPROMISING POSITIONS

When the doorbell rang, I thought I was hearing things. It wasn't until Parish nudged me that I realized I wasn't dreaming.

"Just a minute," I screamed out, walking to the bathroom to relieve myself and freshen up a bit. I grabbed my robe off the back of the door and walked out of the bedroom, pulling the door closed behind myself. I opened the door to Keith's smiling face.

"Hey, baby. Did you get my text?" he asked, grabbing me up and throwing his tongue down my throat.

I heard the toilet flush and the faucet come on at the same time Keith stopped attacking my tonsils.

"Yo, you got company, ma?" he asked. I sensed anger in his tone and hurt in his eyes.

"Yes, Love, I do," I answered. I wasn't trying to hurt him, but he had to realize I wasn't going to sit around and wait on him and Phyllis to get their shit together. I had needs, too.

"Word, Mimi? It's like that?"

"It's like what?" Parish asked, walking down the hall in just his boxers and a shit-eating grin. "Everything all right out here?"

I rolled my eyes in my head and shot Parish the death look. He ignored me, and so did Keith.

"I'm talking to Mimi, my dude. This ain't got nothing to do with you," Keith said to Parish.

"Well, Mimi is busy tonight as you can see," Parish countered.

"That's too bad, my dude," Keith said, walking past me and taking a seat on the couch. "'Cause I ain't leaving. Yo, Mimi, you got anything to drink in here?"

I was still in shock, standing in the open doorway looking out onto the street. Parish reached over my shoulder and pushed the door closed.

"You want to tell me what's going on here, Mimi," they asked in unison.

I didn't have an answer so I diverted their attention to my body. I dropped my robe at the door and strutted over to the kitchen. "I don't know about the two of you, but I need a drink."

I walked over to the cabinet and retrieved my brand-new bottle of Jack Daniel's and a shot glass. I needed to be good and fucked up before I walked my ass back in the living room. Since they both wanted to puff out their chests this evening, may the best man win. I wasn't the one for compromising positions. I leaned back on the cabinet and let the liquid burn my throat and chest.

"How you gonna do this to me, Mimi?" Keith asked, entering the kitchen and grabbing a shot glass of his own. "I thought…"

"You thought what, Keith? That I gave up my BFF status because you threw down something lovely last night?" I didn't mean to sound so bitter, but I couldn't help it. He stood me up and now had the nerve to be mad I'd made alternate plans? I think not.

"Well, yeah," he said dejectedly. "I thought we had an agreement…or rather an understanding…"

"And I think you must have misunderstood. Keith, I'm not…"

Keith had me pressed up against the counter. Grabbing at all of my curves and kissing me even more passionately than Parish did some hours ago. I got lost in his embrace until I heard Parish clear his throat loudly while standing at the threshold.

"So this is how it is, Mimi," he asked. "You gonna play me right to my face?"

"Parish, we are not in a relationship," I said, moving off the counter and standing in front of Keith. "You already know what this is about, and I never committed myself to either one of you. So, y'all can stop the pity-party, get dressed and leave me the fuck alone. I'm a single woman and I don't need this type of drama in my life."

"I already told your ass, I ain't going nowhere," Keith said, grabbing me by my waist and pulling me into his body. "You already know what time it is with me."

"Well, I ain't leaving, either," Parish said, walking over and kissing me like he owned me.

The dual sensation of both sets of hands and both pair of lips exploring my body was too much to handle. When they began peeling off my body stocking and thong, I felt my knees begin to buckle. I regained my composure, eased from between their writhing bodies and played follow the leader as they trailed me to the bedroom. I couldn't believe what I was about to do, but I was too far gone now to stop myself.

"Take off your clothes," I said seductively to Keith as Parish began tongue kissing my lower lips.

When Keith was naked, I pulled him on top of the bed and placed my lips around his shaft. The feel of Parish's tongue and fingers inside me, coupled with the taste of Keith on my tongue had me so horny I needed to feel the real thing. I pushed Keith back, flipped Parish onto the bed and took residence atop his lap. When my gyrations led to low moans, I put my mouth back on Keith and helped him grow to the required size.

Keith jumped down off the bed and retrieved my baby oil off the dresser. When he returned to the bed, he squirted a generous amount on my rotating ass, sliding his oily fingers in and out of my anus preparing me to receive his girth. He oiled himself down and then inserted his tip very slowly and meticulously into my tautness. I bit into Parish's shoulder, trying to relax through the pain. I knew pleasure was just a few strokes away, but it took some getting used to. Parish and Keith had me plugged up like a bowling ball. Just as I was about to give up and call the whole thing off, I was overcome by a feeling of euphoria. Parish's feel-good rhythm coupled with Keith's unfamiliar, but pleasurable rear invasion had me screaming all kinds of obscenities. Listening to our grunts and moans, I clawed at them both—taking their smacks to my ass in stride. My body was sandwiched between theirs. I let out a guttural scream as skin slapped against skin and I came like I never came before. The feeling started from my back and took over my front, turning me into an epileptic, biting my tongue and my eyes rolling to the back of my head.

Once they released their members from their respective holes, we all fell back on the bed spent, satisfied and confused.

"So what now?" Keith asked, still trying to catch his breath.

"Now, I take a shower," I said, climbing down off the bed. "You both have the option of following suit once I get out and then I'm going to bed…alone. As for the two of you, you will be going home to your women."

"You know damn well that's not what he meant, Mimi," Parish chimed in.

"All I know is that I can't do this right now with you two. So play nice while I'm gone." I hurried into the bathroom and clicked the lock. I leaned against the closed door and looked up to the ceiling. I heard Parish mumbling something inaudible and it sounded like he was snatching up his clothes. As I turned on the shower water, I heard my front door slam shut. When I finally emerged from my sanctum, Keith was lying back on my pillows watching the basketball game.

"One down, one to go," I said, crossing over to my vanity and applying generous amounts of lotion to my skin. Anything not to have to face Keith and talk about what had just transpired.

"Didn't I tell your ass that I ain't going nowhere," he asked, throwing his legs over the edge of the bed and sitting up. Now standing, he continued. "I'm going to take a nice, hot shower, then I'm coming out here to have a peaceful sleep spooning with the woman I love." He was walking toward the bathroom, but stopped short once he let those last words roll off his tongue. He looked down, shook his head, smiled and then continued on—leaving me sitting at my vanity sore, satisfied and speechless.

THERE'S NO PLACE LIKE HOME

I knew there was going to be a hefty price for Keith to pay since he didn't leave for home until Sunday afternoon. When he didn't show up for work two days in a row, I began to worry. It wasn't until Wednesday morning that I decided to finally listen to the voicemail message Phyllis left for me on Sunday night.

"I give up, Mimi. I don't know what the fuck Keith is up to, but I'm through. He's been distant and funny acting for the last few weeks and I'm just fed up. He won't kiss me, he won't touch me, let alone talk to me, and I've had enough. He stayed out all night last night and I was going to call you, but by the way he's been acting, I knew he wasn't over there. By the time he came home, I had his things packed and waiting for him by the front door. The funny thing is that he seemed happy to grab his shit and go. I don't know if I did the right thing, Mimi, but I don't know how to fix it…"

She started crying at that point and I couldn't make out the rest of the message. All I knew was now three days had passed and no one had heard anything from Keith. He was not only messing up his perfect attendance record at work, he was fucking with my sanity to boot. I was tempted to call him, but knowing I was partially to blame for him now being homeless, I thought better of it and just bided my time. If he wanted to talk, he'd surface.

By Thursday morning, I could no longer take it. I needed to know where Keith was and if he was all right. Besides, this temp they sent in to replace him was getting on my last nerve. Instead of her assisting me, she was prancing around the office in inappropriate outfits that were two sizes too small. Since the majority of the office was made up of men, I seemed to be the only one who found issue with it, but I didn't give a damn. She couldn't type, she got a third of my messages incorrect, and she was late every single day. I'd had enough.

I went to pick up my phone and Parish was already on the line. "Hello? Mimi?"

"Hey you. How have you been?"

"I've been fine, but you've been unreachable. Why haven't you been returning any of my calls or texts? I know you got my messages." He sounded upset, but I couldn't really let that affect me right now. I was on a whole other mission.

"I'm sorry, Parish. This is not a good time. I was just about to make an important phone call and…"

"So I'm not important? My feelings don't matter? I'm irrelevant all of a sudden?"

"Parish, where is all this coming from? Don't you have a fiancée? Why are you bugging out?"

"Oh, so now I'm the one who's bugging? I just got finished sharing my sidepiece with her sidepiece and we can't even hang out anymore? What happened to the Mimi I used to know?"

"Parish, let me call you later." I hung up before he could even respond.

It's like he and Keith had gone crazy overnight. One minute they were sneaking out on their women with me, and next thing you know, they're acting like they're sneaking out on me with their women. It was all a little much and it made me rethink my call to Keith. I had just hung up the phone when a brief knock at the door revealed the smile I was longing to see.

"May I come in?" Keith asked in that baritone voice that sent chills down my spine.

I nodded and he stepped inside. He dropped in the chair directly in front of my desk. He was suited up, smelling good and looking delicious. I kept my mouth closed and let him take the lead. I didn't want him to know I knew what was going on, unless he felt the need to tell me.

"Sorry I've been out so many days. I was feeling a little under the weather."

"No problem," I said. "They brought in a temp and she's been…"

"A fucking nightmare," he interrupted and started laughing loudly. "Just by the hodgepodge of bullshit she left on my desk, I already know she was absolutely no help to you. I did enjoy her outfit, though."

"Yeah, you would," I said, laughing with him. "She was the worst."

"Well, I'm back now…better than ever. Looking forward to getting caught up and making us some money."

"Now that's the kind of assistance I've been missing. I have these seven files here that need some order, so I'm glad you're back and raring to go."

I handed him the files as he stood to leave. He walked over to the door, opened it, closed it and then returned to the chair in front of my desk. He looked me square in the eyes.

"I want to be totally honest with you, Mimi."

"Okay," is all I said. I waited for him to continue.

"Phyllis put me out and I've been staying at the Regency the last few nights."

There it was; everything was out in the open without me even having to ask.

"I know that must be hard on you, because there's no place like home," I said.

"I guess not, but I've spent the last few days looking for a place," he continued. "Thanks to you, I was able to put down the required deposit, pick up my keys and move into my new spot last night."

"Thanks to me? What do I have to do with all this?"

"Your internship program. You mentored us on financial stability and investing. I've been able to grow an impressive portfolio over the last five years. So, I thank you."

"Well, you're welcome and I'm happy for you," I said rather impressed. "Are you sure you're okay?"

"Yeah, I'm fine. It's going to take a little getting used to, but it's the right thing for me right now. Phyllis and I were done and if she didn't kick me out, I would have dragged my feet leaving. It all worked out for the best. Now I just have to parlay these seven files into a big-ass bonus for your boy." He smiled radiantly and then just stared at me.

"Well, if you're sure you're okay, then get to work. We have a lot to catch up on, and three of those puppies are due tomorrow. So, make it happen."

"Looks like I came back just in the nick of time."

"Yeah, you did."

"Who knows, we may have to wind up pulling an all-nighter." He smiled again.

"If you get to work now, we may be finished by quitting time," I countered.

"Yeah, I know, but maybe I'm looking forward to an all-nighter." He winked at me and made his way out of my office.

I sat smiling at the closed door. When did I let this young one dazzle me out of my drawers and into a full-blown love affair? Keith being on his own was trouble. I had to put my life into perspective quickly, or I'd be heading for heartbreak.

THE CHOICE IS YOURS

The weekend couldn't get here quick enough. Keith was excited about having his own place and invited me over for dinner Saturday night. I turned down Parish too many times to count, and he was now feeling some type of way. Of all my BFFs, he was the only one who wouldn't take the hint. Everyone else stopped calling and texting; most probably erased my info from their phones. A few unfriended me on Facebook; I guess they did whatever it took to work me out of their system. Parish was different. He was determined, and he was starting to frighten me.

I finished wriggling my thick frame into my outfit, and sprayed my body with some smell right. I clicked off the TV, grabbed my purse and made my way to the front door. When I got in my car, I felt funny—like I was being watched or something. I looked around me, but didn't see anyone or anything. I pulled out of my driveway and made my way over to the address Keith had given me. I stepped out of the car and again got that eerie feeling. I quickly shook it off and walked over to the door, knocking heartily. Keith opened it in record time and grabbed me up in a crushing bear hug.

He ushered me in and gave me a quick tour of his scantily furnished bachelor pad. It was cute and cozy. In the corner of the living room was a small dinette set with two place settings, a bottle of wine chilling in an ice bucket and candles lit for ambiance. I smiled as he pulled out my chair and poured me a glass of wine.

"Are you impressed?" he asked, grinning like a big kid.

"As a matter of fact, I am," I said. "Whatever you made smells great."

"Thank you." He disappeared into the kitchen and returned holding two large dishes, one of penne alla vodka and the other of stuffed chicken breasts.

"Where'd you order this from?"

"Very funny. This is all from Keith's Culinary Kitchen. There's a whole lot about the kid you don't know. I'm actually a pretty good cook."

"Really?"

"Yup," he said, filling our plates and then taking a seat across from me. "I grew up a latch-key kid, so it was cook or starve. My mom worked nights so I had no choice. Trial and error turned me into a whiz in the kitchen."

"I'll be the judge of that," I said, picking up a forkful of food and shoveling it in. "Mmmmmmmmm. This is really delicious."

"I'm glad you like."

"Hell, I love it. This tastes amazing. I can't believe you really cooked it. What other tricks do you have up your sleeves?"

"Wouldn't you like to know?"

He smiled, I smiled and we made small talk for the rest of the meal. Once our bellies were full and the wine was starting to take effect, we made our way to the bedroom and got comfortable.

"I'm really glad you came," he whispered into my ear as we lay spooning on the bed, listening to love songs.

"I'm glad I came, too. I'm having a great time tonight, Keith."

"I am, too. Lean up for a minute," he said, pushing me off him gently so he could get up. He walked over, cracked the window and lifted the blinds. "It gets a little stuffy in here sometimes," he said, lying back down and folding his body into mine once again.

"Do you have any regrets?" I asked, trying to figure out if the

Phyllis situation was really over, or would he be going back and forth with it for months and years to come.

"Any regrets like what?" Keith asked, skirting the issue and forcing me to come out and ask him what I really wanted to know.

"Any regrets about the way things ended with you and Phyllis. Are you okay with it all?"

He sighed. There was a long pause before he began to speak. "I'm not going to lie to you. Phyllis and I had a long conversation last night and we came to the conclusion that…" He paused for effect, and my heart skipped a beat. "That we made the right decision… There is no turning back." He began kissing the back of my neck.

"You sure about that? The two of you were together for a long time, and…"

"And time is all we had. We were holding on for all the wrong reasons. Young, bullheaded and determined to prove all the naysayers wrong. In the end, we had to cut our losses and move on. She was tired of my shit and I wasn't happy with hers, either."

"I see. So, what are your plans now?"

"Well, right now I plan to ravage this sexy beast that found her way into my bed."

He kissed me passionately and began removing my clothes. I undressed him, too, and was happy to spread my legs as he kissed my inner thighs and went to work on my love box. I arched my back and thrust my hips into him. His tongue was causing me all kinds of pleasure and just as I was on the verge of coming, I sat up to watch his oral attack. When I did, I almost jumped out of my skin. There was a figure standing in the window staring at us. He moved as soon as our eyes locked. I pushed Keith off of me and ran over to the window, but when I looked out, there was no one in sight. I don't know where he went so quickly, but I know what I saw. Parish was watching us with pure hatred in his eyes.

"You all right?" Keith asked, pulling me back over to the bed. "You're shaking."

"Parish was just at the window," I said.

Keith walked over to the window and looked out as well. He didn't see anything, either. "He was just outside *this* window?"

"Yes. He was…watching us."

"Watching us? For what?"

"I don't know."

"Is there more to the two of you than you're letting on, Mimi?"

"No, Keith. He's engaged, for Christ's sake. He's been getting a little bit more possessive over the last month or so, but I just chalked it up to him being jealous. After that little encounter with the three of us last weekend, he's been relentless with the calls and texts every hour on the hour. I just don't get it."

"I do," Keith said, placing himself between my legs. "He's just as sprung off this good shit as I am."

I got lost in Keith's embrace. His hands were kneading my excess flesh, making me feel beautiful and wanted. He kissed me passionately and inserted himself inside me. Parish was quickly forgotten as I moaned out in pure pleasure as Keith did a slow stroke in and out, loosening my tight walls and filling me completely. I grabbed my own thighs and brought them up to my chest, giving him better access so he could go as deep as he pleased.

"Damn, Mimi, this shit feels so fucking good."

"Mmm-hmm. Yes, baby. It does. Just like that, baby. Just like that…"

He pressed my thighs into my chest and while on his knees continued to pump vigorously inside me.

"Like this," he asked, stroking me lovingly. "You like it like this?"

"Yes, baby. Oh God…you gonna make me cum…"

I moaned and thrashed about. My head was spinning like *The*

Exorcist. Keith was hitting my spot and just as I exploded, he grabbed me tightly and started bucking violently. He didn't even have a chance to pull out before the "bong-bong" filled the room.

"I know better," I said, reluctantly pulling away from Keith and retrieving my phone. I pressed the text envelope open and lo and behold, Parish had something to get off his chest.

"What is it?" Keith asked, standing and walking over to me.

"It's Parish."

"What does he have to say?"

I opened the message envelope and read aloud.

"I don't know what you're thinking, but you're not going to get rid of me this easily. It's either him and me, or just me, but I ain't about to sit back and watch the two of you live happily ever after. You decide. The choice is yours."

I was speechless, but Keith wasn't. He was furious. He started pacing and yelling.

"What the fuck is Parish smoking, Yo? He really thinks you are going to settle for being second best for the rest of your life? I know your worth. You are my number one. And if he thinks I'm going to give you up without a fight, then he better think again."

"Keith, calm down. Parish is all talk. He's not going to do anything crazy."

"Nah, man, he practically threatened us. Your boy done lost it, and I'm not about to play that shit down like he ain't serious. I swear, if anything were to happen to you, Mimi…"

I was so touched by Keith's sincerity. As he talked the veins throbbing in his forearms and forehead were turning me on. I pushed him back on the bed and put my mouth on his sex. I worked my jaws and jerked him off to the rhythm of my heartbeat. I loved the way he tasted, and the freaky shit he mumbled made me go even harder. When he could take it no longer, he flipped me over and entered me from behind. Pressing his hand into my lower back and spreading my ass cheeks apart, he deep dug me until both of our toes were curling and we sang out together in sweet release. Sleep came easily after that. Threat or no threat, great sex is the perfect lullaby.

SOMEONE PLEASE CALL 911

Keith and I were falling into a pretty steady rhythm. We worked together, played together, ate together, slept together at his place or mine, and we soon became inseparable. I stopped harping on our age difference and began appreciating the mature young man I had in my life. Keith doted on me. When he said that I was his number one, he meant it. My every wish was his command and he never let me forget it. We were three months strong and growing.

Parish had eased up on the phone calls and text messages and everything seemed right with the world, until I arrived home to find him sitting on my front porch one Wednesday evening.

"What are you doing here?"

"Wow," he said. "No hello? No long time no see? No I miss you? Just what are you doing here? Where they do that at, Mimi?"

"I'm sorry," I said, approaching with caution. "I just didn't expect to see you…"

"Why not? I mean, it's not like we talk anymore. You don't take my calls. You ignore my texts. Your assistant won't put me through to your new extension at work. What's a guy to do?"

"I don't know, Parish, but I don't think this was your best idea. What's going on with you?"

"Are we going to stand out here on the porch and talk, or are you going to invite me in? I mean, I'm not allowed over the threshold anymore, Mimi?"

"Parish, why are you doing this?"

"Doing what," he asked, leaning against the porch rail. "Trying to spend time with what used to be my best friend, who all of a sudden doesn't know me? What exactly am I doing?"

"Trespassing, for one," Keith said. I didn't see him drive up, and by the way we both jumped at the sound of his voice, I don't think Parish did, either.

"Yo, my man, this is between me and Mimi. This ain't got nothing to do with you."

Parish was now standing and I had made my way over to a very pissed-off Keith.

"Hey, baby," I said, kissing him full on the mouth. "Parish was just leaving."

"No I wasn't," Parish said.

"Yes you were," Keith said, approaching the porch aggressively.

"Listen," I said, with my hand on Keith's heaving chest. "Parish is leaving, and we are going to enjoy our evening as planned."

"That's how it is, Mimi?"

"Yes, Parish. Now, I need for you to go home and let this go."

Parish just shook his head and laughed. He walked off the porch and continued laughing until he got behind the wheel of his car. Keith guided me inside, but he wouldn't close the door until he saw Parish drive off.

"What was he doing here, Mimi?"

"I have no idea. He was sitting on the porch when I got home. You pulled in right after me."

"Well, what did he want?"

"I'm not sure. Why are you giving me the third degree? You can't think I told him to come over here."

"I don't know what to think. All I know is I don't want to see him here again."

"Keith, I didn't want to see him here this time, but obviously I don't have any control over that." I stormed off into the bedroom and slammed the door behind me. Parish must have lost his mind showing up at my house like that, and Keith must have lost his right along with him for even suggesting I had cosigned that shit. I was still pacing when Keith entered.

"Mimi, I'm sorry." He walked over and grabbed me by the arms. "I don't know why seeing him here got me so upset. I know ain't nothing going on with the two of you. But just the thought of someone coming at you like that makes me see red. Baby, I love you and I'm genuinely sorry. You forgive me?"

He was bent at the knees, moving from side to side, trying to make eye contact with me. When I wouldn't look him in the eyes, he threw me back on the bed and pinned my hands over my head.

"Keith, get off of me."

"Not 'til you tell me you love me." He smiled and I melted.

"You aiight," I said, as we burst out laughing. I shook my head. "You make me sick."

"I know I do, but you love it."

His lips came down on mine with such force that my panties were immediately drenched and my girl was thumping uncontrollably. We dry humped for a few minutes until the urge built to overflowing. We ripped at each other's clothes and clawed at each other's flesh, threatening bodily gratification that seemed too long overdue. He filled me up and rocked my body effortlessly. I was so wet. The sensation flowing through my walls made me moan and profess my love for him over and over again. He pumped into my middle, telling me how much he loved me, too. I was underneath him receiving all his good loving when I heard a loud pop. Keith collapsed on top of me. I thought it was a joke until I saw the blood.

"Oh my Gooooodddddd! Someone please call nine-one-one!" I screamed out. "Oh no, Keith, are you okay? Keith!"

No response. I wiggled from underneath him and called the police. The operator told me they were already en route since another call had come in a few moments earlier. I was still cradling his lifeless body in my arms when they broke down my front door and my bedroom became flooded with police, firemen and paramedics. Once they convinced me to put some clothes on, a detective began asking me questions, but I couldn't hear him. My focus was on the tubes and machines they were plugging up to Keith and the faint beep of the handheld monitor the EMT kept checking. When they lifted him onto the stretcher, I stood up as well. If this detective wanted answers, he'd have to follow me to the hospital because there was no way in hell I was leaving Keith's side.

FATAL ATTRACTION

I t was like the doctor wasn't speaking English to me. She said something about unresponsive, a punctured lung, excessive blood loss and a few other clinical terms I naturally blocked out. I didn't want to hear all that gibberish. I just wanted the cold hard facts.

"Bottom line, is my man going to be okay?" I blurted out in the midst of her dissertation. "All I need is a 'yes' or 'no.'"

"I'm sorry, Ms. Jackson…" I guess it's right what they say. In times of crisis, some of the craziest things run through your head, because all I could hear once she said that was Andre 3000 screeching out the chorus… *I'm sorry, Ms. Jackson, I am for real…*

"I'm sorry," I said, shaking my head for clarity. "Can you please repeat that?"

"I said Mr. Myers' prognosis is sketchy at best. We were able to remove the bullet from his lung and extract the excess fluid surrounding it, but right now. it's touch-and-go until we can take him off the oxygen and see if he'll be able to breathe on his own."

"Well, how long will it be before he comes off of oxygen?"

"We will know more in the morning once all the swelling goes down and we get him stabilized. He has been sedated for the night and will be in ICU for at least the next twenty-four hours. You're welcome to stay with him, but he will not be responsive."

"Thank you," I whispered, for lack of anything else to say.

"Is there anyone you need us to call for you? Has his family been notified?"

"Yes. I spoke with his family already."

"Okay, I'll be here until midnight. If you need me, just have them page Dr. Greene."

"I will."

"And stay optimistic. This can go either way, but if he's a fighter, you don't have anything to worry about."

She walked away and I collapsed against the wall. I knew Keith was unconscious and wouldn't know if I fell apart or held it together, but I didn't want to bring any somberness or negativity into the ICU. I wanted to enter those doors confident and in high spirits so he would continue to fight hard to get back to me. I spoke with his mother earlier and assured her if there were a need for her to fly in from California, I'd let her know. I downplayed the seriousness of his condition because I didn't want to break her heart. I also didn't want her to blame me for his predicament, no matter how true that sentiment was. All kinds of thoughts rushed through my head as I cried my eyes out for the man I loved. I finally pulled it together and made my way down the corridor toward his room, which was still surrounded by police. Before I made it halfway, the "bong-bong" sounded and almost gave me a heart attack. In all the confusion, I forgot to silence my phone. I hurriedly pulled it out of my bag and read the screen. The message chilled me to the bone.

"You're next."

I started shaking uncontrollably and the same detective that was asking me questions earlier was the same one who had caught me right before I'd hit the ground. When I finally came to, they had me lying on the bed next to Keith. An oxygen mask was covering my face. I pulled it off and tried to sit up. The detective was on me immediately.

"Take it easy, Ms. Jackson. We don't need you getting excited and passing out again."

"No, no, I'm okay. I'm okay. Where's my phone?" I was frantic. He was trying unsuccessfully to subdue me.

"Ms. Jackson, please."

"My phone, I need my phone. You don't understand."

"Here you go, Ms.," a second detective said as she handed me my mobile.

I snatched it from her hands and pulled the text back up on the screen. "See. This is proof." I handed the first detective the phone.

"Who is P-Lover?" he asked.

I looked at him like he had two heads. "It's *him*. Parish. Parish Petersen. The man who shot Keith."

"When did the text come through?" he continued, jotting notes down in a small black pad.

"Right as I was walking toward you."

"Is the address you gave us for Parish a valid one?" the second detective asked. "We had a car go by there earlier and the place seemed to be abandoned."

"Yes, it's valid. Well, it was valid. I haven't been in contact with him for a few months now, so I don't know what's been happening with him. Did you try to contact his fiancée?"

The first detective flipped through his notebook, then shot me a puzzling look. "We don't have any knowledge of a fiancée. Do you have a name for this woman?"

"Yes, it's Taylor."

"Wait a minute," the second detective chimed in once again, flipping through a notebook of her own. "Taylor," she repeated, flipping through the pages. She smiled when she found what she was looking for. "Is it Taylor Channing, by chance?"

I nodded. "Yes. Taylor Channing. That's right. Why, did something happen to Tay?"

She looked at her partner, showed him her notes and he shook his head. He placed his hand on my arm and sat down on the edge of the bed beside me.

"Taylor Channing has been classified a missing person. No one has seen her in close to three weeks. About the same time you lost contact with Mr. Petersen."

"Oh no, not Taylor." Rivulets of tears streamed down my cheeks. The female detective passed me a box of Kleenex and began in on me again.

"Is there anything you can tell us about Taylor or Parish that you may not have mentioned to us before? Anything at all? It can be the most insignificant thing; just tell us anything. Where do they vacation? Eat…work…hang out…"

"Well, Taylor comes from a very affluent family," I began. "They sort of disowned her when she met, fell in love and moved in with Parish. She mentioned he had a record of some kind, but never elaborated on what that record consisted of. She used to have a place on the lower East Side I don't believe she gave up. She was subleasing it last I heard."

"Do you have the address to this place?" the first detective asked.

"No, but it's listed on sublet.com. If you enter Taylor's name, it will bring up the address and also show a video tour of the place."

"Thank you, Ms. Jackson. Detective Bennett and I will look into this and we will be right back."

"Burns, you go on ahead. I'll catch up. I just want to talk to Ms. Jackson a little longer."

"As you wish," she said, rushing out to check on the info I'd just given her.

"Ms. Jackson…"

"Mimi."

"Mimi. I know this is not the right time to be questioning you, with the man you love lying unconscious just a few feet away, but there's something that's not sitting right with me."

"And what is that, Detective…Bennett, right?"

He nodded and then continued. "Where is your allegiance? With Taylor or with Parish?"

"I'm not following you, Detective, because my *allegiance* is with Keith Myers. Period."

"That's not what I'm asking. How do you know so much about Taylor when it appears that Parish is—or rather was—your friend?"

"Actually, Taylor was my friend. We met at work a few years ago. I was even with her the night she and Parish first met. I was the one who began noticing the change in her. Wanting to be with him and only him. Letting herself and her responsibilities go just to satisfy him and his needs. She left the job a little while after meeting him. She moved out of her place, into his and then started working for a company he recommended to her. I thought she was bugging by switching up her whole lifestyle for him. But it was none of my business. Besides, he seemed cool enough, and he and I started hanging on the regular as well."

"Hanging," he asked, with a raised eyebrow.

"At first it was just hanging. After a while, it became a little more than that. He was the one who actually drove a wedge between Taylor and I. We weren't as close as we used to be, and she just became another fool in love—another victim in my eyes."

"I see," he said, scribbling nonstop in his notebook. "And this Parish Petersen…describe him to me again."

"I can do you one better," I replied, scrolling through my phone. "This is Parish," I said, holding the phone screen toward him so he could see the picture of the two of us taken on the night of my first threesome. Parish looked so handsome in the picture. Who knew his ass would turn into a real-life fatal attraction?

The detective did a double-take when he saw the picture. "Um, can I borrow this for a moment?" he asked, pulling my phone out of my hand before I could respond. He placed the notebook into his pocket and began to walk off. "I-I'll be right back," he stammered.

I watched him leave, then my eyes narrowed in on Keith lying there immobile. He looked so handsome and peaceful. I walked over to him, placing kisses all over his face.

"Baby, the doctor told me that you are going to be all right, and I know you are. You have to be. I don't know what kind of hold you have on me, but I love you so much." Tears were now streaming down my face. "You've taught me how to trust again…how to love again. You've taught me what it feels like to have someone worthwhile in my corner. I will never regret giving you the opportunity to prove yourself to me. My only regret will be if you don't allow me the same opportunity to prove myself to you. You're my heart and I love you, baby." I was overwhelmed with emotion and crumpled onto the bed, crying into his stiff chest. "Please don't leave me, baby."

Sedated or not, I listened to the steady beat of Keith's heart. I climbed into bed with him and snuggled up to him as if he were awake and we were just passing time like we normally did. I knew the nurses were going to make me get up as soon as they entered the room, but I was going to enjoy our closeness for as long as I could.

A MILLION THOUGHTS

I thought I was imagining things when I felt something nudge me in my side, awakening me from a very deep slumber. But the sound of his voice was unmistakable.

"Mimi, wake your ass up."

I jumped up in a panic. Keith was still lifeless beside me. The room was empty except the three of us—me, Keith and Parish. Parish stood next to Keith's bed in black slacks, black T-shirt, leather jacket and a detective's badge hanging around his neck. The gun was not imaginary. Parish had it pointed at my head the entire time.

"Get out the bed," he ordered, gesturing with the gun.

I did as I was told and backed slowly against the wall. "What do you want, Parish?"

"Isn't it obvious?" he asked, moving toward me. "Didn't you get my text?"

A chill ran down my spine, but I wasn't about to let him see me sweat. "No, I didn't."

The gun smashing against my left cheek left me seeing stars and spitting out blood. I crumpled to the floor holding my face.

"Don't fucking play with me, Mimi. You got the text, but chose to ignore it. Just like with all the other ones I sent. I heard when Bennett called it in. Montoya is on the way to Taylor's place on Houston and they'll all be running in circles for the next few hours trying to track me down. Leaving us all alone to do whatever it is we want to do."

"And what is it that we want to do, Parish?" I asked, trying unsuccessfully to mask my fear. "How did you get past security?"

"Security?" He laughed. "I *am* security. Hell, I'm your worst fucking nightmare, Mimi. I'm a nigger with a badge."

It was so funny when Eddie Murphy said those same words in *48 Hours*, but with my man in a drug-induced coma to my right, and me in a bloody heap on the floor, somehow I didn't find any humor in it at that moment. Parish had me questioning everything, because for the first time I realized I didn't know a damn thing about him. A million thoughts were going through my mind. What the fuck was he doing with a detective's badge anyway? I thought he'd been unemployed for the last year or so.

"I see those wheels spinning, Mimi. Don't overthink it. That was your girl Taylor's problem. She was always butting her nose in where it didn't belong. Getting involved in shit she didn't need to be involved in. The one time I needed the bitch to be involved, she flaked out. But that's neither here nor there. Right now, there's only one woman I'm worried about and that's you, Mimi."

He walked over and yanked me up by the hair. I felt tracks unbind from my scalp. I jumped to my feet to avoid further damage. Parish began mumbling inaudibly under his breath. Although I couldn't understand what he was saying, there was no mistaking what he was doing. Bent over the bed across from Keith with my jeans and panties around my ankles, Parish entered me raw. The gun was against my temple and his other hand was around my neck. He was thrusting inside me so deep that it felt like he was in my stomach. I knew I was being raped and I shouldn't have been aroused, but I was. Parish was kissing on the back of my neck and manhandling me in a way that was turning me the fuck on. I forgot about the gun. I forgot I hated him. I forgot my man was in a hospital bed right beside us. I forgot Parish wasn't wearing a condom; I forgot about the danger I was in and got lost in the act. I started throwing it back and moaning softly.

"That's right, baby. You know you love this dick."

Parish moved his hand from around my throat and slid it between my legs, fingering between my thighs, bringing my clit to life. His pelvis was moving double-time and I was imagining how tight his ass must look as he pushed into me with all his might. I spread my legs wider and shifted my hips higher. Parish was hitting my spot and I felt my inner walls tensing. He felt it, too.

"Yeah, cum all over your dick and have my baby, Mimi. Let me make you mine again."

I snapped out of my trance and started fighting against the inevitable. I didn't want Parish to make me cum. That was Keith's job. I didn't want to love the way he was fucking me, but his stroke was mesmerizing. I was too far gone. His hand was back around my throat. His dick was still splitting me in half. His tongue was making wet circles on my neck as he professed his undying love for me. My body started tensing once again. With one final thrust, I cried out, "NO!" and erupted along with the blast from Detective Bennett's Glock 23 pistol.

The shot shattered Parish's shoulder, making him drop his gun and spin off of me. Detective Bennett and his partner were immediately on him, kicking the gun out of the way and restraining him on the floor. Detective Burns quickly covered me up and ushered me into another room where an emergency rape kit was done and an entirely new statement was given. By the time I was able to shower, change clothes and return to Keith's room, my head was spinning.

They had found Taylor in her old apartment badly beaten and

severely neglected. Parish was torturing her, trying to get her to lure me over, but she wouldn't do it. She'd almost lost her life protecting mine, and I wasn't even worth it. I was the worst kind of friend to her, and I knew I had a lot of making up to do once she was released from the hospital.

We later found out the name Parish Petersen was actually an alias. He was a rogue detective that got in too deep while undercover, stealing from the dealers he was supposed to bust and then disappearing with over $6 million in drug profits. His real name was Dwight Darden and Detectives Bennett and Burns were looking at promotions for being the ones to finally bring him down.

A week later, Dr. Greene removed the last of the tubes from Keith's body. Since the swelling had gone down, she was going to disconnect the oxygen mask as well.

"Are you ready?" she asked, looking back at me and motioning for me to come stand beside her.

I did as she beckoned and watched as the mask was taken off. Tears flooded my eyes when Keith's chest began to rise and fall on its own. Dr. Greene beamed.

"Well, it looks like the operation has been a success and Mr. Myers will be just fine. He should be coming out of sedation quite rapidly from here. I have another patient I must check on and then I'll be back to see if Mr. Myers has made any more progress."

"I don't know how to thank you," I said, giving her a very tight and extremely unprofessional hug. She hugged me back.

"No need to thank me. You just take care of yourself and make sure you take care of him as well."

"I sure will." With that she left. A half hour later, Keith opened his eyes. He squinted as he tried to adjust to the light. I waited for him to look around and take in his new surroundings. I waited for him to focus on my face. I waited for that radiant smile I thought

I'd never see again. I waited to hear what was on his heart, because I already knew what was on mine.

"Hello, Beautiful," he said, in a low, raspy voice. He reached up and cupped my cheek in his hand. "I had a dream that I lost you." There were tears in his eyes.

"Hey, Handsome," I said, my own tears falling shamelessly. "I almost lost you for real."

"Never that, baby. I told you, Mimi, I'm not going anywhere and I mean it. As soon as they let me out of here, I'm going to prove it to you once and for all."

"Oh, really," I said with a smile, my mind automatically jumping to sex. "And how are you going to do that?"

"By doing what I should've done day one and marrying your sexy ass. That's if you'll have me. Will you have me, baby?"

I was speechless. Was he asking me what I thought he was asking me? "I thought I already have you," I said in a barely audible whisper.

"You do, but I want to make it official." He grabbed my hand and looked deeply into my eyes. "Mimi, will you marry me?"

"Yes, Keith! Yes, I will marry you," I screamed as tears sprouted from my eyes once again.

I leaned down and kissed my future husband as if this would be the last kiss we'd ever share. We kissed like he was dicking me down right there in ICU—giving me the best he had and more. His kiss made my toes curl and my center moist. My body shivered in anticipation of release.

What started as me catching feelings for a younger man, turned into this old dog being taught a new trick, and remembering love is not a dirty word. In fact, being in love with Keith saved both of our lives, and I planned on spending the rest of my life thanking him in my own special way.

"Keith, you better believe I'm not going anywhere, either. I love you so much."

"I love you, too," he said, kissing my hand.

"I'm yours forever, baby."

"Forever ever," he joked.

"Forever ever… Ever, ever," I confirmed, kissing him passionately once again.

Michelle Cuttino is the "Queen of Plus-Size Fiction," and serves as a body positive advocate, talk radio host, and motivational speaker. She is President of Big Body Publishing and Big Body Broadcasting. She is a columnist for four publications, and a plus-size lifestyle and publishing industry blogger. Cuttino is the author of Love & Happiness, Love Is Blind, *and* Me & Mrs. Jones, *an eBook series adaptation of her screenplay once optioned with Queen Latifah's Flavor Unit Films. Read more at MichelleCuttino.com.*

Let's Connect!
Facebook.com/MichelleCuttino
Twitter.com/MichelleCuttino
Instagram.com/BigBodyPub
Pinterest.com/BigBodyPub
Email: michelle@bigbodypublishing.com

CHECKMATE:
A Cougar's Tale

SHAKIR RASHAAN

Hello, my name is Nicole Berkeley, pleased to meet you.

I'm really feeling your flow and I think we can work something out, if you can play your position.

Yes, I'm married, but you don't have to worry about him. I've got that on lock.

If you can play by the rules, you might get what you want, too. I like to take very good care of my toys.

All I have are three rules:

Treat me like a lady if we happen to be out and about.

Fuck my brains out when I call you to come through.

Keep your fucking mouth shut.

If you can do all of this, you might be a part of my D.O.C.: Dicks On Call.

"Excuse me, would you come join us for a moment?"

That question came from the mouth of Calvin Berkeley, one of the partners of George, Harman & Berkeley, one of the largest Black real estate investment firms in Atlanta and the U.S.

He was also my husband.

We have been married for twenty years now, and he popped the question almost as soon as we walked across the stage with our degrees in hand. He was my heart and soul, although I had my moments where I did enjoy my outside pieces of candy. He was the one who silently invested in the nonprofit foundation that I ran with my right-hand woman, Isabella, who was helping me run the event that we were hosting tonight.

Isabella kept all of my secrets, and I usually rewarded her with perks that were not always of monetary value, even though I paid her extremely well. Truth be told, she was another piece of candy on the other side of the fence that I enjoyed on occasion.

He called over one of the interns at the firm—his name was Shawn—to join us at the table for a cocktail before Calvin delivered tonight's keynote address.

As he made his way over, I sat in my chair, stunned for a few moments. Our eyes connected, and to be honest, I was speechless. This young man—he couldn't have been older than twenty-three— was absolutely breathtaking!

The tuxedo he wore gave him a very debonair flavor, but I could tell by the way he moved that he had a ruffneck swagger about him, too. If I was a little younger—and I wasn't married—I would find out what other flavors he tasted like and keep him for myself.

Wait a minute…I didn't have to worry about all that. Since he's going to be dining with us tonight anyway, I was already scheming on how I would find out what he tasted like.

Shawn took a quick glance at me, and I swore I saw him wink at me before he turned his attention to Calvin. He sat down next to Isabella, and I knew he was sexy because she began to blush profusely like a damn teenager, even though she was in her early thirties. "Yes, sir, Mr. Berkeley, how can I be of assistance?"

"You see, that's what I like, a man that is ready and able to assist with whatever is required." Calvin smiled as he commented to an executive who happened to be sitting with us. "As a matter of fact, there is something that you can assist me with. If you would do me a favor and sit with my lovely wife and keep her company for a bit, I have something to attend to before I give my speech."

I rolled my eyes in my husband's direction. He knew damn well that I didn't need anyone to keep me company. His ulterior motive was to keep me away from the other gentlemen who couldn't stop glancing in my direction the entire evening. If he thought using one of his interns to ward off the stampede looking to fill my dance card, he had another thing coming.

Not that it mattered all that much, especially considering the way my husband and I flowed.

I believe this was where I might need to explain a few things, if you don't mind indulging me?

I would guess I need to explain a few things. For starters, my husband and I were swingers.

Yeah, yeah, don't get too bent out of shape, okay? And contrary to what you might have heard, it actually was my idea.

Yes, you can pick your jaw up off the floor now. It. Was. My. Idea.

We actually started experimenting back in college when we first got together. You know the "key" parties from the late seventies? Well, it was the same concept, but it was within the same dorm instead of houses.

You say you don't know what a key party is? Well, let me quickly explain:

Key parties are when you put your house keys with a tag on them identifying you into a bowl. When you find the person that you want to be intimate with, you tell them what the word is on the key that belongs to your place and you go home together to take care of business.

This, of course, was back in the day when you had to be a part of a couple to get into parties like this, and if you were single, you were S.O.L., but now the singles were allowed to roll out, which was cool, at least to a degree. But I digress.

Anyway, since we're swingers, there were those times where we tended to find different men or women that we might vibe with and decide to kick it to the next level, if that person was game to go with the flow.

That's how Calvin ended up with his current secretary, and how I managed to luck up and have Isabella as my right-hand chick. They understood the rules and played their positions.

The way Shawn kept staring as he tried to reply to my husband, he was going to find out how the game was played, too.

"Yes, sir, Mr. Berkeley, if it is okay with your wife, I would be happy to keep her entertained." Shawn reached his hand over to take mine as he greeted me. "Shawn Terry, and I'm at your disposal, ma'am, if you will have me?"

Isabella poked me under the table a couple of times, which tipped me off that she wouldn't have minded to have a piece of the young-ster, too. That really piqued my curiosity; she hardly ever got this heated over a man. She's always been into me all these years to even worry about dating men on the regular.

I felt my pussy tingle when Shawn said that last little piece, but I wasn't about to be so easily influenced. *Oh, I'll have you all right, if you keep staring at me like you want to beat this pussy up.* "Sure, Shawn, since you're my date for the evening, I would like to know if you can dance."

"Yes, Mrs. Berkeley, I can dance."

"Please, you're my date, no need to be so formal. You may call me Nicole," I corrected as I gave him my hand to lead me to the dance floor. "Besides, my husband must have picked you for a reason. I'm curious to find out for myself."

Once on the floor, some of the more mellow songs began to play from the DJ booth. When we first hit the floor, the deejay played "Seduction" from Usher before changing to "I Wish" by Carl Thomas. I figured he wasn't trying to do too many songs from the present, not that I would have minded so much, but the crowd was over thirty-five, so I think he got the message.

I wasn't in the mood to really do a lot of high-energy dancing anyway, so it was a nice flow and vibe to work with. It also gave me a chance to get to know this strikingly handsome young man.

Emphasis on *young*…

"So, how long have you worked for my husband?" I began my probing to find out what the scoop was.

"I'm actually on a paid internship through the end of the summer, Mrs. Berkeley…I mean, Nicole," he replied as he remembered to call me by my first name. "I'm hoping to become a trainee so I can work my way up. I've never been one to take a handout. I like to put in work."

Mmmm, the way you're holding me while we're dancing, I can think of some work you can put in for me.

I didn't want to have the thoughts that invaded my mind, but the closeness of the dance wasn't helping at all. I felt his hand on the small of my back and I secretly wanted him to palm my ass so I could feel how strong his fingers were. I also couldn't stop noticing he was a lot taller than I am, and I'm five feet nine without heels. That made me wet; I have a weakness for tall men—especially tall Black men.

"Well, my husband must see something in you for him to place me in your care," I commented as I tried desperately to shake the lust-filled thoughts in my head. "Calvin doesn't do a lot of things without thinking them through. He plans for damn near everything."

Shawn grinned, and I noticed a sexy dimple deepen into his cheek, disappearing behind the outside of his well-kempt goatee. "Thank you, Nicole, it actually means a lot that he would trust me with his sexy wife. I hope you don't mind me commenting about you in that manner; I don't want to offend."

"You're definitely not offending me, Shawn." I couldn't help the way I felt; enjoying the attention and fawning that he lavished on me made me feel feminine, sexy. The halter dress I wore for tonight's event was meant to turn my husband's head. I even had the tailor raise the slit in the dress to show off legs that I'd spent three days a week for hours on end keeping shapely and thick.

The only problem was everyone else noticed how great I looked in this dress—except for my darling husband. At least, that's what he led me to believe. He'd been too busy trying to push the Board of Directors into a hostile takeover of a smaller firm for the past six weeks, so he'd been spending a lot more time at the office.

He was lucky we had the type of relationship we had, or I'd have divorced his workaholic ass a long time ago.

Oh, fuck, who was I kidding? He's my heart and soul, and I'll love him forever.

Still, there's only so much a woman of my sensual maturity could take, and something had to give. Placing me in the arms of a man who could realistically become a pleasurable distraction could prove to his detriment if he wasn't careful.

Out of the blue, the deejay switched up and went up-tempo, and hearing the familiar "OH!" before the drums led into the baseline for the "Wobble" song by V.I.C, gave me a chance to get loose and show this youngster what a forty-three-year-old woman could do with her body.

I rolled my hips every chance I got during the step, making sure that Shawn got a good look at my ass whenever he was behind me. I got a little slick and started grinding up on him during parts of the dance, winking and blowing kisses as the entire group began to break a sweat. This was probably one of the sexier line dances that I could remember, and I felt my body come to life, putting my sexuality on full display. I laughed as the other men in the group kept tripping over themselves trying to watch me work Shawn over, but my attention was on my dance partner tonight.

If he played his cards right, he might become a different type of partner.

I tapped Shawn on the shoulder to let him know we needed to take a break from the dance floor so I could get something to drink and cool down a bit. He immediately offered his arm for me to walk with him back to my table. Calvin was already seated and engaged in a full conversation with a couple of the other executives over something. Shawn sat me down and walked to the bar to get something for me to sip on.

"I see Shawn is making sure you have a good time, Nic," Calvin mentioned with a smile on his face. He kissed me on the cheek before moving back to his conversation. I was too busy trying to calm down to get worked up over his quick dismissal of me to get back to business.

Shawn returned with my drink in one hand and bottled water in the other, and I shared the grin he gave me with a smile of my own. "You had them dudes breaking their necks trying to watch you!"

I blushed, realizing that I had made a spectacle of myself in my attempts to keep Shawn's attention. "Well, I couldn't help it; the music was hot and so was the step."

Calvin must have overheard my last comment; he turned his attention to me quickly. "I didn't think you were going to dance tonight or I would have joined you out there, babe."

Really, is that why you were still sitting here while I was shaking my ample ass on the dance floor with your stand-in?

"Oh, don't worry, honey, Shawn was more than up for the task.

I'm glad he was able to keep up with me." I winked in Shawn's direction, watching as he blushed for a moment and chuckled, giving the impression that we were in on the same joke. "He's taken good care of me tonight."

He'll be taking better care of me later tonight if I have my way…

"Well, that's good to hear, Shawn. I like a man in my company who is willing to take care of things for me," Calvin remarked, sparking his yes men to agree. Anything to keep the boss happy, I guess. "Speaking of which, I'm going to have to ask an additional favor of you, Shawn, and I'll be willing to give you the day off with pay. Would you escort my wife home? The driver will take you in the limo. I have to fly out first thing in the morning to handle the last of this takeover."

Shawn raised an eyebrow immediately, and I could tell from his facial expression that he wasn't sure how to answer that request.

"Is there a problem, Shawn?" Calvin asked again. He rubbed his chin for a moment, studying Shawn's body language. "I will make sure I take care of you on the back end if you take care of things now."

I already knew what my dearest hubby was planning. He was testing him. I should have known there was a reason he had picked Shawn, and it wasn't only for business purposes. If he passed this test, there was no telling where the limit would be to his potential, both inside the boardroom…and inside a bedroom of my choosing, among other places.

I tried to wipe the grin off my face before anyone would notice, but Isabella felt me already, playfully tapping and caressing my thigh. I turned to her to find out why she needed my attention so badly. It wasn't like we weren't together last week for some afternoon "merger" discussions.

She mouthed "checkmate" and winked at me.

Yeah, this was nothing more than a chess game.

It was only a matter of time before Shawn would become a pawn, willing to sacrifice for his Queen.

Shawn seemed to shake out of whatever thoughts were in his mind, then glanced in my direction first before turning his attention to my husband. "Mr. Berkeley, I would consider it an honor to escort your wife home, sir."

"That's a good man." Calvin extended his hand to shake with Shawn's. "Now, if you will excuse me, I have a speech to present."

"Rick, take the scenic route home, please?"

"Yes, Mrs. Berkeley."

I settled into the plush leather seating as the Escalade limo pulled away from the building feeling tipsy…and horny.

I'd usually left events in the same manner, only to ride home in the limousine alone, with only my driver, Rick, for conversation to try to take my mind off of my wanton state. One time last year after a benefit event, I was so far gone that I masturbated the entire ride home. I didn't care that he enjoyed the show, either. If I was really bold that night and he could have kept his mouth shut, I would have fucked him in the limo the moment we got to the estate. I even gave him a two-hundred-dollar tip to shut him up, with the unspoken request that he not say a word about what he saw or he wouldn't drive for the firm again.

The second time I showed off for Rick was after a theater event a few months later. He never batted an eyelash, and he kept cool and never let anyone know what I was doing, even though this time around, we rode in an executive Town Car. He got an up-close and personal view that night, and I even invited him during stop-lights to finger-fuck my pussy and taste my juices on his fingers. I almost fucked him once, but fate intervened when Isabella rode home one night, and I wasn't feeling the threesome action that particular night.

Needless to say, he became my regular driver from then on, almost a pseudo-boyfriend of sorts…*almost*. Wherever I went, he made sure he drove me. My guess was he wanted to finally get lucky and fuck me, too. The problem with that plan of his was the fact that he really never opened his mouth to say if he wanted to or not. I mean, if I wanted it, I'd make sure I asked for it.

That's probably why he didn't say much when I got in the SUV with Shawn. Rick knew me well enough over the past year and a half to understand what was about to happen, but I think he was taken aback by the extra passenger in the car. I think he was hoping to have our usual interlude, especially when it had been a few months since the last one. He was even more perturbed when I asked him to roll up the partition to give Shawn and me some privacy, but I didn't care. Tonight, as with any other night that he drove me, it was all about me and what I wanted.

And tonight, I wanted Shawn…and I was going to have him, without an audience.

With all the room in this limo—it was an eighteen-passenger SUV—he could easily put me in as many positions as humanly possible before we ever got home so he could put me in even more positions within the confines of my abode.

I noticed Shawn enjoying the surroundings of the interior. It was not hard to figure out that he had not been in a limo probably since his high school prom. His body language gave me the impression that he seemed a bit overwhelmed, but it was difficult to tell because his demeanor reflected someone who was comfortable in the boardroom and on the street.

There was only one way to find out for sure.

"Did you enjoy yourself?" I turned toward him, showing off my chest. I watched his eyes subconsciously move to appreciate their fullness. A slick smile spread across my face while he focused on them, imagining his wheels turning as he tried to figure out what I was up to. He finally shook out of the trance he seemed to be in and met my eyes again. "I was half-expecting to be in a lot of boring conversations or being a gofer or something."

I stroked the inside of his thigh, narrowing my eyes to reflect the seductive nature rising inside of me as I remained persistent in eye-fucking him from head to toe. "There's nothing wrong with being a gofer, Shawn. Sometimes you have to put in some work to get where you want in life, and you already admitted that you didn't mind putting in a little...*work*."

I slid closer to him, entranced by the intoxicating mix of the cologne on his skin and the slight hint of cognac on his breath. I inhaled deeply, closing my eyes to imagine what it might feel like to have that scent on my skin. My hands slowly caressed the lining of my top, teasingly tugging at the fabric as my nipples began to engorge and make their presence known.

"Nicole, are you okay?"

I was held captive in my own lustful daydream with the leading man in that erotic feature a mere inches away from me. I opened my eyes for a moment, trying to shake the sensual aura that encompassed my body, but it was too late.

I leaned forward and kissed him, my tongue mixing feverishly with his. He hesitated at first, but he adjusted quickly, moving his hands across my breasts before moving to my legs. I opened them slightly so he could feel the heat rising between them, but he went further and softly groaned between kisses when he realized that I had gone commando for the evening.

Almost like he'd been shocked by a stun gun, he pulled away

from me suddenly, moving away from me to the other side of the limo. He tried to make sense of what happened a moment ago, but his eyes betrayed him. I saw the hunger he wanted to sate, so I adjusted my body, pulling my dress above my hips to show him the object of his ravenous desires.

I spread my legs wide, resting my right leg against the headrest, grinding and rotating my hips as I studied his facial expressions. He didn't know if he should do what his body told him to do or if his mind would win out and tell me to cover myself. I reached out to him and grabbed his hand, but he slowly pulled away, wanting to break the connection, but not wanting to break the connection.

I had him where I wanted him. All he had to do was say yes. I took my fingers and slowly inserted two of them between my folds, spreading them apart to show him what he'd done to me all night. "I know you find me sexy, Shawn. I felt it on you while we danced. If you want it, you can get it."

"But your husband—"

"My husband hasn't fucked me in a month, Shawn," I confessed as a few small tears welled up in my eyes. I quickly brushed them away, but I wasn't ashamed of what I was doing. If anything, the tears were out of frustration; I was so close to getting some dick that it began to show in the tears that threatened to streak down my face. "As far as I'm concerned, my husband did me a favor by having you escort me home. If I had my way, you'd have been fucking me in the limo on the way home now instead of talking about it."

I was taking a risk, especially when he wasn't exactly "in the know" about how my marriage actually worked, but from the way he looked at me, the sexy way he winked at me at the table before taking me out on the floor, the way he held me as we danced, the way he grinded against my ass at times when the tempo picked up, I couldn't have been reading his signals wrong, could I?

"I…Nicole, I don't want to break up a marriage. Yes, I'm feeling you—my God, I'm feeling you—but I work for your husband. What if he finds out?"

"You want me, Shawn. I'm giving myself to you, so take it." I cut him off. I no longer cared about anything anymore except getting my body handled. "You're not breaking anything since my husband and I are unlike any couple you've ever met; I promise you that. If you don't want me, I'll get out of the limo when we get to my home and you can have the driver take you home. If you do want me, and I can see from the bulge in your pants that you do want me, you can have me, even if it's only for tonight. The choice is yours."

The gauntlet had been thrown down.

I studied his face as we sat in silence for a few moments. I didn't know what to think, but I didn't want to sit exposed like this forever, so I began to slide my dress over my hips and cover up so I wouldn't look so unkempt when I got out of the SUV. To my surprise, Shawn got out of the limo with me and escorted me to the door.

Walking to the front door was the hardest thing to do. The anticipation nearly overwhelmed me. I didn't know why I felt so nervous; I *really* wanted him. His hesitation in answering my question probably had a lot to do with my nerves, but there was nothing I could do about that until he actually said or did something to give me a clue.

I turned and watched Rick scowling at me, pissed off as he noticed that Shawn was at the front door. Nearly two years as my driver, and he'd never made it that far.

Whatever! I didn't read minds. If you wanted to be a part of my D.O.C. Detail, you either asked or you *get* asked.

I wasn't about to worry about his hurt feelings. Drivers were a dime a dozen, even ones that you'd done some sexy shit with. If he acted up again, I'd have to cancel him and get another.

We finally got in the foyer, and the moment I closed the door, Shawn was on me quickly. His leg spread mine and I worried that I would soak his pant leg if I wasn't careful. He kissed me like his life depended on the reaction he got from it. I wasn't about to give him that satisfaction. Not to sound conceited or anything, but I'd never had to work this hard to get a man to capitulate to my desires.

Despite his hesitation, I got my answer.

"If you want, the guest bedroom is right around the corner," I coolly mentioned after we broke from the kiss.

His incredulous expression silently told me he wouldn't be denied now that his mind was made up. "I'm not exactly interested in the guest bedroom unless I'm fucking you in the guest bedroom, Nic."

"You're so aggressive, sexy, what happened to worrying about my husband?"

"The worry went out the door the minute you showed me that pretty pussy."

He got me wetter by the second with his growing confidence, and I couldn't resist his charms because I'd made up my mind hours ago that I would fuck him. At the same time, I didn't want him to think I was *that* easy.

I tried to walk past him to give the impression that he was gonna have to put in the work that he said he had to do to do what was necessary. And he was going to put in *work*. The way I felt? He might not be able to walk right in the morning because I planned on draining him.

Shawn stopped me cold. "You're not getting away that easily, gorgeous. I'm about to handle that…right now."

Fuck, this was exactly what I needed.

I tightened my legs around Shawn's waist as he slowly forced his long, thick shaft deep inside my essence. I was so high from the wine and Appletinis I'd had all night that I didn't feel him pick me up off the ground and pin me against the wall. He had my legs draped over his shoulders and my ass was cupped in his firm, strong grasp. I couldn't do anything but hold on and take every inch he had to give me. His sheer strength in holding me in that position while he mercilessly stroked me into oblivion was enough to keep me flowing like Victoria Falls.

It wasn't like I was a petite woman or anything. I was a healthy size ten with curves that even a Ferrari couldn't handle properly, so anytime a man could treat me like a rag doll, it was hard not to notice. And the way he continued to beat my pussy up, there was no way in hell I was about to complain about my being too heavy or him getting tired of holding me.

His breathing roughened as he kissed me as deeply as he was inside my pussy, his tongue taking control of mine without trepidation. It was all I could do to keep from passing out from the continuous onslaught that seemed endless from him.

"Fuck, take it, baby!" I screamed, needing this release so desperately. My body hadn't felt so alive in months, and Shawn continued to drive into me with such a fury, I wondered if he was trying to release some of his own tension. "Don't stop! It's so fucking good!"

Shawn growled in my ear, unable to form a coherent thought. He picked up the pace as I grabbed at his shoulders to keep him inside me. My legs began to shake and it was only a matter of time before my body would turn on me and make me sing in octaves that could shatter glass if I wanted to.

"Shawn! I'm…fuck…coming! Shit!" I wrapped my arms around his neck and screamed out, hearing my pleas bouncing off the walls in the foyer and fall on the deaf ears of my newest potential stallion. If the neighbors lived closer together, they would definitely know his name by now, the way I shouted it.

"Nic…shiiiiiit!" he yelled as he pulled out of me, nearly collapsing with me in his arms. He let me down from my spot on the wall and grabbed for the opposite wall to steady his balance. I watched his manhood pulsing, calling for me in its own language to put it out of its orgasmic misery and grant its release.

I didn't have to be asked twice.

I dropped to my knees, pulling the condom off his dick, jacking him off and sucking the head, silently urging him to explode. "Come on, baby, give it to me. Get it off!"

"NIC!!!!!!!!!!" he growled as my hands and tongue brought him over the edge.

"AHHHHHHHHHHH SHIT!!!!"

I took him in my mouth and felt the familiar salty cream slide down my throat. I felt his trembling hand grab at my shoulder to keep his balance, but it was futile as he slowly slid down the wall, collapsing into a heap on the floor.

I kissed him softly, caressing his face for a few moments as he tried to shake out of his impending exhaustion. He looked into my eyes and smiled sleepily, struggling to get to his feet.

"I guess it is a good thing I was given the day off tomorrow." Shawn chuckled as we headed up the stairs to the bedrooms. "I might need some time to recover."

"So, how was he?"

I looked at Rick the next morning like he had lost his mind. He had the nerve to look pissed off that Shawn was allowed to spend the night. He was completely closed up, a slight scowl on his face, and the normal flirting that we did before I got in the limo was reduced to nothing more than curt phrases. I realized he had gotten comfortable with our "relationship," but if he thought he could pull rank or something, he had another thing coming.

He even had the nerve to try and flex in front of Shawn like he had clout or something.

"How was who?" I asked in mock anger. "If you mean the gentleman that my husband *asked* to escort me home, he was fine sleeping in the other bedroom."

"Bedroom, right." There was no turning back in that moment. He seethed as he looked in Shawn's direction, giving the idea that he wanted to challenge him.

"Is there a problem, Rick?"

"No problem at all, *Mrs.* Berkeley."

"Good, now if you would be so kind as to take Shawn home, I would appreciate it."

"Yes, I'll make sure he gets home," he mumbled under his breath.

As I watched Shawn pull off in the executive car, I had to wonder what in the hell had gotten into Rick to be checking me like I'd made some sort of twisted vow to him. Hell, I wasn't wavering in my commitment to my legal husband, so I wasn't about to lose sleep over a man losing his mind over some pussy that he's only tasted off his fingers from time to time. I was damn near gonna give him a piece just to see if he could handle it, but I saw that he didn't take too kindly to competition for my attention.

Jealousy did not work in my world, and it certainly did not work to be a part of my detail.

That was okay with me, though; I was getting a little bored with him anyway. The conversation wasn't stimulating me anymore. I made a mental note in my head to try a different driver for a benefit a couple of nights from now. I guess it was my own fault, though. I shouldn't have let Rick get attached like that, but he was willing to keep things between us, so in a sense I got comfortable with him just as easily.

I walked back inside the house and made my way to the shower to wash the sin off my body. Not that I really wanted to, of course, but I wanted to feel cleansed before my mid-morning nap.

From the moment the water hit my skin, my mind instantly shifted back to Shawn and last night. I imagined the water was his hands caressing every part of my body, making me feel lustful, sexy, willing to do whatever he wanted to do. I was so tempted to take the attachment and turn on the stronger jets to get myself off, but I wanted to handle that once I lay on the bed to moisturize my skin. Besides, it wasn't like the shower didn't get its share of fun, either.

After we headed upstairs, I suggested that he take a shower before heading to bed, and I would do the same. After all, we did put in some serious work downstairs and sweated out the clothes we wore. It was such a spontaneous moment and such a turn-on that I felt like I needed to get myself off again.

I disrobed while the water warmed up in the shower, and before I opened the door, Shawn popped up out of the blue, buck naked and hard as a rock all over again.

Thank goodness I had to wash my hair that night anyway. He took me doggy-style before I had a chance to protest or say a word of anything. I had to use my hands against the wall of the shower to brace myself as he pounded into my pussy like a fucking jackhammer, growling like a beast in heat, almost gaining strength from hearing my unbridled screams as the water cascaded unmercifully down our bodies.

My pussy tingled at the thought as my hand made its way down to my sore and swollen folds, softly massaging them as I finished lathering my body. *God, that boy was so damn good*, I whispered to no one as I stepped out of the shower and grabbed my towel.

I moved to my wonderfully large, California King-sized bed with cocoa butter lotion in hand and began my pampering routine. I always loved my bed. I picked it out personally because of its dark-brown lacquered oak pilasters that held the canopy top in place no matter how rough the sex got on the mattress. I had a thing for snakes, so the serpentine design that slinked its way down each post got me wet every time I touched them. Of course, the plushness of the mattress was to die for, and came in handy when I wanted to go the distance and not worry about my knees taking too much damage.

There weren't too many women who admitted to their love of masturbation, especially when they got some on the regular. Don't get me wrong; I fucked my husband like a porn star—when he's home long enough for me to fuck him, of course—but that really had nothing to do with it. Sometimes a woman had to get in touch with herself and really *feel* what turned her on so she could tell her lover or lovers exactly what got her off. Even when I put it down on him or he worked me like a part-time job, I still found myself quickly slipping my fingers between my thighs once he went to the bathroom to shower.

Once in bed, I tried my best to make sure every inch of my body was silky smooth, but my mind continued to replay the images, and my body responded quickly. I fingered and pinched my fully engorged nipples, so sensitive that if anyone spent any amount of time sucking and nibbling I would certainly explode.

I tugged lightly at my right nipple, feeling it stiffen between my fingertips and thumb as I rolled and tweaked. My other hand moved down to my still-swollen labia, my fingers finding my clit immediately. I smirked as my clit responded to the thoughts of taking Shawn's thick, sweet juices down my throat. I wanted something in my mouth badly, but once I felt my juices slide down into the crack of my ass, and there was no turning back.

Then I remembered my B.O.B.

Actually, "he" wasn't battery operated, per se.

"He" was my Hitachi Wand. When I needed to really have a mind-blowing climax, "he" *never* let me down!

I picked it up and turned it on. I swore my entire arm began to tremble with the intense vibration. Instantly, I grinned; this was what I needed to make me explode! Nestling "him" between my thighs, the vibration shook me immediately. I didn't care if it actually touched my clit; I couldn't wait for the familiar buzz to take me over the edge. "He" really began to take hold of my pleasure, resting just beneath my clit and ever so snugly against my slick, wet slit.

I didn't bother to stifle my screams as "he" began to put in some real work. My head jerked back against my pillow with each jolt through my clit. My back arched uncontrollably and for a moment, I thought I might pass out from the intensity surging through my body. I fought every urge to close my legs around "him" and ride the express to orgasmic bliss while simultaneously trying to keep from pushing "him" away from me. The pleasure threatened to make me see stars. Oh my God, it felt so fucking good!

Never before had I felt my clit rise from its hood so quickly. Both of my hands were holding, trying to keep control of "him" as best they could. I rolled my hips and moaned loudly as "he" pressed deliciously between my clit and my misty, slippery opening. Before long, my mind replaced "him" with Shawn, which only intensified the pleasure I felt coursing through me.

Fuck me, baby; come on, that's it, harder, baby! I continued to shout at Shawn, knowing full well he was at home relaxing from the workout we went through last night. *Damn, that's my spot; get it, baby!*

The waves began to crest and I was ready for the mind-blowing crash as I held "him" in place for what seemed like an eternity. My hips undulated, desperately trying to catch the wave at the right moment so I could scream to the heavens that I was *there* and there was not a force on this planet that could stop the deluge.

I was near the point of no return…I was ready to welcome the thousand little deaths with open arms and legs, when I heard an unexpected voice slam through the clouds and thunder with the force of a sledgehammer.

"If I'd known I would come home to this, I would have come home sooner."

"I thought you were out of town?"

My husband stood at the foot of our bed with this slick smile on his face. His eyes locked with mine as I struggled to cover up like I was a teenager who had been caught by her father when she thought she was alone in the house. He was the last person I expected to walk in unannounced, especially when I thought he was gone first thing this morning.

"I canceled the flight and handled the merger by video conference," Calvin replied, looking somewhat disappointed that I wasn't exactly happy to see him.

I was in the middle of the mother of all orgasms, only to be rudely and abruptly interrupted out of the blue and caught by surprise. I didn't know any woman that would be *happy* after that.

I noticed the dejected look on his face and tried my best to recover a little bit by showing myself off and hoping he would get the hint. "Come here, honey, don't you want a taste while it's nice and slick and smooth for you?"

The answer to that question came in watching him wink at me before walking into the bathroom to shower.

Really?

"So, you're just going to turn it down like you can get it anytime you want!?!?!" I angrily shouted into the bathroom after him. Normally, it wouldn't have bothered me, especially when I just got fucked so well by Shawn last night, but I was honestly feeling greedy and it had been a few weeks since the last time we were intimate, much less had sex. "What's so important that you don't have time to handle your wife?!?!"

"Honestly, I wanted some of you, Nic." He turned in my direction, offering up a defeatist smile. "But you kinda ruined the mood when you looked at me as if I'd just taken away your best friend."

I wanted to crawl back under the covers and hope for a do-over. *Damn. Smooth move, Nic.*

"Come on, Daddy, please? I haven't had that good dick in so long." I tried to sound like I really needed to have him, which wasn't a complete lie. It looked like it had started to work when his cell phone rang. *Fuck.*

He walked to where he'd left his phone on the bed, ignoring the look on my face, imploring him to ignore it. "What time do they want to meet? Okay, tell them I'll be on video conference in fifteen minutes."

As he hurriedly turned on the shower, I tried again to persuade him, doing my best to not sound needy as hell, but I knew I was going to fail miserably. I needed him to balance me. "Can I suck him while you're in the video conference like we used to? I promise I'll only suck you deep when you're not talking."

The look on his face was priceless as he stopped in his tracks to consider my proposal. He was mine for the taking, even if it was a 68-and-I'll-owe-you-one-later.

I walked to him prepared to suck him so deep he would forgo the shower and fuck me instead…when the funniest thing happened.

My cell phone started ringing.

Dammit!

Only one person would have had the nerve or the guts to call my cell phone when I wasn't at the foundation, and that was Isabella.

"Yes?" I snapped as I picked up the phone.

"Mrs. Berkeley, I'm sorry to interrupt, but there's a Samantha Gibson that has been trying to reach you about a fundraiser that you committed to for later on this weekend," she calmly responded, even as she knew from my tone that I did not want to be disturbed. "She had some last-minute changes that she wanted to go through with you, and she didn't want anyone else."

"Fine, Isabella, please give her my work cell phone number, please?" I huffed, irritated that once again work would keep my husband and me from screwing each other's brains out.

About ten minutes later, Samantha Gibson was on the other side of my Bluetooth.

Sam and I go back about twenty years or so when we were in college together. We crossed together as sorors and kept up with each other ever since graduation. Her husband was a big-time art director; every so often, I would sponsor fundraisers for the gallery that he owned, which was becoming the hottest ticket in the circles we ran in. We used to do some wild shit when we were younger, though; going to swingers clubs, private parties and things like that. We never really grew out of it, sometimes doing some same-room activities of a lewd and lascivious nature, one as recently as a couple of weeks ago, if you get my drift?

But that was then, this was now, and we were supposed to be up-standing pillars of high society and such. You know, the ones that everyone was supposed to look up to?

Yeah, right.

The truth of the matter was I kept Samantha close so I could keep up with what she was doing. She was always up to some-thing, and when she found out about my wanton proclivities, she wanted in on the action, sort of a "sisters in sin" type of situation. I knew better; she always wanted what I had, and that included my husband, despite the high-powered one that she was married to.

Friends close, enemies closer…

As far as my association with Samantha Gibson was concerned, she was a frenemy until the bitter end.

"What's up, girl; I wanted to run these changes by you for the gallery's exhibition on Saturday," Samantha chimed over the earpiece. "I sent the guest list to you by email just now, and I wanted to make sure that all was on the level."

I looked at the list, and there was nothing that would make me do a double-take, so to speak. I had a suspicion that I was about to be set up for something, but I wasn't sure what it was. Sam didn't have to call me about this mess.

"Okay, Sam, what's the call really about?" I cut in while she tried to monologue. "You could have sent this and kept it moving."

There was a quick pause before Sam went into gossip mode. "Okay, Nic, I could never put one over on you. Word on the street has it that you were escorted home by a fine piece of meat last night and he didn't leave until earlier this morning."

It wasn't hard to figure out whose "word" got on the street. Rick ran his mouth to the boys at the limo service. Traitor. I made a mental note to have him replaced as my driver as soon as I hung up the phone.

"Well, if you must know, Calvin had one of his interns escort me home, and he slept in one of the spare bedrooms downstairs," I lied through my teeth. I was damn good at it, especially considering the past sidepieces I'd had over the past ten years. "And don't bullshit me, Sam. I already know who put the word out there. He's a little pissed that he thinks that I fucked him last night."

"Well, did you?" Samantha continued to press me. "I know I would have had him saddled up and ready to ride, based on the description alone!"

"Yeah, like I'm going to tell you if I did or didn't, so you can try to rope him in, too?" I seethed. "I thought you were comfy with that new artist that your husband put on the fast track to superstardom for the past few months."

"Chile, please, you know how it is with artists," Samantha scoffed. "I got bored with him within a month because he can't fuck worth a shit. All that body and he had no idea how to work it. Sad."

I giggled to myself; I remembered having some of those over the years. "One-and-dones," I called them.

I continued my explanation of what had happened to keep her at bay. "Anyway, he was a gentleman, and I had my former driver take him home after he tried to check me like he was Calvin. He must have found out and decided it would be fun to burn me. He doesn't know who he's fucking with. I'll have him blacklisted before the weekend gets good."

"Former driver? Damn, remind me not to ever get on your bad side."

"Well, when you stop trying to figure out my movements, you won't have to worry about getting on my bad side, Sam."

"Whatever, trick, we've been doing dirt for too long for you to start making threats."

She had a point, and I knew it. We kept each other's secrets buried deep. I would probably regret it one day, but I wasn't about to worry about that now. Although I never signed a pre-nup because we were broke as fuck before Calvin began to build his empire, there was no need to. But that didn't mean that I didn't have a lot to lose if she decided she wanted to reveal a couple of indiscretions that he didn't know about. We may be swingers, but that doesn't mean the ability to cheat wasn't possible.

If Samantha tried to burn me, she'd compromise herself in the process; we had a propensity to share the same men from time to time, and that included some of the ones I kept buried in the closet.

Look, I never said I was a saint, okay?

She couldn't afford to divorce her husband any more than I could afford to divorce mine. The only difference between us was her husband made his millions before she married him, so she had a pre-nup hanging over her head.

That didn't stop either of us from stacking the stable.

"Okay, so I fucked him. Happy?"

"Yes, bitch, I'm happy; I had been dying to tell you about the piece I had last night, too. I wasn't about to be the only whore in the city."

As I listened to her yap about the newest artist that she seemed to always have a weakness for fucking, I waltzed into my husband's office while he was in the midst of his video conference, dropped to my knees and crawled under the desk while no one noticed I had entered the room, and began to give him a more satisfying oral presentation than the one that he was listening to. He tried his best to push me off without giving me away to the other folks on the feed, but I wasn't about to be denied. I got what I wanted, and I wanted his beautiful dick in my mouth until his video conference was over.

"Sam, I'm gonna have to call you back. I forgot about this oral presentation and potential merger that I needed to take care of. I'll see you on Saturday, okay?" I whispered low enough for her to hear me and hung up before she could respond. I had more interesting matters to take into my hands.

Oh my God, I loved the way he smelled when he was freshly showered. The freshness of the body wash on his skin stirred my already awakened senses. I wished I could explain how much satisfaction I get out of sucking dick, especially my husband's dick, but the reason was his reaction to me doing it turned me on so much, my pussy began to ache at the thought of it.

I ran my tongue down the length of his hardness and took it into my mouth as he continued his video conference, trying desperately to keep from alerting anyone to my presence. I sucked it as it swelled in my mouth, pressing the head against the back of my throat. I knew it excited him to have this naughty, nasty action going on under his desk as he tried his best to keep his wits about him, but it wasn't about him anymore. I did not appreciate being dismissed when I was upstairs and I wanted to be greedy with my husband after almost having the most intense orgasm. My plan was to take my dick the moment the meeting was over, getting my back blown out if I got what I wanted.

I was gonna get what I wanted, whether he wanted me to have it or not.

I struggled to take a deep breath around the thickness in my throat and swallowed hard. I loved the way it filled my throat. I felt my juices flowing down my thighs as I tasted the salty warmth of his pre-cum on my tongue, and I knew it would only be a matter of time before his pending eruption would welcome my waiting mouth.

"Meeting is adjourned, ladies and gentlemen; I will see you later in the week," I heard him say as I heard the monitor turn off and a low growl escape from his mouth.

Yeah, now the real fun could begin!

My inner slut showed herself as I felt his palms find the back of my head as I hungrily suckled my husband. He slid from under the desk and stood up, watching in amazement as I never let go of his dick nor did I stop sucking him. He was going to bend to my will this time. I took his hands out of my hair, subtly letting him know that he wasn't in control right now and I would let him know when he could take over. His grunts became more intense as he tried to take my hair in his hands again, but I slapped them away each time, never once slowing my strokes.

I grabbed the base of his shaft with my left hand, cupped his balls with my right hand, and lavished them with my tongue as I stroked his dick. I nearly went crazy when he managed to grab a fistful of my hair and tore my ravenous mouth from his balls and forced it back onto his head. I knew then he planned to give me what I wanted, and I wanted his eruption, all of it. Realizing that we were alone and no one could hear either of us, I pulled back defiantly and spat on it. He pulled my hair back and exposed my face so he could slap my cheek with it. Damn, he was so nasty, and the smile on my face and the hunger in my eyes only encouraged him further. It made a delicious sound as I kept my mouth open, waiting for him to force it back in before I could catch my breath, burying it again deep down my throat.

His movements became much more deliberate now that he wasn't constrained from the meeting any longer, and the pace quickened. His grip on my hair tightened as he pressed my face into his groin and I felt his dick pulsating on my tongue. He groaned and threw his head back in a grimace as he exploded down my throat. Tears came to my eyes as I gulped and gasped for air at the same time. He released my hair and I fell forward into a steady suckle as I drained every drop he had to give. I heard him sigh and felt his body relax in the chair. I finally withdrew my mouth and licked the length of his spent member again. I grinned up at his spent expression as I relished my victory.

That's what he got for trying to keep my prized possession from me.

He looked down at me once he gathered his strength, staring into my eyes, piercing my soul the way he used to when we first dated so long ago, and I swear I fell for him all over again. I might be a cougar, and I had my pick of the litter from time to time, but there was only one man on this planet that could tame me, and he was that man. Moments like this reminded me that he could take what was his anytime he chose.

"Yeah…I definitely…need to come home like that…more often."

"You better, you never know what you may come home to, baby."
I smiled. "Want some more?"

"Give me twenty minutes."

"Good evening, Mrs. Berkeley, my name is Jalil."

My new driver for Saturday night's art exhibit at the Gibson Gallery was a different kind of flavor, and that was a good thing.

He was tall and thick, like "brick wall" thick, and if I didn't know any better, he could easily double as my bodyguard if the occasion called for it. When he held out his massive hand to help me into the car and never once tried to sneak a peek at legs that were on display in the dress I wore for tonight's festivities, I was taken from then on. Southern gentlemen were a rare breed these days, especially among the brothas, so to have this young man go through all of the extras that only a lady would notice was a breath of fresh air.

It made me realize just how much different he and Rick truly were, and it was only his first night.

It also made me wet…really wet.

"Hello, Jalil, nice to meet you." I smiled as his hazel eyes met mine. I knew I was in trouble; his stare was intense. "What happened to Rick? He was my regular driver."

Jalil gave a hunch of his shoulders. "He was told his services were no longer required; that's all I know, Mrs. Berkeley. He also recommended that I be your replacement driver because I knew how to keep things secret."

I smiled; I already knew what had happened to Rick. I simply wanted to confirm that the company valued its contracts over blatant disrespect of its clientele. "Do you know the place we're heading to, Jalil?"

"Yes, ma'am, I've driven to this location before. It was during the last big opening that Mr. Gibson put on. It was crazy to say the least; I had to shove a few photographers out of the way for that particular client." He smiled as he reminisced. "She was very grateful for the assist."

The mischievous grin on his face tipped me off, so I opened up a little with the next question. "Was she grateful in the tip that she gave you, or was it something more than a tip that she gave you?"

Jalil glanced through the mirror and saw the grin on my face and instantly he knew what the deal was. He tried to suppress the wider grin that threatened to spread across his thick, kissable lips. "A gentleman is never supposed to tell, Mrs. Berkeley, but I imagine that my body language gave me away."

"How old are you, Jalil?"

"Thirty, Mrs. Berkeley."

"Please, now that things are out in the open, you can call me Nicole when it's the two of us, Jalil."

"Umm, well, thank you, Nicole, I didn't expect that, but only if you're okay with me being so familiar like that. I love driving; it gives me the opportunity to meet interesting people."

"Not to mention the beautiful women that flirt with such a handsome and charming gentleman such as yourself?" I began to lay the groundwork and he didn't even know it.

He grinned again, trying to keep his eyes on the road, but that was a bit hard to do when I kept raising my skirt to show more of my legs. "Umm, Nicole, umm, if I didn't know any better, I would say you were trying to seduce me."

"That depends. Is it working?"

"Yes."

"Can you play your position?"

"Yes."

"Good, because if you can, you never know what opportunities it might bring you, Jalil."

"I think I might enjoy being your regular driver."

"We'll see how well you work it. If you can fuck me as well as you drive me, you'll enjoy being a lot more than being my regular driver."

"What the client wants, the client gets, Nicole." He pulled up, got out of the car and walked around to the passenger side to open the door for me. I knew it was part of the routine, but after the conversation we were engaged in, I felt the genuineness of his gesture, complete with a sexy grin and a lingering hold on his hand as he lifted me out of the vehicle. "I'll be ready when you are, Nicole, with anything you need…anything. Text me."

"Watch it. If you play your cards right, I might take you up on that offer."

I walked into the gallery, scanning the area to see if I could find Samantha or her husband. It wasn't like either of them to really not be seen, especially at an exhibition opening. I finally spotted someone, much to my pleasant surprise.

It was interesting to see him here. That was for sure. "I didn't expect to see you here tonight, Shawn."

Taking in the sight of my conquest from earlier in the week, all street and thugged out, only made me want him more. The only thing I had to do was get over my feelings as I observed the woman on his arm, grinning like she was the cat who swallowed the canary. Samantha must have thought she was pulling some sort of power move or something, but she should have known better than to try to stake a claim after I'd already laid the foundation.

"It's good to see you, too, Nic." Shawn smiled and let his eyes linger over me for a few moments, taking the grin off Samantha's face for the moment. "You look good enough to…well, excuse my

French, and I hope I don't embarrass you or your friend, but, yeah, you look absolutely lickable."

I couldn't contain the grin on my face, and the squeal was threatening to rise to the surface as I watched the color begin to leave Samantha's face. I decided to ask the question of the evening, simply on general principle. "So, how do you and Mrs. Gibson know each other, Shawn? I'm curious to know."

"Well, your husband told me that you would be here tonight." He gave away another disarming smile that had the potential to turn my body temperature up a few more degrees. "He felt since he couldn't be here tonight due to a stockholders' meeting that I should be here to accompany you on his behalf."

Samantha's face contorted. "You told my security that you were here because the new artist was a good friend of yours and he personally put you on the VIP list. Not to mention you wanted to see the sexy woman that helped put this together."

Shawn turned toward Samantha and gave her a look that should have cut through her icy stare. "Honestly, Mrs. Gibson, your security dude got you mixed up with Mrs. Berkeley. I never spoke a name, but I knew exactly who I was referring to."

She shook her arm from his like she'd been electrocuted. "I think I have some other guests to attend to," she flatly commented before walking off in a hurry. She barely heard my goodbye to her and never acknowledged with a reply.

That's what she got for trying to get like me.

I turned my attention to Shawn, who by now had slipped his way to my side and was blatantly staring at my ass. "Enjoying the view?"

"I would if I lifted that hemline a few inches."

"Oh my, someone's been in a mood all night."

"Your *friend* tried to put me in that mood. Thankfully you showed up before she tried to show me her 'private collection.'"

I laughed, lightly tapping my hand against his arm. "I think she figured out who you were and tried to make a play to take you away from me."

His eyes flashed for a moment. In the next moment, he was back to his smooth-as-silk swagger. "That would be a neat trick. Why would I want to mess things up when they're just getting heated?"

"So, you're telling me you like it heated?"

"The hotter, the better, sexy."

"Be careful what you wish for, playa."

"I'm not scared…bring it, mami."

I whipped out my cell phone the second he said it. Going into text mode, I sent the message that I wanted to convey.

Start up the limo, sexy. I feel like a little no-holds-barred action right…now.

I didn't bother waiting to go home.

I directed Jalil to drive to a condo that Calvin and I owned in a gated community so we wouldn't be disturbed. It would also be easier for him to leave the limo outside without anyone disturbing it. I made him call his dispatcher to let him know I needed him for the rest of the night and to take him off the schedule. He couldn't stop smiling; that phone call netted him about half a grand for work that didn't require driving.

I had something else in mind for him…and Shawn.

"Take off your clothes, boys, you're not gonna need them for a while," I ordered as I slipped off the dress with one slick motion. I licked my lips as I watched grins spread on both of their faces, their eyes taking in my body from head to toe.

The condo was more intimate than the house, and for obvious reasons. You don't need a lot of space when you're only going to stay overnight or less than a week at a time. Even the bedroom was more intimate than the spacious surroundings that I came home to every night. It was perfect for the sin we were about to indulge in.

I pulled Jalil to me first. He needed to be warmed up since it was his first time with me. I never gave him the option to say no when I pushed him down on the bed and slipped the condom on over his quickly rising thickness. He shuddered once I slipped down over him, and I gasped at his girth. He was bigger than I thought, but not enough to want to get off this ride early.

One time for the rodeo…

I rode Jalil reverse cowgirl as I made eye contact with Shawn. He'd already gotten hard after watching my face twitch and wince as I adjusted to Jalil. I mouthed for him to come closer as Jalil began to get comfortable and work his dick from underneath me.

I was beyond the ability to speak because Jalil was really stretching my walls, but I had enough to know Shawn was close enough for me to feel his head caressing the inside of my thigh as I rode hard. I took his shaft into my mouth, slicking it with my saliva quickly, hearing his familiar moans and growls when I was doing a good job sucking him off.

"Mmmm, damn, Nic, that's it," he repeated. He took my nipples in his fingers and began pinching them hard.

I gasped through sucking him, fighting the urge to scrape my teeth along his length. My body took over from there, jacking and sucking Shawn off while grinding my hips to fuck Jalil into oblivion.

"Shit…fuck me…damn…harder!" I tried to yell at Jalil as I took Shawn's dick out of my mouth between each command. Jalil followed suit, holding me in place as he increased the pace, working his dick like a piston in an engine and hitting my G spot each time up.

"He's gonna make you come, isn't he, baby?" Shawn looked down when he realized that I couldn't concentrate on sucking him anymore. I nodded my response, no longer trying to speak. "Give it to him, baby; let him know he's working your pussy."

I took Shawn's member from my mouth and screamed my arrival on cloud nine as Jalil continued to pound into me. A few moments later, I finally felt him shudder and grunt, a sated grin on my face knowing that he'd finally came.

I got off Jalil and immediately bent over in front of Shawn, taking his pulsing dick and sliding it inside me. I didn't want to come down from the orgasmic high I was on and my body was on fire. "Fuck me, baby, give it to me good!" I yelled as I slid the condom off Jalil and began sucking him to get him hard quickly.

I wanted him ready for what I wanted them to do next.

Shawn felt like he had been fucking me forever as he took hold of my hips and pulled me into him mercilessly. I could barely keep my balance and concentrate on getting Jalil hard again at the same time, but I was flattered by the point Shawn was trying to make. He wanted to show the new guy how to fuck me properly. My body tingled on the verge of another orgasmic release, but this time I let go completely as Shawn tried his best to fuck me into the middle of next month.

"Yes, baby, yes!" I yelled out, watching Jalil's eyes as he took in what his pseudo partner-in-sin was doing to me.

Before Shawn could come, I pulled away from him and slid back on top of Jalil. I eased down slowly to readjust to his girth again before turning around and grabbing Shawn to bring him close.

"I want you in the other hole."

"Are you sure?"

"No-holds-barred, sexy. Take it."

He didn't have to be told a second time. Shawn bent me over, close enough to kiss Jalil.

He took a moment, and I couldn't figure out what he was doing, but I soon found out. I felt warm liquid trickling over the crack of my ass. He eased in slowly, taking his time getting the head in, and I felt the painful pleasure that came with the pressure of sliding it inside of me. I started to get dizzy and I gripped the sheets in anticipation of being completely filled by both of my studs in a few moments.

"Shit...it's so fucking tight." Shawn gritted and groaned as he slid his entire length in my ass.

Jalil continued to lock eyes with me as he tried to kiss me while we were so close. I avoided his advances as I concentrated on the friction they created in both my holes. It was enough for me to scream out again, hearing the sounds reverberate against the walls.

Shawn started pumping into me first, trying to get my ass to open for him, with Jalil following soon after, finding it difficult to move the way he wanted to until they found a rhythm with me. As Shawn moved out of me, Jalil moved in, and I felt like they were attempting to churn the creamiest butter on the planet the way they moved in sync, each trying to be the first to trigger the eruption building slowly inside of me.

"Damn, boys, keep fucking me! Shit!"

Shawn pulled me up slightly, wrapping his fingers around my throat. I don't know how he lucked out and figured out that I went crazy from being slightly choked, but he got the message quick when I began to strain against his fingers and move against his dick.

I don't know what hit first, the anal climax or the vaginal, but the moment one hit me, the other one hit me just as hard. My body wouldn't stop trembling, and I began to see stars from closing my eyes so tight to brace against the force of the orgasms. Any attempts at words became unintelligible sounds that I knew neither of them would make out.

Shawn growled out first, spurting inside my ass before he pulled out and collapsed on the floor in a heap. Realizing he was no longer burdened, Jalil continued to pump inside of my pussy until I finally rolled off him to the other side of the bed because I couldn't take any more. I continued to tremble from the aftershocks as I grabbed the comforter to cover myself before the adrenaline rush wore off and the heat left my body.

Shawn crawled onto the bed beside me as Jalil slid off the bed to grab his suit and get dressed. I was too exhausted and high to figure out why he was leaving, and feeling Shawn's body close to mine was enough to safely drift into a coma-like sleep.

"Bitch, you could have stayed at the gallery opening!"

Samantha was lucky I didn't pay attention to the caller ID the next morning when she called. I was actually expecting a call from Isabella sometime this morning to handle our Sunday recap and start setting up for the next work week.

"Do you kiss your husband with that mouth, or do you keep it nasty for your boy toys?"

"I don't know if I should be pissed or jealous that you left me in the middle of that nonsense to go fuck *your* toy, Nic."

I laughed for a moment and let a moan escape my lips for good measure as Shawn was tonguing my clit while I was on the phone.

"Slut."

"And proud of it, trick, now what did you want besides to try and pick a fight?"

"Like I said, you could have stayed at the gallery opening for at least a few hours or something, damn," Samantha huffed over the earpiece. Shawn continued working the hell out of my clit with his tongue, so it was becoming a more difficult task in listening to her bitch and moan. "If it was that pressing, I would have given you the loft to do your business. I could have gotten mine, too."

"Damn…mmm, shit, baby."

"Are you fucking while you're talking to me, Nic?"

"Nope, but this man is definitely putting me in the mood to fuck his brains out. Suck on that clit, baby," I continued to encourage Shawn in an effort to get Samantha off the phone. "Can you please hurry up before he makes me come and you get an earful?"

"Damn, bitch, let me know when you're done and call me back!" Samantha yelled before the line went dead.

I looked down at the fine piece of man between my legs slurping and suckling my wetness, and I couldn't help but smile to myself. I was definitely a lucky bitch on a lot of levels, and it could only get better. I had already figured out plans for Jalil when my phone rang again.

I didn't recognize the number, so I was hesitant to answer it. Shawn felt my body tense up and tried to keep working to get me to relax, but I couldn't until I answered this call. I don't know what compelled me to do it, but I did.

"I had hoped that you would have been home by now, but I can tell from your voice that you're still a little 'busy.'"

My husband's tone was unlike anything I'd heard before. He sounded cryptic, which wasn't like him. I froze and sat up in bed, trying to get my bearings and get out of the orgasmic fog that I enjoyed.

"Calvin? What's wrong, honey? You don't sound like yourself," I asked, my concern growing with each passing second. I didn't know what to think.

"Everything is quite fine, Nic. In fact, they've not been better," he replied. He was way too calm for my comfort level. "Is my intern there with you?"

Shawn got up from where he was on the bed with a quizzical look. I shooed him away as I tried to focus on the call.

"Yes, he's here, baby; why do you ask?"

"Because I want to see him, too, since this involves him." His monotone nature had me on edge, and it wasn't the way I wanted to start off my morning.

"What's this all about, Calvin? You're beginning to scare me." I scrambled to figure out if I had done anything wrong, trying to find anything that would give him the wrong impression.

"There's a car waiting for you downstairs, baby. I should expect to see the two of you in the next hour," Calvin instructed. "There are some things that need to be brought back into focus."

"I can't say I'm not surprised."

The pensive look on my husband's face left me in a bit of a quandary.

He sat in our living room, casually in his lounger as the television played a chess tournament on one of the overseas satellite channels.

You see, my husband was an avid chess player when he was younger. He even made it to the national finals in high school. With chess players, they always think two or three steps ahead of their opponent. I always kept that in mind, even when I slipped up from time to time and had a few D.O.C.'s "off the grid," so to speak. It was part of the reason I didn't do it a lot; trying to outthink someone who loves to strategize damn near every aspect of his life can be damn near exhausting and not even worth the trouble.

That was why I found myself trying to figure out where his ice-cold demeanor came from. "What are you talking about, Calvin?"

"Out of all the ones that have been around over the years, this was the one that kept your attention the most." Calvin smirked as he switched his gaze from me to Shawn. "I sure can pick them, can't I?"

He was speaking in riddles and it was unnerving to say the least.

"You know, it confused me for the longest, especially considering he's only been around you for the past couple of weeks or so," he continued to monologue. "I saw a lot of potential in him from a business perspective, but never once did I think that he had the potential to replace me."

"Calvin, he doesn't—"

"What, he doesn't compare to me?" Calvin cut me off, shutting me down almost immediately. "Obviously he does, since you called out *his* name while you were masturbating…something you swore only my name crossed your lips when you let yourself go when no one was watching."

OH. SHIT!

He recognized the panicked expression on my face and I knew the situation was about to change drastically. His facial expression never changed, and his body language remained stoic. He had only been this way one time before, and that was when he found out about my sexual interest in women without so much as telling him. He caught me in the throes of passion with a woman who I had only meant as nothing more than a fling, but I was into my desires back then, regardless of the consequences.

Transparency…anything less than that was grounds for unspeakable retaliation. It was the one thing that was his deal-breaker. He had always told me about the women that he had interest in in the past. It wasn't something I wanted to hear back then, and I almost resented him for it, but I also knew what I consented to because I loved him—I still love him.

He wasn't perfect. He had a few slipups earlier in our marriage, also. We've survived all of that to come to this moment in time.

The way he looked at me, I knew the one rule we agreed to after we had come clean with everything back then had been broken.

I didn't tell him what Shawn represented. I never told him the reason why he had become a favorite in my stable.

Shawn reminded me of my husband.

It was an ugly truth I was not prepared to face, much less admit to the love of my life. The problem with that truth was I inadvertently screamed it out when I thought no one could hear me.

Except…he heard me. He simply never told me he had until now.

"Calvin, listen to me, we can get through this." I tried to reason with him, knowing that it might be my last conversation before lawyers are involved in something extremely messy and contentious about a week from now. "I know I slipped, but believe me when I say that he is not you, baby. You have to believe that. Look into my eyes and tell me if I'm lying."

"I know you're not lying, baby, but you crossed the line that *we* established long ago." Calvin continued his calm and collected responses. I think I would have been better off if he had blown up and thrown a tirade and broken some things or something.

However, that wasn't Calvin. He was too measured for that.

The walls between us all were so thick you would need a laser to penetrate them. Shawn never said a word during the entire exchange, which was a smart move, to say the least.

"Here's how this is going to go down," Calvin finally spoke after what felt like an eternity of deafening silence. "You two are going to continue to do what you obviously do best, starting now."

Shawn's confusion showed quickly. "Wait just a minute! You're *forcing* me to fuck your wife? What kind of sick, twisted game are you playing?"

"Oh, this is no game, Shawn, and there's nothing twisted about it. I've known you two have been fucking since that night at the benefit." Calvin shifted his focus as I saw his eyes narrow. "I didn't get to where the fuck I am to have some snot-nosed wannabe get the drop on me. Why do you think I asked *you* to take care of my wife? I don't make decisions unless I know how to control the pieces on the board, and I can—and will—control you until I see fit to no longer control you anymore."

I didn't expect this twist at all. It was the ultimate checkmate: either do what he wants or suffer the consequences.

He nodded at my acquiescing behavior, and continued speaking. "You're going to fuck my wife, and you're going to enjoy it. You're also going to take the promotion that I am going to give you first thing in the morning so that you can have the freedom to fuck my wife without worrying about the financial shackles that limited you and forced you to fuck my wife in my house without my permission."

"I didn't do shit!" Shawn protested loudly. "You can't blackmail me like this!"

"I don't think you're realizing what you've gotten yourself into, and no one held a gun to your head as long as you *thought* I didn't know or care," Calvin retorted. "The choice is yours. You can either take the promotion and the perk of fucking my wife, or you can refuse and I'll have you blacklisted to the degree in which you'll never work in the industry again. Your degree won't be worth the paper it's printed on."

"Shawn, take the offer. You enjoyed fucking me, didn't you?" I turned to him, trying to calm the wildness in his eyes. "It's only until he calms down. Trust me, he's just pissed at me, and he has every right to be. Go along with it, please?"

I didn't know what came over me at that moment, but I dropped to my knees before he could protest further and took his dick out. He was half hard, which tipped me off that he wasn't as opposed to what had happened. His mind might have been on one thing, but the way his dick got hard at my touch, his body was focused on another, and that was immediate pleasure.

He tried to act like he was not into it, even with Calvin watching the whole time. I heard Calvin call from behind me, "Fuck my wife, Shawn; you've been doing it this whole time. Show me how well you've been fucking her so I can see if the proposal I've suggested is worth it."

I leaned forward and stuck out my tongue to capture the glistening evidence of his arousal. I circled my tongue around his head, spreading the salty nectar evenly over it before closing my mouth softly over the skin and gently circled my head to get a corkscrew effect. My tongue continued to dance and swirl, provoking a low growl from him.

Looking upward into his eyes, I suddenly opened wide and slowly worked the length of his shaft into my mouth. I gagged for a brief second because I hadn't deep-throated him before, paused to regain my composure, and then bobbed back down. There was no way I was going to not take it all. I kept at it until I had his length completely engulfed and then released him. Gasping loudly, I looked over to my husband, who seemed to change his demeanor all of a sudden.

"Mmmm...I'd really like to fuck you." I maintained eye contact with Shawn as my hand slid up and down his slick shaft. I looked back at Calvin and sweetly cooed, "Can I fuck him now, Daddy?"

His eyes were fixated on what I was doing to Shawn. I saw the smile spread across his face and realized that he had gone from being pissed to being aroused beyond words. He slowly shook his head, silently encouraging me to continue sucking Shawn off.

I tugged at his balls and gripped his slippery manhood aggressively with my other hand, slowly stroking him. I held my mouth open in front of my hands, teasing him to enter. He was too far gone to worry about the acrimony that preceded this lustful interlude as I pulled hard at his balls with each tug of my hands, causing him to rhythmically lunge forward into my face. Suddenly, I leaned forward and plunged his dick back into my warm mouth. My tongue danced around his girth as I slowly and softly worked it in and out of my mouth, making the entire length easily disappear down my throat.

I changed positions, getting on all fours to continue sucking and stroking Shawn, showing my ass to my husband in a deliberate attempt to get him to fuck me. I arched my back and gyrated slowly as my mouth worked around him. I quickened my pace as I felt Shawn's hands grabbing the back of my head, letting me know he was close to coming. I continued to work him when I felt my pussy being probed by my husband's fingers.

"Damn…Daddy, get it, show him how it's done."

Shawn saw Calvin mount me from behind and watched as my body trembled from his entry into my wetness. I tried with all of my might to expedite the inevitable and get Shawn to come, but Calvin's movements, the sounds of his dick sliding in and out of me and my juices flowing with each stroke, and Shawn's fingers in my hair pulling harder were more than I could handle. I braced for the overwhelming crescendo of a violent orgasm. I loudly informed my sexy men that I was going to come, sinking Shawn's dick back in my mouth to stifle the screams that were sure to come. I shook violently and buried my face deeper into his pelvis as I felt the first wave of my climax rolling through my tightened legs. I cried out as I started to squirt.

"Fuck me, Daddy, fuck me!" I yelled after pulling Shawn from my mouth to breathe. "Shit, baby, get it!"

I heard Shawn moan again, deeply, his dick trying to take control of me. It felt like he wanted to wrest power over me away from Calvin and it added to his intensity. He suddenly lifted from me, pulling his dick from my hungry mouth, and I tried to focus again, pulling at him to come back to me. His eyes forced me to submission, hypnotizing my entire being. I wanted desperately to say something, anything to him, but my voice was taken from me, and I was breathless at the sight of him stroking his shaft, beckoning me to beg for it to plunge deep inside my walls.

I wanted him to come back to me so I could finish him, make him come for me, keep me in this blissful zone that I didn't want to leave. He finally returned to me, slipping his dick back in my mouth. I suckled him deeply, hungry for more.

I felt my legs being forced wider as Calvin pulled out, but by then, I was completely at my hubby's mercy to have him fuck me senseless. He grunted loudly as he slid back in, like a starved and cruel beast ready to gorge, pushing his dick against me, rubbing it over my pussy, getting it wet and slippery with my juices. Then I felt it pushing deep inside me, stretching my walls painfully. I looked back and saw his face, cruel and unyielding as I cried out with both pain and pleasure, grabbing my hips to push his dick deeper inside me.

Calvin was seconds away from erupting inside me as I continued to pump Shawn's dick until he growled loudly that he was there. I welcomed his spurts as he sprayed all over my face, falling to his knees as the exhaustion took over. Considering we had gotten some extra fucking in before Samantha called earlier this morning, he was definitely done for at least the next few hours.

"OHHHHHHH FUUUUUUCKKK!!!" Calvin bellowed as he came deep in my pussy. I felt every drop flow through my walls as he collapsed on top of me. He finally rolled off and moved to my side as I wiggled my ass against his slowly shrinking shaft.

"Give him the job anyway, Daddy, please? He's worth the trouble, and he'll treat me well, won't you, Shawn?" I cooed again, staring in Shawn's direction to get him to comply. "We don't need those extra provisions, do we? It won't happen again, Daddy, I promise, but he reminded me of you; you can't deny that he doesn't."

Calvin nodded, unable to form a coherent thought. I looked over at Shawn and was greeted with a half-smile as he nodded to answer my question.

I planned one final move to bring this impromptu chess game to a close. It would be a game-changer; I had never stuck my neck out for any of my previous D.O.C.s before, and it was not likely that I would ever do it again, so I had to make this one count.

"I'll be a good girl from now on, I promise." I snuggled against my husband as he kissed my lips. I looked over at Shawn as he gathered his clothes to dress before looking up at Calvin again. "Don't punish him for something I did, especially when you know it will make me happy and hungry for you more when you've helped another brother make it to where you are."

My final plea began to have its effect as his body relaxed and I no longer felt the tension as he held me in his arms. "You're lucky you're so damn sexy, Nic," he replied, kissing me again before turning his gaze toward Shawn. "But I wasn't playing, youngster; you had better treat her right, or it will be the shortest promotion you've ever heard of."

And just like that, the queen takes the pawn and the king in one swift and deft move.

Checkmate.

Known for his mind-twisting plots and unique prose, Shakir Rashaan rolled onto the literary scene as a contributing writer to Z-Rated: Chocolate Flava 3 *in 2012. His raw, vivid, and uncut writing style captured the attention of the Queen of Erotica herself, Zane. A year later, Rashaan made his debut with*

The Awakening, *opening to rave reviews and a "recommended read" accolade in* USA Today's *"Happy Ever After" literary blog. The follow-up in the Nubian Underworld series,* Legacy, *has garnered even more success, and its third installment,* Tempest, *picked up yet another "recommended read" from* USA Today's *"HEA" blog, making the series one of the most unique in the erotica genre.*

The Kink, P.I. Series, *which include the first three installments,* Obsession, Deception *and* Reckoning, *has drawn high praise and comparisons to the* Easy Rawlins *series, bringing a different and exciting paradigm to the mystery genre. A few new projects are also being developed under the pen name, P.K. Rashaan. With his prolific writing prowess and openness on his social media platforms, Rashaan has plans to be a mainstay within the erotica genre and beyond.*

Shakir joined USA Today's *"Happy Ever After" literary blog as a regular contributor in 2015. You can find him there for his "Manly Musings" blog, where he dishes on the latest movies, television shows and books, all from a man's perspective.*

Shakir is a Phoenix, earning his Bachelor of Science degree in Criminal Justice/Communications from the University of Phoenix. He currently resides in suburban Atlanta with his wife and two children. You can learn more about Rashaan at http://www.ShakirRashaan.com.

Twitter: http://twitter.com/ShakirRashaan
Facebook: http://www.facebook.com/Shakir.Rashaan
Instagram: http://instagram.com/ShakirRashaan
Email: shakir@shakirrashaan.com
Blog: http://www.medium.com/@ShakirRashaan

YOU SHOULD LET ME
Love You

ANNA BLACK

MADISON

"Give it to me. Make me cum," I had begged my husband. It didn't do any good. I wanted him to go deeper and make me cum hard. I wanted to only want him and for him to only desire me at that moment. I wanted that newlywed fucking; that fuck that had me at work with a love hangover. Unfortunately, after twenty-plus years of marriage, he couldn't deliver like he used to and I was so over him and my marriage.

I had known there was someone else; someone half my age, but I'd imagined he'd get tired of spending all of our hard-earned money on that toddler and make things right with me.

"Baby, fuck me harder—make my pussy scream! I wanna cum all over your dick," I moaned, trying to encourage him to do my pussy right. The harder he tried, wasn't hard enough, and when his body jerked, I knew it was over. He came not even six minutes into it. I rolled my eyes. This was some ole bullshit, but I wondered why I even cared.

"I'm sorry, baby. I can lick your pussy if that's what you want," he said. I gave him a push to get off of me. He didn't move fast enough.

"No, I don't want you to eat my pussy, Kirk. I want you to leave Ashley and come back to our marriage. Since you have been fucking that teen, you don't touch me the way you used to, and when you come at me with these pity fucks, it's horrible!" I shot. He finally rolled off me.

"Madi, don't start this shit again. I asked you for a divorce, but you refused to give me that. I love you too much to hurt you, Madi. I just want to move on. And I'm not excited to fuck you because I'm not into you anymore. Don't you get it…I don't want this anymore!" he grumbled. Right then, I had made a big-girl decision. I had to let that shit go. I had to accept that he and I had run our course, and it was no more Kirk and Madison.

"I'll give you the divorce, Kirk, so I can be free to fuck men who want to fuck me. You and Ashley can live happily-ever-after for all I care, but it won't be in my house. And you will tell your daughter the fucking truth about it all! You fucking left me!" I yelled and got up. I knew it was best, but I tried to hold on to something that didn't want to hold on to me.

Kirk and I were over several years ago and I was too scared of what people would think to admit it. Now, I was done and ready to move on to someone else. I just didn't know who, but I knew it was going to be someone other than Kirk's tired, trifling ass.

Kirk and I were once a power couple. We owned businesses and had made an extraordinary life for ourselves, and then he goes and ruins it with a younger woman, who I know for a fact couldn't suck dick better than me, because Kirk told me. Now he was playing sugar daddy to a twenty-two-year-old, gold-digging, black Barbie and that pissed me off.

Despite how much it felt like yesterday, that had happened two years ago. Now here I am sitting in an airport headed for Chicago at the absolute worst time of the year. I hated winters and the weather reports were terrifying, but I had to go.

I got off the plane and headed to baggage claim quickly to retrieve my luggage. I wasn't in the best of moods that afternoon. I didn't want to be in Chicago. It was freezing and our reason for moving to Arizona in the first place was to be where I could sit by the pool the majority of the year if I wanted to. Kirk and I owned a couple of hotels together in the downtown Chicago area that were doing well, but one stumbled on to some management issues, and it didn't take Kirk long to figure out the general manager was not only doing a poor job, but he was lacing his pockets with our money. I wanted to scream when the words floated from Kirk's lips. I looked at him with a blank stare for a few moments, hoping he was joking.

Kirk had his hands full with our other business matters, and a trip to Chicago was too much to add to his plate, so sending me was the only option. I was a freelance photographer and had a more flexible work schedule, and sadly, more time on my hands. He and I had managed the property together years ago when we'd first married, and even though I didn't want to make the trip, I gave in. It took a little arm twisting and a whole lot of persuading, but ultimately I decided to be a good ex-wife and go and handle our business.

The trip was only going to be temporary; to recruit and train a qualified candidate. After I thought about it, a brief trip home wouldn't be so miserable. I only dreaded the brutal, bone-chilling climate, but it wasn't like I could fix the business problems from Scottsdale.

I retrieved my two designer suitcases from the belt and fished around my purse for the key to my lock to get my coat and hat. I squatted to open the larger suitcase and thought to myself how happy I was that I hadn't gotten rid of my entire winter wardrobe. I planned to do a little shopping, but for the most part, I had packed enough items from my storage to get me through the trip. I was all set to leave, but there was no one in sight with a sign up with my name on it. Kirk and I visited Chicago frequently to visit our family and friends and always had a driver there to meet us upon arrival. I pulled out my phone to make sure Kirk remembered to make arrangements for me.

"Kirk, did you remember to get a car for me?" I belted as soon as he said hello.

"Yes, baby doll, you know I set that up when I booked your flight," he answered promptly. I then heard ruffling, so I assumed he was going through his rolodex for the number. "No one's there yet?"

"No, I don't see anyone. I didn't go outside or anything," I said.

"Hold on," Kirk said. I heard the loud dial tone of his desk phone and assumed he hit the speaker button. I looked up and spotted a young man coming my way holding a sign alongside his body with my name on it.

"Wait, Kirk. I think this is him," I said. He came closer. *'HEEELLL-LOOO!'* I said to myself when I got a closer look at him. "Kirk, I'll call you back," I said quickly, ending the call. He stopped and put up the sign with my name across his masculine chest. I swallowed hard. This baby god had to be my daughter's age, and I knew I was wrong for looking at him like he was a piece of meat, but he was too fine. I shook it off and approached him thinking, his mother would probably want to whip my ass for wanting to spank her baby boy. I knew me and his momma had to be close or even the same age. "I'm Madison Washington," I said after clearing my throat, and then, BAM! He hit me with his sexy smile.

"Hello. I'm so sorry I'm late. It was crazy traffic," he explained.

"You're fine… I mean…ummm, it's fine," I stuttered. His voice was even sexier than his smile, and I just stared for a moment.

"Can I get those for you?" he asked. It didn't dawn on me that he was talking about my luggage. I was too busy looking at his lips. He stood over six feet, and even though he had on a heavy coat, I imagined him having an athletic build underneath. His medium-brown skin was smooth and clear and his beautiful long lashes laced the top and bottom of his eyes. His brows were thick and shaped to perfection and they laid sleek under the brim of his Chicago Bears hat. I imagined he had a nice grade of hair. He had a thin mustache and goatee, and he was definitely the type I went for back in the day when I was in my twenties.

"I'm sorry," I said, looking at him confused.

"Your bags, ma'am," he said. The word "ma'am," for the first time stung like a bee. I was forty-four and assumed he was at least twenty-five—at least I hoped, but either way he was too young for me to be lusting after.

"Oh yes, my bags." I smiled, handing them over. I went into my purse and pulled out my shades and was glad I flew like I was going on a date instead of in my oversized sweats and hair scarf. I usually flew comfortable, but I knew I would be greeted by my staff at check-in and I wanted to look like the owner's wife—well, ex-wife. I looked gorgeous at forty-four. I still looked fifteen years younger than what I really was and I knew my twenty-four-year-old daughter would have a mouthful to say if she knew I was checking out a man close to her age. "Lord have mercy," I said softly as I followed this work of art out of the airport doors.

"This way, Mrs. Washington," he said, as if I wasn't already following his lead.

"It *was* Mrs. Washington, but now I'm happily divorced, so please just call me Madison," I insisted. He opened the door for me. I got in. I did a quick mirror check before he got in and quickly removed my heavy coat to get comfortable. I fluffed my hair and he got in. It took a moment for us to pull off because there were cars everywhere, but I didn't mind. I just checked him out in the rearview mirror.

"Are there any other stops you want to make before going to the hotel, Mrs. Washington?" he asked as he pulled out of the parking space.

"No, straight to the hotel is fine. And please, it's okay to call me Madison," I repeated.

"Yes, ma'am," he said and hit the button to raise the center window. I stopped him. "You can leave it down." He pressed the button to retract it. He looked up and my eyes were staring, so he smiled.

"So tell me, is this your first time visiting the Windy City?" he asked, now giving me the same eye contact in the mirror.

"No, I was born and raised here," I said. Now we were both watching each other.

"Really, what side?"

"Southside," I replied.

"So what brings you back? Visiting family, business, or pleasure?"

"Mostly business. I'll be visiting family and I'm hoping for a little pleasure," I said, giving him my sexy girl smile. I hoped he knew what I was implying. I got on the plane that morning with thoughts of getting in and getting out; now I added getting my pussy wet to my list. I knew he was a lot younger and I never thought of getting with someone so much younger, but hell, I was now divorced after a twenty-four-year marriage, and my first sex encounter with a man half my age, didn't sound so bad in my mind.

"A little pleasure too, huh?" He flashed that boyish grin again. I felt my pussy tingle. I hadn't had any in six months, and I hadn't had it *good* in even longer. Things with Kirk and me went sour when he started fucking a younger woman. I knew she was with him for the money because his lovemaking began to play like a rerun of a minute man after only a few years of marriage.

"What do you do for pleasure?" he asked.

"Well, I travel a lot. I enjoy taking pictures and reading from time to time. That other thing I used to love doing for pleasure, I haven't done it in a while," I admitted.

"How long will you be in town?"

"A couple weeks," I said, knowing it may be a little longer.

"How much of that time are you willing to use in pleasure?" he asked.

I then thought he knew I was checking him out and I hoped this wasn't his first rodeo ride with an older woman. He was a bit cocky—I could see that in his demeanor and in how he looked at me in the rearview. He looked damn good and I knew in this business, he may have encountered plenty of women, and I wondered if he thought I was as sexy as I thought he was.

"It depends," I replied.

"On what?"

"If it's good," I said, and then reached for the champagne and opened it. We were stuck in traffic, so why not.

"Is that an invitation for a test drive?" he asked.

"If I said yes, would I get a yes to that invite?"

"Definitely."

I smiled even brighter. I filled my glass before I spoke.

"Before you speak too soon, I gotta be honest. I'm forty-four," I exposed. I hoped I wouldn't turn his sexy smile into a disappointed frown.

"You certainly don't look it," he replied.

"I'm aware of that, but I need to know would that be a problem for you?" I asked nervously. I put myself out there, and if he said my age was a problem, I'd be too embarrassed.

"Should it?"

"I don't know…what—you're twenty-six, twenty-seven," I asked. I didn't want him to think that I thought he was more of a baby than he actually was.

"I'm twenty-four, and as sexy as you are, forty-four is no problem."

I took more than a sip when he said that. *Did he just call me sexy?* I smiled to myself. Excited, I asked, "Okay, so…wait, what is your name?"

"Jerome. Jerome Taylor," he said.

Jerome Sexy Ass Taylor, I thought. "Nice to meet you, Jerome." I added more to my glass.

"You too, Madison. I know it's cliché, but everyone calls me J.T.," he said. We both laughed.

"I figured that, but Jerome works for me, or I can come up with another name for you later," I flirted. He smiled shyly. We continued to make small talk. Finally, we pulled up to the hotel. The bellhop got my bags. I asked him to wait a minute and I rushed inside. When I announced myself, the staff hurried into their positions as if things were going well. I knew it was all a front. If they were doing the right thing, I wouldn't have had to be there. After I received my keys to the master suite, I rushed out the door to Jerome.

He got out of the driver's seat and came around and stood in front of me. I was trembling, but I handed him a copy of my room key while I still had the nerve. "What time should I expect you?" I smiled. I had never done anything so risky in my life, and I was hoping I'd be able to go through with it.

"I'm off at six, so about nine."

I nodded. I stepped in closer to him. I could smell the mint on his breath. I knew it may not have been professional, but I wanted to taste his tongue. After slight hesitation, he gave me what I wanted. I closed my eyes and enjoyed the sensations his tongue gave mine. I wanted to fuck him right then and there.

"Can you make it sooner?" I expressed, after he planted the last gentle kiss on my lips.

"I'll try," he pledged.

I finally let him leave and then rushed inside to get acquainted with everyone. I got all of my first-night business out of the way and made sure room service knew to have my room stocked with champagne, whipped cream and strawberries. I ran myself a nice hot bath and soaked until the water chilled. I rubbed myself down with my favorite fragranced oil and slipped on some lingerie. It wasn't the sexiest number I owned, but it would do for that night. Shopping for my young stud some eye-catching teasers were now on my to-do list.

At 8:27 p.m., I heard the door open. My heart stopped for a moment or two. When he walked in, my hands began to shake and I began to have second thoughts. He moved in my direction quickly and ran his hand gently across my collarbone.

"I've been anxiously waiting to touch you," he whispered. I wanted to fan myself. I wanted to ask questions, but it wasn't time for all that.

I swallowed hard. "What are you going to do to me?" I whispered back at him. My nerves were going crazy. Him standing that close to me, had me quivering.

"Make you want to want me every moment that you're here," he said in my ear. He began to glide his tongue down the side of my neck. I then began to wonder if he had someone.

"Is that right? Will you have that much time on your hands?"

"I can be available if you want me to be…this is all on you. Remember, this is my test run." He caressed my arm softly. He kissed me deeply and his fingers found their way to my pussy. I opened up for him. He gently played around in my area in a soft circular motion before licking his fingers. I wondered if he was making sure it was okay to put his tongue on my clit, or if he just wanted to taste my juices. Either way, I was okay with that.

"Take this off," I instructed. He took a step back, not putting a lot of space between us. My heart was pounding out of my chest. He pulled his shirt over his head, revealing a sculpted chest and rippled stomach. I bit my bottom lip at the sight of him and wanted to see it all. "These too," I demanded, tugging on the rim of his jeans. Within seconds, his jeans and boxers were off. Chest chiseled, stomach ripped, dick enormous, and overall beautiful. "Damn, baby," I hissed, thinking out loud.

"Now you," he said. I let my straps fall and slowly slid my nightie down. I wasn't afraid to show him my naked curves because my body was thick and in great shape. My stomach barely had any traces of me having Amber twenty-four years ago because I didn't have stretch marks. "Damn, baby, you are sexy as hell. Turn around and let me see all of you," he instructed.

I did a sexy spin for him. He pulled me into his body and kissed my neck from behind. He grabbed my tits firmly and massaged them. I reached behind to touch him. The action had just begun, but I was so hot, I wanted to feel him. I wanted him to please me like never before.

I broke loose from him and anxiously pulled him toward the room. He stopped me and pinned me against the wall. He pushed his tongue inside of my mouth and I enjoyed kissing him. Wet, hard, long and sensual was how he ravished my mouth. At that moment I could not remember a man kissing me so well.

He kissed my skin, heading south. He didn't forget to please my nipples on his way down. He got to my neatly trimmed pussy and pushed my left leg up. He put his mouth on me and began to send waves through my body, applying the right amount of pressure on my clit. He lifted my thigh over his shoulder and after sucking my clit a few times, used his free hand to open me up. He pushed his tongue inside of my pussy. I wanted to cum with him inside of me, but he was on a mission to make me cum in his mouth.

"Baby, it's right there, and I don't wanna cum yet," I refuted, but he pinned me harder to the wall with his lips pressing into me. "Jerome, baby, I'm there," I screamed, and then began to shiver. I released, and he came up smearing my juices on my stomach and tits as he made his way back to my mouth.

We kissed deeply and I wanted more of what he had to give. I caught my breath and we went over to the bed. I asked him to lie down, but he said, "No, get on your knees," and I did. He grabbed his dick and caressed my face with it. The heat from his flesh warmed my skin. He teased my mouth for a minute before he let me take him inside. "Aaaahhhh," he moaned and I looked up at him, and he had his head back with his eyes shut. I wanted him to play with my hair while I pleased his dick, so I reached for his hand and placed it on my head. He pulled back and I licked his head, not wanting to give him composure time because I wanted to make him cum as hard as he had made me cum a few moments before.

I wanted to relieve him, revive him and feel him deep inside of me again. His dick jumped, and I knew he was ready, but when he pushed it back into my mouth, I realized I was wrong.

Surprisingly, he could hang and I was up for this pleasure match. I took him deep and then I pulled back and sucked the shit out of the tip, and he finally backed off. "Ooooh shit, baby, hold on." He winced. I knew I had him. He reached for me and pulled me from the floor. "I want to feel your pussy," he groaned, and then kissed me deeply, again.

"How do you want me baby?" I asked, breathing heavily because I was so fucking hot and turned on.

"Lay down." He nudged me. I was surprised he chose missionary. He went back into the other room and came back with a Magnum. I had three under my pillow. I had gone into the hotel's gift shop and purchased them right after I got settled in.

"I have condoms, baby," I whispered. I reached underneath the pillow and pulled them out. We laughed.

"We'll need those too," he teased, opening the condom. I watched him roll it on. He climbed on top of me and after a few moments, he had my legs spread so wide I thought he'd break me. My pussy was aching for him. I anticipated him entering my body. I exhaled when he finally slid inside of me and instantly filled my body with pure pleasure.

"Awww, baby. That's so damn good," I moaned. My pussy hadn't felt that way in ages.

"Can I go deeper?" he asked, pumping me like a skilled lover. His thrusts were perfect and I could feel the passion with every down stroke. "Yes, baby, yesssssssss!" I moaned. I took all of him like an eager lover was supposed to. My desire for him was so strong at that moment, it felt like we had been lovers forever instead of first encounters.

He pressed deeply into me. So deep it pained my insides, but felt so good at the same time. "Aaaahhhh, aaaaahhhhh, ummmmm, ummmm," I moaned, dealing with the pleasure and pain he rewarded me with. My eyes bulged when I felt my clit tingle. "Ahhhhh, ah-hhhhh, ahhhhhh, baby, I'm coming," I screamed in shock. That had never ever happened to me in all my years. I'd never came from penetration. Oral…yes. All the time, but never penetration. I figured the juices my body released excited him more because he pumped hard and then he came down and began to slow roll it inside of me. He sucked my neck and whispered, "Baby I'm close," but then he went back up and pushed my legs back again. His sweat rolled down his chest and stomach. It was so damn sexy.

"It's good, baby, it's good, baby; your pussy is so damn good," he moaned softly, and then he slowed.

"What's wrong, baby?" I didn't want him to stop my love injections.

"Turn over," he ordered.

I flipped over quickly. All I wanted was to feel him inside of me. He slid back into my wetness. His skin slapped so loud against mine, I knew someone could hear us. I felt his sweat dripping on my ass. My hair was even soaked. When he was ready to release, he held my waist in place and pushed deeper inside of me. He let out a sound that I wanted to hear again and again. He kissed my back softly and slowly released the grip he had on my waist. He pulled out and we both collapsed.

"So did I make the pleasure cut?" The first question to roll from his tongue.

"Oh baby, you definitely did." I smiled. We lay there and relaxed for a moment before he went to flush the condom. We grabbed robes and decided to sit in front of the fireplace. With champagne and strawberries, we talked about our backgrounds and got to know each other a little better. He serviced my pussy one more time before we called it a night.

JEROME

I left Madison that morning after kissing her goodbye, feeling high. It was crazy when I really thought about the reality of the matter. It didn't feel like I was with an older woman nor did it feel like she was a stranger. Being with her felt no different from being with a woman my age. I couldn't believe she had me just after one night. This woman was incredible, and I knew my friends and family were going to have negative things to say, so I decided to keep it to myself since she was only going to be in town for a couple weeks. I didn't even want to tell my boy, Warren. One night had me open for a woman twice my age and I'm glad I didn't hold back because it was just that damn good.

Her face—beautiful, her body—sexy, her personality—perfect, and lastly the sex—bananas. I was looking forward to seeing her again. I mean honestly, I didn't want to say goodbye. I thought about calling in, but she insisted I go and handle my business. She had a busy day herself. Room service came with our breakfast. We ate, got it in again and showered. She kissed me twenty times at the door before she allowed me to go. I must have been trippin' because I've had plenty of women, plenty of ass, and many, many one-night stands with women I met on pickups, but none I wanted to call back. That was not the case with Madison.

She wasn't your typical forty-four-year-old woman. My mother was two years older and Madison looked nothing like my mother.

Don't get me wrong; my mother is beautiful and elegant, but Madison was sexy and sensual. She gave head like she invented it and her pussy was tighter, wetter, and better than a lot of women I'd had. I was questioning my sanity. I asked myself, *'What the fuck?'* about fifty times after I accepted the key and have been asking myself, *'What the fuck?'* ever since I left her suite that morning.

I walked down the halls to the elevator, waiting for one of my boys to jump out with the camera crew. I thought for sure I had been set up. After I made it to my Infiniti, I realized it was real. I had fucked a woman twice my age and I wanted to fuck her again. I was shaking my own damn head, wondering what had gotten into me. How did I feel such an attraction to her that quickly?

Once I made it to work, I thought the thrill of the day and traffic would distract my thoughts of Madison, but I was dead wrong. I was the first one to run to clock out that evening. I chatted with her a little bit during the day when I was free, but she was busy and we didn't get too much conversation in. I rushed up to my condo, showered and changed, then headed over to the hotel. When I walked in, the fireplace was lit, and the melodious sounds of R&B filled the room. I looked around for her, wondering where she was since I had alerted her that I was on my way up.

I went over to pour myself a drink. She walked in.

"Hey," she said. I turned around. She was just as lovely as she was the night before.

"Hey, you," I said, rushing over to kiss her lips.

"I am so happy to see you. It's like the hours stood still today." She smiled radiantly.

"Oh you missed me, huh?"

"Yes, to be honest. I did. It's crazy, but I did."

"I missed you a lil' bit, too," I teased. She playfully hit my arm. "I'm joking, babe." I kissed her again. "So what's all this?" I asked, noticing the table was set with covered plates.

"Dinner. I figured we'd eat, chat a little, and do what we did last night and this morning," she proposed. I was down, but I wanted things to go down in a different order.

"How about you let me hit it real quick," I said, lifting her dress. I rubbed her ass and my dick instantly got hard. "And then we chat while we eat…and *then* do what we did last night and this morning, after that," I returned. Before she could dispute, I pushed my tongue into her mouth and lifted her up. I carried her to the sofa and gently sat her on the back of it. She wrapped her legs around me and I licked her down her neck to the center of her breasts. I slid both her bra and dress straps off her shoulders, exposing her erect nipples. I was impressed that her tits were not sagging, and the definition in her arms and legs was evident she worked out. I teased her nipples and put my hand up her dress and played around in her pussy, and it didn't take long for her to get wet.

"Take this off," she said, unbuttoning my shirt. After I removed it and my tank, she undid my belt and jeans. My jeans dropped to my ankles. I had to bend down to get the rubber out of my pocket. We kissed and she grabbed my dick in her hand and stroked me, but I was ready to enter her body. I rolled the condom on and grabbed her ass, pulling her body into mine. I slid on in.

"Aaaaahhhhh, baby, that feels nice…ooooh that's good," she panted. She wrapped her body around mine and I lifted her off the sofa.

I carried her over to the armless chair and sat down. She began to ride me so smooth and easy. Her body felt so good, I was going nuts. "What are you doing to me, Madison," I whispered as I sucked on her neck. "Work that pussy, baby," I cheered as she rolled harder. She looked me in my eyes and I stared back, challenging her gaze, wondering what in the hell had come over me in less than seventy-four hours. I felt like she was already mine and I didn't want anyone else at that moment.

"I'm there baby. I'm there!" she screamed. She did a back-and-forth move, mixed with a circular motion before slowing her rhythm. She giggled a little and gave me a soft kiss, but I wanted more.

"Let me bend you over," I requested. She went back over to the sofa and bent over resting on the arm of the sofa. I spread her ass cheeks and pushed my way back in and went to work. A few steady pumps were all it took to send my soldiers into an explosion, and I was more than satisfied with what just went down. I pulled out and headed to the bathroom to flush the plastic. "Baby, fix me a drink," I said, and inched my way to the bathroom. I still had on my tennis shoes and my jeans and boxers were around my ankles.

"Okay," she replied. I paused and watched her pull her straps back on her arms, thinking this woman had put something on me. When I came out, I snatched my tank up from the floor and joined her at the table. "So are you seeing anyone?" she asked.

"No," I truthfully replied.

"I wanted to ask last night, but I was too nervous."

"Why?"

"I don't know. I figured since this is only going to be a fling, why ask something so personal?" she said.

I don't know why I didn't like that word 'fling.' "So do you have flings often?" I questioned curiously, because honestly, I was digging her.

"Absolutely not."

"I just didn't want to assume."

"Jerome…I mean I'm forty—" she tried to say, but I cut her off.

"I know how old you are, Madison. Our ages shouldn't be an issue or a subject matter. We are both grown-ass people who enjoy each other," I declared.

"Okay, I won't mention it again." She smiled.

"Okay, now let's eat," I said, realizing our food had gotten a little cold.

"Let me heat that up for you, baby," she offered.

"No, let me," I said. I took our plates over to the kitchen. The suite was a huge open-floor concept with living, dining, and kitchen open to each other. It was nice. I wanted to ask about her position, but I didn't want her to think I was interested in her dough. "Here you go," I said, putting her plate down in front of her. I took a seat with mine. "So you own this place?" I asked casually.

"Yes, my ex-husband and I bought it fifteen years ago. It went under a major reno about two years ago when we settled our divorce, and since we get along so well, we have continued our business relationship."

"Well, it's nice…very upscale," I complimented.

"Thank you…as soon as I can get a new manager in here and get things underway, I'll be leaving this freezing city," she said, laughing a little.

"Anxious to leave already, huh?"

"No, I just don't like it here when it's cold," she whined.

"Well, I can keep you warm."

"I'd like that."

I smiled at her. She had this chill persona and I liked that.

"So what if we become more than a fling before your departure," I asked out of curiosity.

"Well, I don't know, Jerome. I live in Arizona and having a long distance romance is not something I'd like to do." She took a bite of her steak.

"I see," I sighed and turned my attention to the plate. I knew then to pump my brakes, because even though I knew it was too soon, I was feeling her.

"I didn't mean it like that, Jerome…it's just I was married to Kirk my entire life, and if I fall in love again, or fall for you, I'd want to be where you are and not so far away," she explained.

"Well, it's just day two, so we do our *thang* and figure out what's next when we have to. All I know is you are sexy, smart, and beautiful. If I fall for you, I don't want you to up and leave." I took a drink.

"Come on, seriously, Jerome. You could see yourself with someone my age?"

I dropped my fork. "Madison…" She cut me off before I could finish my thoughts.

"No seriously, Jerome, be honest with me, because the last thing I want to do is sit here and set myself up to be crushed by a young, sexy-ass, twenty-four-year-old man that is only here for a moment to have a good time."

"Wow, Madison, seriously? I'm sitting here asking you questions about us being more than just a fling…you think I'd be asking those questions if I was just playing with you?"

"I don't know, Jerome," she said. Her eyes got glossy. "I don't want to be a fool, you know. I don't want this to end with me being hurt. It's bad enough I'm opening up to a man my daughter's age, and to be crushed by you, would be a bad thing. So not a good look," she expressed.

"Okay, Madison, look at it from my side. You're like two years younger than my mom. I'm putting myself out there, too. You think I'd want to be hurt by someone I know others would talk shit about if they knew. It's still early and we have a couple weeks, so let's just enjoy it and see how it goes. Can you do that for me? I know this is like day two, but in this short time, I am really feeling you, Madison. So for me, can we just see how it goes?" I pleaded, taking her hand.

"Yes, that sounds like a plan."

I caressed her cheek.

"You are just as sexy, just as fine, and just as hot as a woman my age," I said sincerely.

"Thank you." She blushed. We went back to our food. Room service came afterward and cleared out the uneaten food and dishes. We sat and talked for hours. That night we didn't fuck again. I just held her all night. She came into my shower the next morning and I set her right for the day, before I headed to work.

MADISON

I had hired a new GM and she was good to go, but I wasn't. It was going on week three and I had already changed my flight once to stay an extra week. I didn't want to leave him. Jerome was smart, kind, thoughtful, and considerate. When we were together, it's like we were the only two people in the world. We'd spend every moment we could together. I knew we did it to ourselves, but each day that went by made it harder and harder for me to leave. I had been in Chicago for a month and my family wanted to know what was keeping me there since they knew winter wasn't my thing. I had a man that kept me warm at night, so I didn't have any more complaints about the cold.

"Hey, Saturday night my cousin is having a birthday party at this club out south. I want you to come with me," Jerome said.

Shocked, I answered, "Jerome, I thought we agreed to keep our relationship discreet."

"I know, baby, but I think we shouldn't have to do that anymore. I mean, you're my woman, and I want to show you off."

"I don't know, Jerome," I said apprehensively.

"Why not?"

"What will people say?" I asked afraid. We didn't go out much because it was cold and I didn't think I was ready to hear the whispers of people who thought I was a "Cougar."

"Who gives a shit what people say, baby? Look at you…you are sexy as fuck, and my boys are going to envy me when they see what's been taking me away from them the past few weeks. They know I'm seeing someone, and it's time that they meet you," he said.

I let out a deep breath. "Are you sure that's what you want, Jerome?"

"Baby, I'm sure. I want you to meet my family, and my mom."

"Hold the phone," I protested.

"What?"

"I can't, Jerome. I can't meet your mother…baby, are you crazy?"

"Madison, it is going to be fine. My mom is cool. Trust, she'll be cool," he said.

I wasn't convinced. Saturday rolled around quickly and when he picked me up, I was nervous. By the time we pulled up, I no longer had butterflies. I was nauseous and I knew I'd pass out.

"Baby, I don't think this is a good idea. I'm not ready to meet your family and friends," I cried.

"Relax." He took me by my hands. My hands were shaking. "Why are you so nervous?"

"Because I am twenty years older than you," I whined.

"And I'm twenty years younger than you. If anything, we'll both be embarrassed," he said, smiling at me. "Trust you'll get more props fucking a hot-ass younger man than I'll get fucking a sexy older woman. Now come on, baby. I got you and I'm going to be with you all night."

I relaxed, shook it off, and got out. We walked in, hand in hand. We found a seat at the bar.

"Jerome!" someone yelled out. He turned around.

"Warren, man, what's up?" I knew that was his best friend. Jerome told me a lot about him.

"You, man…you've been hiding out. I hope this young lady is worth it," he said.

My thoughts were, *not young, but old.*

"Yes, she is worth it," he said. He grabbed my hand. "I'd like you to meet Madison."

I extended my arm and the look on Warren's face was a surprise, but a pleasant surprise.

"This is Madison?" he asked. From his reaction, I got approval.

"Yes, this is my baby," Jerome boasted.

"It is a pleasure to finally meet you," he said and kissed the back of my hand.

"You too," I said. He chatted with Jerome a little longer and before I knew it, I was meeting everyone. So far there were no evil looks and I could tell Jerome's family and friends were cool.

"Baby, my mom just walked in," he said. He rushed over to greet her. I turned to the door and my heart began to pound out of my chest I was so nervous.

"A shot of Patrón," I ordered quickly. I was glad he handed it to me before they approached.

"Baby." I turned to them. "This is my mom, Maxine. Momma, this is Madison," he introduced.

"Nice to meet you, Maxine." I extended to shake, but she looked at my hand like I had shit on it.

"How old are you?" she boldly asked. She rested her hands on her hips. She gave me major attitude and since she was full-figured and from the Southside, I became terrified.

"I'm ummm…I'm…ummm," I stuttered nervously.

"Gurl, I'm just *messin'* with you. Get up and give me a hug," she joked. I swallowed hard. "J.T. already told me that you were damn near my age, but he didn't tell me you were gorgeous," she teased. I stood and gave her a hug. Jerome allowed her to take his seat next to me. He ordered us a round and his mom turned out to be so cool we exchanged numbers. A couple hours later, after we danced and I met everyone, I was tired and ready to go.

"Baby, are we leaving soon?" I asked.

"You're ready to go? My fam was talking about hitting this other spot," he said.

Just then it hit me again that I was twice his age.

"Another spot? Baby, it's almost two," I said, looking at the time on my cell phone.

"Two, baby…it's early. Don't tell me you're ready to take it in." I hated it, but I was. "Listen, I can grab a cab and you can go without me. I don't mind. I'm tired, baby." I pouted. He gave me a quick kiss.

"Since I don't live far, I'll take you by my place and I'll just hang out for a little while longer, then I'll be home."

That was fine with me. "That's fine." I nodded.

When we walked in, I kicked off my shoes with the quickness. I worked out every day, but I hadn't danced that much in a minute. My feet were throbbing. I pulled off my coat and tossed it onto the sofa and began to undress as I headed to his bedroom.

"Okay, baby, you know where everything is. I'll only be gone like an hour or so. I'm gone show my face and then I'll be home," he said. I stood in front of his dresser in my undies to remove my jewelry. "Damn, Madison, you're making my dick hard, baby," he said, standing in the doorway watching me. I saw him in the mirror readjusting his dick in his pants.

"Well, you have a choice to make. Head," I said, and licked my lips in the mirror. "Or the club?" I turned around to face him. I gave him my sexy pose and he looked at his watch.

"Okay, head," he said. He removed his coat and dropped it to the floor. He rushed over to me and kissed me passionately. Even though our skins were cold to the touch, we were both burning hot inside. I quickly undid his belt and his jeans and went down into a squat and bobbed up and down on his massive dick. I slurped loudly and he pulled my hair and my neck snapped back. He grabbed his dick and said, "Stick out your tongue, baby." When I did, he slapped his dick against my tongue before forcing it back into my mouth. He began to pump his dick inside of my mouth harder than ever. I gasped trying to keep up, but I felt I'd choke if he didn't slow down.

I looked up at him. I figured he saw the tears from him nearly choking me, running down my face. He pulled away and then pulled me up.

"Come here, baby," he said, breathing heavily. He knocked everything on the dresser to the side and lifted me on top of it. It was rough, but I liked it. "Open your legs," he instructed. After planting a few kisses on my wet cheeks, he went to my nipples, sucking on them strong and hard. I wondered if the liquor was to blame for all the roughness.

"Oooowwwwweeeee, baby, you're hurting me." I winced. He was biting on my nipples with more pressure than usual.

"I'm sorry, baby, I'm sorry," he said. He kissed me again. "I'd never hurt you, Madison. I love you, baby," he breathed into my ear. My heart stopped. He said he loved me.

I held up my hands to his chest to stop him. "Jerome, baby, don't say that if you don't mean it." I loved him, too, but was terrified to say it.

"I mean it, Madison. I love you and I want you to stay," he said, pushing his tongue back into my mouth. He pulled my ass into him and he slid in, this time without the latex separating his flesh from my flesh. He felt so good inside of me. He stroked me nice and slow. I moaned in his ear and he picked me up from the dresser without pulling out. He laid me on the bed and then he undressed completely. When he got on top of me, he looked me in my eyes and I said it back.

"I love you too, baby, and I want to stay with you, Jerome." He pushed my legs back and reentered my pussy. We made love until our bodies gave out and the next day, we didn't leave our love nest. We ordered in and made love over and over. I knew I'd have to either stay in Chicago or convince him to move to Arizona. Either way, being without Jerome was not an option.

Two weekends later, we were out again, and I took a nap earlier that afternoon so that I could hang and not give out like an old lady. I danced and met a few more of Jerome's friends. After a little while, I started to feel uncomfortable. This wasn't a family gathering like before and no one was even close to my age. It was a bunch of young adults partying like I used to back when I was in my twenties. The music was bumping, drinks were all over, and the women looked like they were on a music video set.

I leaned into his ear. "Baby, I'm going to run to the ladies' room." He gave me a point. I headed to the restroom. I was so happy when it was my turn because I had to wait in a line to piss.

"Did you see that old-ass bitch Jerome is with?" I heard a voice say. I paused. I was about to exit my stall, but instead stopped to listen.

"Gurl, yes…I'm looking like, are you fucking serious. That bitch is like fifty or sixty," the other said. They roared with laughter.

"I know, right…I mean, her body is tight for someone her age, but she has to be lining his pockets *wit' dat chedda* for him to have her up in here tonight." I tried to peek through the opening in the door to see who was talking about me. I could see one, but not the other.

"Well, maybe he's a male escort now and done left his daddy's limo business." She laughed loudly at her own jokes. They continued to carry on with their insults and snickering.

After they exited the ladies' room, I walked out of my stall and went over to the sink to wash my hands with my head low enough to taste the water that ran from the faucet. I didn't want the other women to notice that I was the one they had been talking about. I stood outside the bathroom and took a few cleansing breaths before I headed back to Jerome. Before I made it back to his side, the same chick I had peeped out in the restroom, was in his face, flirting and touching my man way too much.

A few seconds later, they headed out to the dance floor. I headed back to my stool and watched my man get his groove on with a girl that looked more age-appropriate for him. They danced a couple songs and I saw her slide him a card or something before he headed back my way. I turned and pretended I didn't witness the exchange. My eyes burned, but when he embraced me from behind and whispered, "Hey beautiful," in my ear, I put on my big-girl smile and let it go. After a couple more dances and drinks, we were ready to head out. I caught that same chick eyeing my man as we were leaving.

When we got into his truck, I was silent. He detected something was wrong.

"Baby, you aw'ight? You're pretty quiet," he asked.

"I'm fine, Jerome," I said.

"No, you're not. What is it? Are you mad because I danced with Sage?"

"No," I answered, and figured Sage was the one that was dogging me in the bathroom with her little friend.

"I was gon' say…chill on that. Sage and I have been cool since forever. I ain't checking for her or no other woman, baby. I'm all yours and everyone knows it, so don't sweat that," he said. I just looked out the window. I didn't reply because it didn't matter. I was not in the mood to compete with any woman. I didn't have the time for foolishness and if Jerome wanted someone his age over me, I wouldn't blame him.

When we got back to my suite, he wanted some pussy, and even though I didn't deny him, I didn't participate much. He passed out after filling my body with his juices. I lay awake and made a decision to leave the next day. I weighed all the pros and cons of our situation, and I felt that I was truthfully robbing him of everything. I was taking away his chances of growing old with someone, and definitely taking away his chances of becoming a father. My cycle had stopped being regular after Amber, and even though we tried for years to have another baby, it never happened. After I turned thirty-five, Kirk and I put a lid on the baby business, and now I hadn't seen a menstrual in two years or so. I just didn't want to take that away from him. I had experienced so many things and he belonged with someone his age. Not my old ass.

The next day, I was nervous as hell and didn't know how I would tell him I was leaving. I went on line and changed my flight to leave that evening. I slowly packed up the things I really wanted to take back to Arizona and didn't worry about everything else because the suite wasn't a rentable suite. It was set up for me and my family when we visited so no one occupied it when we were away. When Jerome got into the shower, I called down and told the front desk to have a car ready for me by five. I pretended to be working on something for work when he had asked what I was doing. I was writing him my farewell letter. Around 4:45 p.m., I hinted I wanted some Portillo's. I knew he'd go out to get it for me. When he made his exit, I put the note on the table and scrambled to get my things to head downstairs. When I grabbed my purse and headed for the door, he walked back in. He scared the shit out of me. I was standing there with my bags.

"Baby, I forgot my keys—" he said. "What's going on? You trying to sneak out on me?" The expression on his face was the sight I didn't want to see.

"I'm sorry, Jerome," I whispered.

"No…you gotta fuckin' come better than that, Madison! What the fuck? What happened between yesterday and today, baby? Was it the club? What…why…why are you packed to bounce? Why would you just leave me without a word!" he yelled.

"I couldn't face you, Jerome. I left you a letter," I said, now shaking. I knew it wasn't the right thing to do to someone.

"A note, Madison…a fuckin' note. I'm not worth a face-to-face truth!" he continued to yell. He went over to the letter and snatched the paper from the table. He quickly read through it. I stood in that one spot trembling. "No, no, no, baby, you got it all wrong. Listen… this is not what it is, okay. I don't want anyone my age. I want you, and you are not cheating me out of anything, baby. Please don't do this," he begged, moving closer to me. "Baby, I know there are some things I will have to sacrifice to be with you, and I don't mind, okay. Don't leave me like this, Madison. Baby, when I say I love you, I mean it. I've never felt this way for any woman and if you leave, you are going to rip my heart into pieces," he cried. I heard him, but I felt that I'd hurt him in the long run if I continued to stay.

"I'm sorry, Jerome…I am, baby. And I don't want to hurt you… I just don't see us having a happy ending. I don't want you to ever resent me or look back and wish you had of chosen someone that can give you children. By the time you're thirty, I'll be fifty, and then you're forty, and I'm sixty. My number is going to climb so much higher than yours too fast, and I can't do that to you, Jerome. That would be selfish of me to do that. I can't." I tried to walk away, but he grabbed me and held me so tight. He put his face close to mine and I could feel the love he had for me, but it was still best for me to go. I didn't want to take away his life.

"Madison, I'm begging you not to walk out that door. If you want me to come to Arizona, I'll move, baby. If you don't want to stay here, we can go, but I don't want to live without you. You have to reconsider, baby. I've never in my life begged a woman to be with me. I've never loved a woman like I love you, Madison. I'm telling you, I can handle this. I can handle us and I want us to be together as long as we can be," he said, allowing a tear to fall. It was breaking my heart.

I didn't want to leave him this way, but there was no other choice. I kissed him softly and caressed his face. "I love you, Jerome. Too much to stay. Take care of yourself and you will find someone that will make you happy. You will fall in love again, get married, and have babies with someone that can, because I can't. I can't give you that life, Jerome. Trust me, baby, this is ripping my heart apart. But last night, I watched you have fun, dance, and mingle with women that are your age. I'm old enough to be your mother. I should not have let things go this far, and I'm sorry, but it's best I go," I said lastly. I hurried out the door.

"Madison…Madison…Madison, don't do this!" he cried behind me, but I kept going. I stood in front of the elevator. He came out into the hall. "Baby, please come back inside and let's talk this out. Please don't leave me like this. I can handle whatever it is to come, Madison—baby, I love you," he cried. I stood in silence, willing the elevator to hurry. When the doors opened, I stepped in and hit the lobby button. He stood there and watched the doors close.

When I got into the limo, I broke down. I cried harder than I ever remembered crying in a very long time. I was so tempted to tell the driver to go back, but I'd only prolong the inevitable. Jerome was a good man and he deserved someone that could give him a long life of love, and because I had him by twenty years, it wasn't me.

JEROME

It had been four days since Madison left. I couldn't function. My heart was aching something bad and I had never experienced heartache in my life. It was a bitch. I called and called and called and texted, and she didn't answer. I called from other numbers, blocked my number, left her tons of messages, but she didn't reply. I tried to see where she was coming from, but it pissed me the fuck off that she took it upon herself to decide what was best for me. I was a grown-ass man and I could decide what was best for me, and it was her. I loved and missed that woman so much my entire body ached. I found myself crying at the drop of a dime, and nothing but her return would take away my pain.

There was a knock at the door and I raced to it, hoping it was her. When I opened it to my mother, I was unpleasantly surprised.

"Momma, what brings you by?" I asked, standing in front of my door. My place was a mess and I didn't want my mother to see me like this.

"Can I come in?" she asked. I hesitantly stepped aside. "Your father called me and said you haven't been to work in a few days so I came to check on you," she said, looking around. I flopped down on the sofa and my mother pushed some clothes out of the chair to sit.

"She's gone, ma. She left me," I said, unable to hold back my tears. My mom got up and embraced me. I cried in her arms like a little boy, but I didn't care.

"Shhhh, baby, it's okay. I know it hurts," she said softly. "Heartache is the worst, son, but it will get better." She held me until I was calm. For a while, I was too choked up to talk, but my mother sat with me patiently until I was ready to open up. "What happened, baby?" she asked tenderly.

"We hung out on Saturday night. I danced a couple songs with Sage, and I didn't think it was a big deal, you know because we dance with other people when we go out, but when we got into the truck on the way back to her place, she was oddly quiet. I tried to talk to her, Ma. And the next day things felt funny. I knew something wasn't right. I went out to get something to eat and forgot my keys. Went back up, and she had her bags, heading out. I begged her not to leave me, Ma. I told her that I could handle our thing and that I knew I may be giving up all these experiences that she thought I was entitled to, and she still left. She wrote this," I said, handing my mother the letter. She read it.

"Listen, J.T. You and your brother are grown men and you know I don't get involved or tell you boys what to do. When you told me how old Madison was, I wasn't happy, but I saw your face, baby, when you spoke of her and how you were with her. I told myself that I raised you into the man that you are, and that you can handle your own business. I'm sorry she left, son, but I can understand all the reasons she did. I know from this letter that she loves you," she said. I still didn't understand.

"Ma, if this is love, I'm afraid to know what she'd do if she hated me," I said confused. You don't leave when you are in love. You endure.

"Okay, let me put it to you this way. She loves you enough to put your happiness first. In ten years, you both will be ten years older, and her ten years older will still be twenty years older than you. What if you change your mind about kids or if she gets sick. These are things Madison considered," she said. It started to make a little sense, but I still didn't like it.

"Mother, I hear you, but she should have allowed us to cross those bridges when we got to them. I could have had a change of heart, and then again, I may not have. The thing is, I was willing to take that chance with Madison, and now she's gone," I said, lying back. All the points my mother made were valid, but it didn't take away any of my pain.

My mom hung around to clean and cook me dinner. I promised I'd eat, but my appetite hadn't returned.

"Call your father because the company is called Three J's Limo Services, and one of the J's haven't been to work, and you know I don't do your father like that. He and I ain't cool," she joked, giving me a motherly kiss.

I stayed home a couple more days and didn't give up on Madison. I called her several times and continued to leave her messages, trying to convince her to give us another chance.

MADISON

I couldn't move and I hadn't left my bedroom in days. Every bone in my body missed him, and I wanted to talk to him so bad, but I had to stand by my decision. Jerome was like a triple scoop of double Dutch chocolate ice cream, buried under bananas, fudge, caramel and strawberry syrup with whipped cream and almonds. It was entirely too sweet and hard on your thighs, but you wanted it all anyway. I missed him more than I missed anything or any person in the world. My heart ached so badly and I questioned myself over and over. Did I make the right decision? Did I make the right call? Was it precipitous to just determine what our conclusion would be? All I knew is I loved him more than I loved Kirk. I loved him more than I loved all of my favorite things in the world and deep down, I wanted him and what we had back.

I wondered if he was okay. I knew in time he'd be fine and find him a Sage, or a Brittany, or a Chiquita…I don't know. I just knew it was meant for him to be happy and I wasn't sure how long I could be that for him. I listened to his voicemails constantly like they were a complete CD. I cried my eyes out as his words penetrated my heart, even after hearing the same message thirty times over.

I'd picked up the phone to call him but put it down. I had to be strong for the both of us. I knew eventually he'd stop calling, and soon he'd have another woman in his life to make him smile. I had to concentrate on nursing myself back to sanity, because at that moment, I didn't know my left from my right. All I knew to think and speak was Jerome.

Six months had gone by and the calls finally stopped. I was back to a semi-normal life. I thought of him constantly, but there were no more daily breakdowns. I was back to taking pictures and had gained the twenty pounds I had lost the first two months postbreakup. I started to take my daughter's advice and get back out there and date. It was hard because I compared everyone one to Jerome. At first I tried to date guys my age. What a joke that turned out to be. The ones I tried to date didn't have a sexual appetite like mine, and it was just plain old boring.

Mike, one guy that I was kind of digging, was fine. Things were going good until I learned that Viagra was his source of a stiff one. We had sex twice and it was decent, not Jerome of course. The first night he slept over at my place he didn't have his blue pills with him and he couldn't get it up. He finally confessed that he had to pop a pill to get going, so the next morning after, I closed the door behind his limp-dick ass and deleted his number from my phone.

I tried, but I still thought of Jerome every day. I wanted to call him, but I told myself that I'd be wrong to set him back after so long, so it was better to leave it alone. I went back to being dateless and spending my days reminiscing on what I had with Jerome, wondering if I'd ever get over him and what we had.

JEROME

"Hold on, Jerome. I need my purse." Sage stopped me and I looked at her like she was crazy. She spent the last three months chasing me and now that I have her in my bed, ready to push my dick in, she asking for her purse.

"Your purse, Sage…right now? What's so important that you need your purse *right now?*" I didn't want my dick to go down. I had just put the condom on and I didn't want to waste it.

"Just get my purse, *niggah!*" she spat. She had a big ass to go along with her big-ass mouth and I didn't want to hear her shit so I got up and got her purse from the dresser. I tossed it to her and stroked my dick in my hand while she fished around in it. She came out with a little black case.

"What the fuck is that?"

"Brian, meet Jerome. Jerome, meet Brian," she said, switching it on. It was a little vibrator and I was down with that. I climbed back on top of her and pushed her legs open to slide in, but she stopped me again.

"Hold on, baby, hold on," she said. She put her toy in place and closed her eyes. "Now," she whispered, and I finally pushed inside. I was stroking her and it was feeling good since I hadn't had any in six months. I looked down at her and she was gorgeous, I'll admit, so I leaned in to kiss her. She just kept giving me little pecks. I tried to push my tongue in her mouth and she gave me a crazy reaction. "Un-uh, I don't kiss, boo boo. That ain't my thing," she hissed. I tried not to let her throw my rhythm off.

"Is it good?" I asked since her eyes were closed and she seemed to be enjoying Brian more than me.

"Yes and my pussy is about to explode," she panted. I felt her orgasm. Her pussy got even wetter and my dick got harder. I went up and grabbed her thighs and began to pound her right, but she lay there lifeless. I was trippin'. I pumped faster and harder trying to burst one to be done, but it's like my dick wasn't satisfied enough to shoot. Faster and harder, I pushed and pulled and all I did was produce more sweat. I slowed and stopped, then slid out. She turned onto her side. I went to the bathroom and pulled off the rubber and flushed it. I headed to the kitchen, hit a couple shots of Hennessy, and when I went back into my bedroom, she was up examining the pictures of Madison.

"I thought you and this old broad broke up months ago?"

"Yes, Madison and I broke up a while back," I said, picking up my shorts and stepping into them. I ignored her ignorant-ass comment.

"So why do you still have so many pictures around of her?"

"Because this is my fucking house, Sage, and I can," I spat.

"Hold on, niggah, bring that shit down…I was just askin'," she said, rolling her eyes.

"Whatever, Sage. Are you staying or going?"

"I want to stay," she said softly. I fell back onto the bed. She came and sat down.

"Listen, J.T. I've been feelin' you for a while now and I would like to have a chance with you, but if you're not over your thing with Madison, I understand. I won't bring her up or say anything else about her. I just want to try and help you to move on."

"I'm over Madison, Sage. But to keep the peace, keep your comments about her to yourself, and honestly, I'd rather not discuss her," I said. She slid down into bed with me. She pushed her ass against me and my dick began to swell again. I wanted some more. I went underneath her tank and started to squeeze her tits and pinch her nipples. She grinded her ass against me. I pushed my shorts down underneath my erection and got another condom. I rolled it on and we stayed on our sides. She lifted her right leg to give me access and I pushed my way inside of her. She was still wet from the round we had minutes before. I was pumping my pole deep inside of her fat pussy, enjoying her, and then I heard that damn vibrator. I didn't say anything, only concentrated on getting my nut. I didn't care if she was moaning in response to my dick stroking or from Brian vibrating on her clit. I was only interested in a release. I was backed up and even though Sage's pussy was good, I didn't shoot hot shit until after I closed my eyes and imagined I was lying behind Madison, softly stroking her tight pussy.

I finally exploded and had to catch the words, "oh Madison," from spilling out of my mouth. I exhaled several deep breaths, happy to have had that nut, but unhappy about who it was with.

I foolishly continued to be with Sage for another two months. It was the second week of November, my twenty-fifth birthday was coming up and I wondered what Madison had done for her forty-fifth. Her birthday was November 2nd, twenty days before mine. I called to wish her a happy birthday, but of course she didn't answer. I didn't say all I wanted to say, just said, "I remembered today was your birthday and I hope it's a great day for you. Happy Birthday." I wanted to say, *"Happy birthday, baby. I love and miss you so much."* I decided to move on with my life and to keep Madison in my memory bank. I secretly wished her well.

MADISON

I hurried and answered my phone when I saw Maxine's name light up. My heart dropped into the pit of my stomach. I thought something had happened to Jerome. That would be the only reason for her calling me after all this time.

"Hello," I answered nervously.

"Hey, Madison. How are you doing, girl?" Maxine sang into the phone. I began to breathe again. No way was he hurt with that tone.

"I'm fine, Maxine, how are you? It's been a long time," I said, flopping down on my bed in relief.

"It has been and I am glad you answered my call."

"Well, to be honest, Maxine, my heart stopped beating when I saw your name. I thought something had happened to Jerome and I just froze. I was scared to death," I honestly admitted.

"Well, that sounds like someone that still cares to me."

"I do, Maxine, you know how much I loved Jerome, but you also know that was destined to fail."

"*Loved*. Do I hear past tense?"

"Love, loved, loves…what difference does it make? We are done," I said, pausing. "So what's up? What do I owe this honor?"

"Well, I called for two things. First, I called to tell you that I respect your decision to leave J.T. and I know your reasons were honorable and great, but I think that you were premature and a bit selfish."

I had to set her straight immediately. "Selfish, Maxine? Leaving him was the most selfless thing I've ever done for anyone in my life. I sacrificed all the love I have for him, for him to be happy."

"Is that what you really think, Madison?"

I was getting angry. "Yes, Maxine. That is exactly what I think!" I snapped.

"Okay, Madison, here we go. And you betta not hang up this damn phone!" Maxine barked. Even though she was all the way in Chicago, she scared me. "I understand your intentions, Madison, and I know you meant well, but love and sacrifice in my book is sticking your neck out and facing all obstacles head-on. You are so right; the age gap between you and J.T. is huge, but my son is a good man—young, but a good one. He is responsible, intelligent, and is not a bad decision-maker. He loved you and instead of you giving him the choice to make, you made it for him. That was selfish and unfair. Just because we are older, it doesn't always make us wiser. If you loved him enough to walk away, you should have loved him even more to stick it out with him through it all. Madison, the future is so hard to call, and all things are unforeseen, so you treated my son unfairly and you hurt him to the core. Although I respect your decision, I don't agree with it."

I hadn't stopped to see it that way. I was speechless because she was right. I'd spent so much time trying to convince him that he was all the man I needed, but treated him like a child by doing what I thought was best for him. I felt ashamed and sorry.

"Maxine, you are right and I'm so sorry I did that to him. He must hate me now," I said, letting the tears fall.

"Well, Madison, that I can't confirm. You'd have to ask him that."

"I don't know if I could even face him, Maxine. The day I left, it was so horrible, and every time I play that scene in my mind, I break down and cry."

"Do you still love J.T.?"

I couldn't lie. "Maxine, you know I do. I cannot let him go, no matter how hard I've tried. I think of him every moment of the day."

"Well, the second thing I called for was to invite you to his twenty-fifth. I am throwing him a party and I'd like for you to come, if you can make it. His dad and I are willing to pay for the ticket," she generously offered. "I know it would be the best birthday gift we could give to him. Once you see him, just talk to him, Madison, and see how he feels."

"When is it?" I asked.

"Not this Saturday but the following."

"I'll come," I agreed, hoping it was the right choice. "And I can handle my ticket, Maxine," I assured her. We went over a couple more details and afterward, I called my daughter. She had become my best friend since the breakup. When she said I should go and give it a try, I was convinced it was the right thing to do. I didn't know what would happen when I saw Jerome, or how he'd react, but I wanted to see him.

I got to Chicago the day before the party and I called Maxine to let her know I was in town. I promised her that I'd be there and she finally let me off the phone with my tenth, "I promise." I decided to shop and find me something sexy to wear and when I was about to leave, the bell of my suite rang. I almost leaped out of my skin when I opened the door to a beautiful surprise.

"Amber, baby, you didn't tell me you were coming into town."

"I wanted to surprise you. I thought you needed some moral support," she said. I squeezed her tight. I was so happy to see my baby girl. It had been a few months since she'd come out to Arizona to spend time with me when I was at my lowest. She lived in

Vegas with her husband and we tried to see each other often, but occasionally time didn't allow.

"I'm surprised. I was on my way out to look for something to wear to the party tomorrow. I mean, I want to be sexy." I winked.

"Well, come on. Let's go find you a dress that's going to make him come crawling back to you," she said. We went out and shopped until I found the perfect dress and shoes. Afterward, we had dinner.

The next evening my daughter and I were dressed to kill. When the car arrived to pick us up, I had jitters the entire ride.

"Mom, relax. You are beautiful and if Jerome loved you like you said he did back then, things are going to be perfect," she said, taking my hand.

"Are you sure, Amber? Baby, I hurt that man and I'm so afraid he's going to spit in my face." Amber laughed.

"Mom, stop being so dramatic." I trusted her. Perhaps I was over-reacting a bit. When we pulled up, I called Maxine and told her I was there. She told me to come in. When we walked in, it was crowded. Maxine greeted me.

"Oh my, Madison, you are just as beautiful as I remembered. J.T. will be here soon, so have a seat and have a drink."

"Okay, Maxine…this is my daughter, Amber," I introduced.

"Hey, Amber, you look just like your mother. Both of you are gorgeous," she complimented.

We quickly found a table in the reserved section. I was a ball of nerves and I downed two glasses of wine before he finally walked in. I blinked several times, because Maxine didn't tell me he was involved with that Sage girl. I got up and hurried over to her.

"Maxine, why didn't you tell me about her?" I said in a panic.

"Her who?" she asked.

"The girl on your son's damn arm!"

"Because I don't know who *her* is," she said. I believed her. She rushed over to J.T. and they exchanged hugs. I watched him intro-duce Sage to his mom. Why did I bring my ass all the way to Chicago, not considering the possibility that he could be with someone else? I rushed over to Amber.

"Amber, we have to go," I said, shaking.

"Mom, what's wrong?" she asked concerned, but not getting up fast enough.

"He's not alone, Amber," I said, giving a point. She looked over in his direction.

"Mom, you are not going to run out of here because of her, are you?" I looked at her like she had lost her mind.

"What do you mean? I'm supposed to be like 'hey,' in front of his girlfriend?"

"Hell yeah…Momma, trust me. She ain't got shit on you," Amber said. I had never heard that language come out of her mouth before. I shot her a look. "I'm sorry, Momma, but you came from another state, so put your 'S' on your chest and go speak to the birthday boy. Don't worry, Momma, I got ya back." She winked. I was terrified. How was I going to compete with this young beauty? I straightened my dress and headed in his direction. After a few people were done talking to him, I approached.

"Madison," he said with eyes bigger than saucers. I knew he was shocked.

"Hi, Jerome. Happy Birthday," I said. He just stared like I was a ghost. He was about to take a step forward in my direction—I too in his, but Sage quickly reappeared and grabbed his arm.

"Baby, you gotta come see your cake," she said, and then she looked at who he was staring at—*me*.

"Madison," she said with a frown on her face. The disappointing look that I thought I'd get.

"Hi," I said to her.

"Can we have a minute?" Jerome said.

Sage snapped.

"HELL NO!" she yelled.

"SAGE!" he yelled on her level. She looked at me and gave me an up-and-down and moved on.

"I'm sorry to just show up," I said nervously.

"You should be," he snapped. "I mean…what are you doing here?" he asked, and now I knew he was not happy to see me.

"Your mom invited me," I answered nervously.

"Well, I'm uninviting you. You need to leave!" he barked.

"I understand you're with Sage now, Jerome. I didn't come here to make waves."

"Well, what did you come for, huh? To take another stab at my heart!" he yelled with venom. It was time to make my exit.

"You know what, this was a bad idea. I'm sorry. I'll go. Just let me get my daughter and we will leave." I turned to walk away, but he stopped me.

"Wait, Madison, your daughter…you brought your daughter with you?"

"Well, she met me here. I wanted you to meet her, but I see it's not a good time," I said. His demeanor changed.

"I'd like to meet Amber. You talked about her so much, I'd like to meet her," he said. I nodded and he followed me over to our table.

"Jerome, this is my daughter, Amber. Amber, this is Jerome," I introduced. When she stood to shake his hand, he hugged her.

"It's nice to finally meet you. Your mom spoke so highly of you. You are just as beautiful as your mom described. Like a carbon copy of your mom," he added. Amber smiled.

"Well, I've heard a lot about you and I'm happy that my mom put on her big-girl shoes and came."

"Yeah, it was a shock to see her. It was nice meeting you. Take care of your mom. She's a great woman," he said, moving away quickly.

"Okay, Mom, what just happened?" she asked.

"He wasn't happy to see me, Amber, and he asked me to leave."

"Oh no he didn't!" she said ready to go after him. I grabbed her.

"No Amber, it's okay, baby. I did this and I understand how he feels. It was wrong for me to show up here, so let's just go. I've had enough for one night," I said. My eyes welled and she took my hand.

"Okay, Mom, but don't let a tear fall. Straighten up and go say goodbye to Maxine. Walk out the same confident and beautiful woman you walked in as," Amber advised. I dabbed the corner of my eyes with a napkin and went and did just that. Maxine apologized over and over again and I assured her that it was fine. After that, we left.

JEROME

"Ma, why?" I asked as soon as I got her attention.

"J.T., you know why and if you don't, baby, I'm too damn busy to explain it right now. Annndddd!" my mother said, putting the bowl of potato salad down. "If you ever loved that woman, or if you still do, this is your last chance to make it right. So you better be the man I know you are and make the right choice," she scolded, and then turned to fuss at her girlfriend Carmen for not placing the trays of food on the table right.

I turned to find Madison and of course she was already gone. I then had to deal with Sage, and Lord knows I didn't want to. I decided to wait until after my party and give her the news once we got back to my place. I didn't want her to ruin my party or for my family to drop a beat down on her. I pretended that all was well, but all I could think of was Madison. I was so eager for the party to be over and to have the talk with Sage I didn't know what to do. I tried to go easy on the liquor, even though it was my birthday, because I wanted to be in my right mind when I broke up with Sage and went to Madison. I had so many emotions going on inside of me at once and I couldn't think straight. I wanted to strangle Madison; at the same time I wanted to hold her. I wanted to cuss and fuss as well as hear her out. I wanted to tell her she was too late, and then tell her she wasn't. I didn't know what to feel and as I silently rode home with Sage, I knew she knew.

"So are we going to play this game or are you going to tell me what the fuck is going on in that head of yours?" she spat with that ghetto-ass look on her face that I hated so much.

"Sage, I have a lot going on in my head right now, so please just let me have this moment to sort some shit out in my mind," I said as calmly as I could. Arguing—wasn't in the mood. Fighting—not this night. I wasn't for it. Sage and I had a crazy relationship and it was truly dysfunctional. I put up with her because she was there. I didn't need her to be there, but she made herself available for me to screw and have a hot bitch on my arm when we were out.

"Yea, whatever, niggah. You got the wrong bitch and I ain't stupid. You can take all the time you need, niggah; just drop me off at my place. I'm not gonna let you dump me for some old tired BITCH!" she yelled to the top of her ghetto-ass lungs.

"That's cool," I replied, letting her cuss, yell, and bitch all the way to her place. I pulled up in front of her building and she spat some threats about having some niggahs jump me. As soon as she slammed the door, I hit the gas. I hopped on the Dan Ryan and headed downtown to Madison's hotel.

"So what now, Mom?" Amber asked.

"I don't know, baby. We can hang in Chicago for a few more days. You know my sisters will never let me live it down if you came to Chicago and didn't see them. Then I head back to Arizona and take it one day at a time," I said.

"Sounds like a plan. And for the record, I refuse to go by Aunt Greta's. Last time I went by, I swear I couldn't get into the front door, Momma. Your sister is a hoarder and you need to call the people on her," she joked. We erupted in laughter.

"I know, but since your grandma died, that's what comforts her,"

I said. We continued to laugh. "So do you wanna hit the lobby bar or call it a night?"

"I'd love to, but I told Sean I'd Skype him and model the lingerie I bought today when we were out. So I'm going to head to my room," she said, getting up.

"Okay, but that was TMI," I joked. I realized my baby was now a grown woman and that she did grown-up things with her man like I used to do with mine. I gave her a tight hug and I closed the door behind her. I hit the stereo remote and turned on some music and started to turn out the lights. I decided to soak in a hot bubble bath to relax and cry because I blew it. As I headed to the master suite, the bell chimed. I wondered what Amber forgot.

"What'd you forget? I know your room has a—," I was saying. It was Jerome. I was so surprised to see him I just stood there and stared at him. I couldn't speak so he stepped in, grabbed my face and kissed me passionately. "I'm sorry...I'm so sorry for what I did to you," I cried when he put his face in my neck and held me tight. "I love you. I never stopped loving you," I said. He pushed the door shut with his foot.

He stared at me and his eyes had a thick gloss. They said all he wanted to say to me. I caressed my skin and then he slid his hands under my dress and grabbed my ass firmly with one hand and then pushed my dress off my shoulder with the other. He pushed the other side down, exposing my bra. He put his face against my chest and moved it from side to side on my skin. He then pushed his face inside of my bra to expose my erect nipples. He devoured them and I could hear him sniffling. My eyes welled and a tear fell. He looked up at me and I could see how emotional he was. He finally let a tear fall. I reached and wiped his face. He grabbed my hand and kissed it, then held me. "Baby, take off your coat," I said. He obliged. I adjusted my clothes and we stood there admiring one another. I wanted him to say something, but I figured it was just too hard. "Jerome let's sit," I offered. He joined me on the couch.

"I'm scared," he finally said.

"What are you afraid of?"

"Giving my heart back to you," he confessed. I swallowed hard. He had every right to be afraid.

"I know, and if that's something you decide not to do again, I won't be angry with you. I'll understand," I said honestly.

"Then what do I do, Madison? Say goodbye to you now or give my heart back to you? If you can't promise me that you will keep my heart safe—say that…tell me the truth and I'll leave and move on with my life. I'm tired of loving you, Madison. I'm tired of feeling like I feel about you for you to simply show up out of the blue and set me back. I feel like you are deliberately trying to mess with my head. What did you even come back for, Madison?"

"You," I revealed as a tear fell. "I was wrong and I was selfish. I tried to convince myself that I was doing it for you, Jerome, but the honest to God truth is, I was doing it for me. I was afraid that I'd grow older and eventually you'd leave me for someone younger. The last night I was here, I overheard that chick Sage in the bathroom calling me old and saying things about you treating me like charity. I got scared and I took the coward route, Jerome, and I'm sorry. If you don't want to forgive me or give us another chance, I will have to live with your decision, but I hope that you would give me another chance to show you how much I love you. You can trust me with your heart again, baby. I am now begging *you* to stay with me. I was wrong to walk out on you like that and I am willing to move here or whatever you want. It's your call. I'll do whatever you want; just please take me back," I pleaded.

He sat in silence. My heart was racing and I hoped he wouldn't get up and walk out on me. He wiped his eyes and rubbed his head. He turned to me.

"If I was cruel, I'd make you suffer, you know dat?" he teased. I exhaled. "You don't have to beg me, Madison. I'm still yours and I forgive you. We will figure out what is best for us. We will figure out if we want to be here or in Arizona. I want to be with you, Madison, until whenever, so no more making decisions for me, you got that?" he said. I would have agreed to anything.

"Loud and clear, baby," I said, kissing him. I climbed on top of him and straddled him. I kissed him like I missed him.

"I deserve to be with you, Madison. I never once made your age a factor. All I wanted you to do was let me love you," he said.

"You're right. And even though I did make a big deal about our age, I know now that I deserve you, too. I'll spend the rest of whatever time we have making it up to you. I promise," I said, meaning every word.

"I know you will, Madison, and I trust you. Now can I get some birthday sex? I miss making love to you more than words can say."

"You don't have to ask."

We didn't make it to the bedroom. He managed to do things to my body that night that made my thighs shake uncontrollably. He gave me more multiples than my pussy could take for one night. My jaw muscles and throat were sore when we finally threw in the towel. Neither one of us wanted to get knocked down in our lovemaking match. We exhausted every move and position we could come up with that night until my pussy was cardboard dry and his dick couldn't stand up anymore.

We made magic that night and after six months of having a long distance love affair, I was back in Chicago for good. Kirk tried to warn me that it wouldn't last since he and his little Ashley didn't make it, but they didn't have what Jerome and I shared. And after ten years of marriage and one five-year-old son that my daughter carried for us from Jerome's artificially inseminated sperm, we are still fucking like we are both in our twenties. The subject of age has never been mentioned again.

Anna Black is a native of Chicago and the bestselling, award-winning author of the Now You Wanna Come Back *series. Her desire to become a published author didn't develop until her late twenties. She didn't take her writing seriously until several close friends and family members encouraged her to go for it. After signing with Delphine Publications in November 2009, Anna became a bestselling author for her debut release,* Now You Wanna Come Back, *within a matter of weeks. She has since released several novels, short stories and compilations under her own publishing house, Black House Publishing which was launched in May of 2013. Her most recent novels include* I'm Doin'Me *and* The Side Effects of You *(Urban Books/Kensington). Anna currently lives in Texas with her daughter Tyra and her adorable dogs, Jaxson and Jasmine.*

Get To Know Anna Black!
Twitter: *http://twitter.com/annablack72*
Instagram: http://instagram.com/annablack72
Facebook: www.facebook.com/Romance Author Anna Black
Website: www.anna*black.net*

DIVORCE
Party

JADA PEARL

"Mrs. Lyric Robinson-Washington, you are seeking a divorce on the grounds of adultery and mental abuse. The court has found that you have proved your allegations and has awarded you the following: the main residence, the Benz, full pension rights, four thousand dollars a month in alimony, and you may also take your maiden name, Robinson, back," the judge stated to her and her estranged husband who was now fuming.

Lyric bowed her head and said a silent prayer of thank you. She didn't even really care about the material stuff. She only wanted her sanity and her last name. The other things were mere bonuses for being married to Vincent for so long. If anyone deserved it, she did. Although they had some good times, they didn't seem to outweigh the bad. Throughout the entire twelve years they were married, she suspected Vince of cheating on her, although she could never prove it until she caught him at the end. Vince belittled her by calling her fat, ugly, and anything else that would deflate the already low self-esteem she had at that time. It took for her to go see a therapist to feel like a woman again. She was down a hundred and fifty pounds, a stronger woman mentally, and she felt like celebrating. Her divorce party tonight would give her just the release she needed. She spoke with her lawyer in the hallway for a moment and then headed toward the exit. Hearing her name called, she turned and then rolled her eyes as her now ex-husband ran to catch up with her.

"You know you don't deserve any of my money," he spoke with disdain.

"Well, the judge didn't see it that way," she told him. Turning to leave, he grabbed her arm. "And what the hell do you think you're doing?" she asked him, yanking her arm from his grasp.

"Oh, I get it, you think you're all high and mighty now that you have lost some weight. Must feel good to have some sex appeal again."

"You wouldn't know the first thing on how I feel, weight loss or not. I was always beautiful and I am glad I know my worth. I let you tear me down and that will never happen again," Lyric told him while looking him in the eyes silently after she made her statement. She wanted him to know that she meant business. All Vince could do was stand there and not say anything because he could tell that she meant it. Walking away, she left him standing there.

Vince watched his ex-wife leave. He would never admit to her that he liked how she looked now. It took for him to hurt her for her to get there.

Walking toward her car, Lyric's cell phone went off as she got into it. Hitting the button in the console, she spoke. "Hey, Erin."

"Hey, so how did it go?" her best friend asked.

"Better than I expected. I still have my home, my car and some alimony, plus my Robinson last name back. I couldn't be happier."

"Congrats. So are you ready to celebrate?" Erin asked.

"You know I am. Too bad it's only ten in the morning. I need a drink now. I didn't eat breakfast this morning so I am going to go head to The House of Pancakes for breakfast. You want to join me?"

"I wish I could. I have a meeting in thirty minutes, plus, you know I am only working a half-day so that we can party tonight."

"Right. Okay, girl, let me go eat and I will see you later at the shop." Ending the call, she headed to her destination. Lyric owned

Pastries and Cream where they specialized in homemade gelato and all types of pastries. She had begun to make herself known and had landed a feature on the news last week.

Lyric took a seat at her table. She started glancing over the menu but instantly raised her head when she heard his voice.

"Good morning. My name is Tyriq and I will be your server. Would you like something to drink?" he asked with a voice that could melt panties.

"Um, I...I will just have a cup of coffee, with cream and sugar," she told him once she could finally speak. She stared into the sexiest bedroom eyes. She could tell he worked out even though he was in uniform. She noticed he was staring at her. Smiling. She instantly blushed. Her reaction must have been common. When he smiled, she noticed two deep dimples in his cheeks. When he walked away to get her coffee, she tried to concentrate on deciding what it was she wanted to eat. She tried not to look up when he came back but failed terribly. He stood over her and waited for her to begin. When she looked up, he was smiling that smile again.

"Are you ready to order?"

"Yes. I will have a two-egg-white omelet with spinach, cheese, mushrooms, turkey bacon and toast, please." She handed him the menu.

"Do you mind if I ask you a question?" Tyriq asked. Lyric nodded. "You look very familiar. Have we met before?"

"In my dreams we have," she attempted to mumble. When he laughed, she realized he heard her. She wanted to sink through the floor. "I'm sorry about that. No, I don't think we have."

"Don't be sorry. I'm flattered." He winked at her as he went to place her order.

Lyric managed to finish her breakfast without further embarrassing herself. She gave him a good tip and left the restaurant.

Tyriq watched her leave, noticing how well her body moved. He wished he had asked her for her number. Then he realized why she looked familiar. He had seen her on TV last week demonstrating some desserts. She owned a bakery. At least that's what he thought he remembered. Tyriq worked the rest of his shift with her on his mind. He had a gig tonight and he was looking forward to it. His band had been signed to perform at a local nightclub three nights a week. Things were moving up for them and he was just waiting for it to happen.

Getting to the club for rehearsal, he and his band were told there were two parties and one special party for a friend of the owner, Donald. They would have to take requests if asked.

Lyric walked into her shop at exactly 4:15 p.m. Erin, Nicole, and Donna would be there in a little while to start the celebration. They would all get dressed at the shop and head over to Club Intense. The owner was her father's best friend and he told her he had a new up-and-coming band performing that night. He reserved her area in VIP, knowing she loved live bands. Plus he had her area set up special for her divorce party. As she finished setting the wine out, all three of her girlfriends walked in together, ready to get it started.

"Who's ready for a drink?" Erin said, reaching for the bottle of wine.

"A toast," Donna said, breaking into Lyric's thoughts. She held up her glass.

"Yes, to new beginnings and better endings!" They clinked glasses and then enjoyed the light food she had prepared for them. She told them about the guy at the restaurant. "Girl, I wish y'all could have seen him. He had a six-pack for days, and his eyes, OMG. He looked kind of young, though."

"So and what does that mean?" Nicole chimed in.

"It means I don't date jailbait, that's what it means."

"Girl, please. If I am not mistaken, wasn't the woman you caught Vince with in her twenties? Men do this shit all the time and they are considered as just being men."

"Why are we even discussing this? All I know is his name. It's not like we exchanged numbers. Furthermore, I may not even see him again," Lyric said, ending the conversation. Finishing her glass of wine, she finished getting ready. Afterward, they left in the waiting limo.

The club was packed for a Thursday night, but they were immediately directed to VIP. Champagne, food, and alcohol awaited them. They were joined by six more of their friends and the party went into full swing. Lyric turned toward the stage to check out the band and her mouth fell open. Looking even better than this morning was Tyriq. He was dressed in black slacks and a royal-blue dress shirt. The brother could sing.

"Damn, look at that man up there. He is fine. What's the name of this band again?" Donna shouted. All the ladies turned to see who Donna was referring to.

"Damn, ain't he a sweet thang. And you know I love me some fresh meat," one of her friends said behind her.

"That's Tyriq singing," Lyric said, barely audible, but Donna, Nicole, and Erin heard her clearly since they were the closest to her. They appeared shocked.

"Lyric, did you say what I thought you said?" Erin spoke loudly so she could be heard. Lyric nodded.

"Yes, that's Tyriq. The guy I met this morning."

"If you won't make a play for that fine-ass man, I will."

"He is too young for me."

"Says who?" Erin asked.

"Do you even know how old he is?"

"No, I didn't ask all that."

"Humph, he look just ripe to me," Donna said and all the women high-fived and laughed but Lyric. She never took her eyes off him. Now he was looking directly at her while he sang a ballad. Tyriq continued singing but came off the stage. He walked in their direction and the women went wild behind her. Once again she felt like disappearing through the floor. When Tyriq stood in front of her, taking her hand and serenading her, she wanted to die. When the song ended, he whispered in her ear, kissed her cheek, and headed back to the stage. Of course they all rushed her when he left.

"What did he say?" one of the ladies asked.

"He said I looked beautiful." Taking a long swallow of her drink, she began fanning herself. It was the first time she even thought about going down that road. Could she?

The ladies went back to acting crazy. A few men came to their area to ask them to dance. Donna and Erin were the only ones to accept. Just as the band announced they were about to take a break, Lyric decided she needed to hit the restroom. The line was long so Lyric decided to use the private bathroom in Donald's office.

Tyriq watched Lyric head toward the restroom. She wore a fire-engine-red dress with a split up to her thigh. She had all the men watching her and she didn't even realize it. He was surprised to see her, sitting in VIP. He felt his soul open when he was singing to her. He had to talk to her before she left. Donald came up to him and asked for a copy of the song list, then remembered it was in his office and asked him to go retrieve it. Walking into the office, he was greeted with a soft thud to his body. Grasping the woman so she wouldn't fall, he was happy to see it was Lyric.

"Whoa, I'm sorry. I didn't think anyone was in here. Donald sent me up here for a list," Tyriq told her. He didn't want her to think he was following her.

"I'm sorry. I just came up here because the ladies' bathroom was crowded. I will leave you to what you were about to do," she told him, trying to walk around him. He made her nervous and she needed to get away from him. He blocked her path and smiled.

"I have about fifteen minutes before we go back on. Can we talk?"

"And what exactly do you want to talk about, Tyriq?"

"Well, for starters, I want to know if you liked my singing," he said, giving her a full dimpled smile.

Lyric shook her head. She knew he was messing with her. He walked closer to her and on instinct, she took a few steps back.

"What are you doing?" she asked. His eyes began undressing her. He licked his lips and her panties grew moist. *Lawd, it should be a crime for a man to be this fine and sexy*, she thought to herself.

"*What am I doing*, is definitely the question you should be asking," he told her in a deep, sultry voice. When Tyriq was standing in front of her, he leaned in and grazed her lips. Seeing that she hadn't moved, he licked her bottom lip and forced her lips open, placing his tongue in her mouth. Deepening the kiss, Tyriq felt her responding to him. His body reacted immediately. He could feel his member grow as she moaned in his mouth. Breaking the kiss, he went straight for her neck.

What was she doing? Lyric wanted to stop him, but his kisses felt like heaven. She had never been kissed with such intensity. Vince never was a romantic type, but she did love the man, until he hurt her. Tyriq tongue-caressed her bare shoulder as he continued to the dip in her breasts. His other hand ran to the open split in her dress. She wore no stockings, as the weather was too warm. Capturing her mouth in a kiss again, he moved his hand to her panties, running his finger over the material. She trembled under his touch. Kissing her harder, he moved the material over some and felt her wetness coat his fingers. She opened her legs and Tyriq explored more. He played with her clit and Lyric's knees almost buckled. Tyriq made sure to hold on to her. He ended the kiss just as Lyric's body shook from her orgasm.

Tyriq's eyes were glazed with desire. "Now that's what I call sexy," he told her as he sucked her nectar from his fingers.

Catching her breath, she watched him and it turned her on. Vince would have never done that. Lyric stood and fixed her clothes. She looked at Tyriq again as he grabbed the list off the desk behind her. She had to know, even though at this point she knew she didn't care. "How old are you?"

Tyriq laughed and his eyes gleamed. "How old do you think I am?"

"I don't know, thirty?" She took a guess.

He shook his head and licked his lips again as if he was replaying their moment. "Nah, sweetness, I am twenty-six. I will be twenty-seven in May."

Lyric wanted to gasp. Why did she ask? *Twenty-six! What the hell am I doing with this baby?* she thought to herself. He was the same age as her nephew. Tyriq's phone beeped. Checking it, he placed it back in his pocket and gave her a card.

"Time for me to head back, but thank you for this quick and delicious experience. I knew this morning I wanted you. It's just the beginning for us." He winked at her as he sniffed his fingers again, smiling, and he was gone. She stood there for a moment. What had she gotten herself into? What she did with him was no way in her character.

Joining her friends, she saw how they were all drunk. They asked her where she'd been?

"The line was long, then I ran into an old friend," she lied to them. She refused to tell what happened. The rest of the night went on without a hitch. Tyriq locked eyes with her continuously throughout the night. She exhaled.

The night had ended and they were headed to the hotel suite where they would be staying for the next three nights. She took his card out of her purse and read it. *Tyriq A Masters, Balladeer.* It included the band's name, *Soulfully4U.* Before she lost her courage and her good sense, she opened her phone and sent him a text.

Just wanted you to have my number. Lyric.

She blew out a breath and closed her screen. The three-bedroom suite was beautiful. The ladies had a nightcap before heading to their sleeping areas. As Lyric was undressing, her phone went off. She looked at the screen. Tyriq wanted to see her. She texted back where she was and said she could meet him at the pool. She grabbed her glass and finished the drink off before she headed out.

Tyriq smiled as she came in his direction. She was wearing a baby doll nightie and a long sheer robe with heels. *Damn, this woman is on fire and thick in all the right places.* He licked his lips. "My goodness, you are absolutely beautiful," he complimented. They sat together in a corner, out of direct view of anyone.

"So, Tyriq. What am I going to do with you?"

"You ask me that in what you're wearing? It is taking all my will-power not to undress you and have my way with you."

"You do realize I am old enough to be your mother?"

"Maybe, but you're not. And it's a good thing because I would never do this to my mother," he told her as he brazenly lowered her robe and exposed her breasts. As he took one in his mouth and sucked her, he rubbed her areola of the other. She took a huge breath and held it as the electricity went through her from her feet to her head. He pulled her on his lap and lay back on the chaise, never breaking his contact with her breasts. Lyric grinded her body on him as her panties got wetter and wetter. She moaned and whispered his name. Tyriq pulled her head down and kissed her hard. She felt him hard on her sweet spot. She shivered. Never had she felt such raw passion for someone she barely knew.

Tyriq ran his tongue over her body, removing the baby doll. She was nude from the waist up. He kissed and sucked her shoulders, her chest, and stomach. He leaned her back on the chaise and removed her panties, lifting her hips toward his face. He bent over and ran his tongue over her clit, becoming intoxicated from her scent. He began rolling his tongue over her clit and feasted on her juices for what seemed like forever to Lyric. She came repeatedly and was still wet.

"Damn, sweetness, I've never seen a pussy this wet," he admitted. He kissed her, allowing her to taste what he'd just experienced. Lyric sighed in his mouth. Tyriq pulled her back onto his lap. She didn't realize they were both nude until now. He quickly sheathed himself and lowered her down his shaft. He was thick and he went slowly so that her body could adjust to his size.

Lyric once again trembled. She held on to his chest as they both met each other stroke for stroke. Tyriq kissed her to shield her loud moans while he himself was trying to keep from reacting to her. He loved when a woman showed how much she enjoyed the sex and he knew she was. Tyriq felt Lyric tighten her walls on his shaft and he lost it. She began bucking on him and riding him harder. He wasn't expecting her to take the lead, but he was enjoying it. She arched her back and he could tell she was almost at her brink. He grabbed her buttocks and thrust harder, twisting some until he felt he had hit her G-spot. She screamed in confirmation that she was cumming. Tyriq followed suit.

They both lay there panting hard, neither saying a word. After Lyriq was able to catch her breath, she looked at him again and asked the same question she had asked before they started this. "What am I going to do with you?"

Tyriq kissed her and laughed. "I am sure we can think of a few things!" he told her, glancing down at their nude sweaty bodies. They lay there for a few more minutes before getting dressed. They sat in the midst of their sex smell and actually had a decent conversation for the next hour. It was nearly four a.m. when she told him she should get back upstairs. "When can I see you again?" he asked her, giving her a small kiss on her hand before releasing it.

"I am here until Sunday. Just call me," she replied. They parted ways and she went upstairs to shower again. When she got in bed, she heard her phone go off. Looking at the text, she smiled. Tyriq told her that she was the first older woman he had ever attempted to talk to and that he was willing to show her he would be worth it all. What he didn't know was that this night alone was worth it all. She had never experienced such an intense sexual encounter in her life. She had met Vincent when she was in college. She was a virgin when they got together. So in her entire life, she only had three lovers: Vince, a one-night stand with an old friend, and now Tyriq. She had missed out on a lot, she thought, as she fell into a deep sleep.

The moment she woke up, Lyric's thoughts went straight to Tyriq and what they had done last night. While they were eating breakfast, Donna caught her off guard.

"And where did you disappear to last night?"

"Wh…what do you mean?" she stammered.

"Well, I came to check on you and you weren't in your bed."

Thinking quickly, she tried to blow off Donna's questions as the other two friends had stopped eating and were waiting for her reply. "I went to get some ice and then decided to get some air as well. I wasn't gone that long," she replied with a straight face as to not give herself away. She didn't dare tell them she saw Tyriq last night. She loved her friends, but this was something she was keeping under wraps.

Donna eyed her but didn't say anything else. She continued eating, pretending to be all into her food. The ladies had decided to do some shopping and then catch a movie. As they were headed into the movies, her cell phone went off. She read the message and blushed.

See you tonight. Same place and time.

She sent a quick "yes" and turned her attention to her friends and the movie. The ladies had decided to party in the room. They had food, music, and plenty of liquor. They played Truth or Dare and shot games. Checking her watch, it was almost time for her to meet Tyriq. Everyone was passed out except her. She was the only one who could always hold her liquor better than the others. She showered quickly, then slipped into some night shorts and a tank. She covered with a robe and headed to the pool area. She was surprised to see Tyriq already there waiting for her. He had on gray cargo pants and a crème-colored polo. He looked delicious. Soon as she walked over, he took her in his arms and kissed her. After a few minutes, she broke the kiss. They were both breathing hard. "Wow, now that's a hello."

"I have been thinking about you all day."

"Have you now? And what were you thinking?"

Arching his brow, he asked, "Are you sure you wanna know all that?" Catching his devilish implications, she smiled at him.

"Yes. I asked."

"Well, how about I show you instead?"

"You still have my attention," she replied.

He walked around her and began kissing the back of her neck. He held her stomach as he grinded his shaft in her backside. He kissed her back slowly as he removed her robe. Letting her straps fall to the side, he tongued her shoulders. "You smell good," he whispered, getting on his knees and planting kisses down her back and buttocks. He bent her over the chair, slid up her body, and all she felt was the electricity between them. She heard him opening the condom wrapper. As he moved the flimsy material to the side with his hand, he gradually made his entrance. Her juices coated his tip instantly. Her body pushed back and she let him fill her.

Tyriq lifted her body some as he thrust into her. It was the most exquisite feeling. He kept doing this until she was about to explode.

He released her and she tilted and opened her legs a little more. He took the hint. He began to thrust harder and deeper, grabbing her hair. "Your pussy is so wet. My goodness, you are making it hard for me to concentrate," he said, pounding into her. The only sound that could be heard was the slapping of their skin. When she thought he was about to cum, she pushed him back and fell to her knees, taking him inside of her mouth. She sucked and slurped on his shaft. He grabbed her head and told her he was cumming. She arched her mouth so she could deep-throat him, and soon after felt his release. She swallowed his seed down, making sure she didn't miss a drop. He tasted like candy. "Damn, now that's what's up." He pulled his pants up and pulled her into his lap. They fell back onto the chaise that was next to the table. "You know I can get addicted to you?"

"Well, we both know that can't happen. I think we both know what this is?" She looked him dead in the face.

"And what is that?" he said.

"Sex."

"Oh, so you just want me for sex?" he asked, feigning hurt feelings. Lyric looked at him and took a moment to respond. She didn't know how to take his comment. This was all new to her.

"Well, isn't this what this is about?"

"Just because it started that way doesn't mean that it has to continue that way."

"Okay, so explain to me what you want, Tyriq. I am almost half your age. What do you think you could really offer me outside of great sex?"

"I could offer you a lot of things if I was given the chance. Haven't you ever heard that song, 'Age Ain't Nothing But A Number'?"

Lyric laughed. She had to because she didn't know how else to respond. She wasn't going to admit to this young stud that she wasn't experienced with men that much.

"Yes I've heard it. But that still doesn't tell me what you want from all this."

"What I want is simple. I want you, and I want to be able to show you how serious I am. If withholding this is a first step, then I can do that as well."

Lyric didn't respond. Could she see herself dating him? It wasn't like he didn't have anything going for himself. He obviously wasn't in the streets. Even with all that, she had to look at what people would say. Would they say she was going through a midlife crisis because of her divorce? Or was she trying to prove a point because Vincent had done exactly what she was contemplating on doing.

Returning to work the following Monday, she was in her comfort zone. She had completed a party order when a bouquet of assorted color roses was placed in front of her. She looked up to see Tyriq holding them. She instantly blushed. "What are you doing here?" she asked, not hiding the surprise in her voice.

"You know I asked myself that same question as I headed here. I missed you," he said, sounding very sincere. Lyric noticed that her staff and customers were watching them. She excused herself and led him to her office. Closing the door behind them, he took a seat as she placed the flowers in a vase.

"Tyriq, I have to admit. I didn't think I would see you again."

"Yea, I can feel that. It took a lot for me to even come to this. But

I told you I wanted you in my life and not only as some sex toy."

Knowing that she did like him, she also missed the contact they had. She had already made her decision. "I will agree if you agree to let us do this discreetly. I am not ready to have my friends all in my business."

"You sure that's why you want the discretion? Or are you ashamed of our age difference?"

"No, no, that's not it. I just need to be able to handle all this. And look at you, no woman would ever be ashamed of you," she said, motioning to his body. He was wearing a gray T-shirt that clung to him and black jeans. His dimples became more pronounced as he smiled at her comment. It made her heart melt. He walked toward her and lifted her chin. They were lip to lip.

"The only woman I want is you," he declared, connecting their lips. The kiss felt different than before, as if it was filled with more than merely lust. She exhaled and deepened the kiss. As he moved in closer to her body, there came a knock on the door. Her assistant manager called her name on the other side of the door.

"Lyric, you have an urgent request call on line three."

"Okay. I will take it in here, Vera. Thank you," she yelled back. Looking over at Tyriq who was now wearing her lipstick color, she smiled. "I have to take this. Do you want to come over for dinner tonight?"

He licked his lips and kissed her briefly. "Send me the address, sweetness, and I will be there. Enjoy the rest of your day," he told her before heading out of her office.

She picked up her phone. "Lyric speaking, how I may help you?"

She tried to keep a professional demeanor. The rest of the day was filled with special orders and maintaining her shop. She barely had time to think about her morning conversation with Tariq. Since being on the news segment, her business had tripled. She had to have a meeting with her two managers regarding expansion and hiring additional staff. The building next door was vacant and would provide the perfect space to accommodate the needs of her store. She would leave the hiring up to them, as they both had been with her since she had opened her bakery's doors.

Before heading home, she had stopped by the store for the ingredients that she would need for tonight. She started dinner and then headed to get dressed. She chose to wear a maxi dress for the occasion. As she was finishing up her makeup, the doorbell rang. Looking at her watch, she noticed Tyriq was early. She didn't bother to look out the peephole and just opened the door. Her smile turned into a frown when she saw that it was Vince and not her date. "Vince, what the hell are you doing here?"

"Is that your way of saying you don't want to invite me in?" He still managed to step around her and walk into the house. He strolled into the living room and saw it was set for a romantic dinner. "Guess I interrupted your plans," he said with a smirk on his face.

"Actually you haven't interrupted anything because you are leaving. Whatever it is that you came here for can wait until tomorrow. Now go!" she told him, pushing him back toward the door.

"Wait a minute. I just wanted to talk to you. See how you've been."

"Call me tomorrow if you are really that interested," she said, closing the door in his face. She leaned up against it and didn't move from her position until she heard him walking down the steps. Why was he bothering her? The last thing she needed was this mess. She made her way toward the kitchen to get the food out of the oven when the doorbell rang again. Thinking it was Vince coming back, she yelled as she was opening the door, "You just don't take no for an answer!"

Tyriq looked behind him and then held his hands up. "Well, I think I can now," he said, laughing.

"I'm sorry. I thought you were my ex-husband. He just showed up unexpectedly."

"Oh, okay. Is it okay for me to come in?"

"Of course." She stepped aside and he walked in. He whistled as he gained entrance, scoping out her home in the process. Lyric loved black art and the house was filled with it. Tyriq went to stand by a common "WAK" piece. It happened to be his favorite. It was called "Black Love."

"This is my favorite piece from this artist. You have quite an impressive collection."

"Thank you. I've been collecting art since my early twenties. I absolutely love to see how they speak through pictures." Lyric handed him a glass of wine.

Tyriq noticed a book on the coffee table and picked it up. It was a book of writings. The pages had been typed in a book format, but he could tell it hadn't been published. "Is this your work?"

"Yes. When I'm feeling a little stressed from work sometimes, I use it to write my thoughts, and that's what it has become over the years."

"Do you mind if I read some?"

"Not at all. Dinner will be ready in about ten minutes," she said.

Tyriq sat down on the couch. He had a feeling he was being watched and looked over toward the window. Seeing no one, he went back to reading. Lyric joined him by sitting on his lap. She drank her wine as he read in silence.

On the outside, Vince was standing in the shadows, steaming. He had no reason to be mad that she was seeing someone. In fact, he was still seeing Angela, the woman with whom Lyric had caught him. What he wasn't expecting to discover was that Lyric was seeing a young dude. He guessed he couldn't be any more than thirty. He watched them together until his cell phone went off. It was Angela asking where he was. He didn't tell her he was stopping by here. Ever since the divorce was final, and now seeing Lyric for the first time since they'd separated almost a year ago, made him miss her. Not to mention that she looked like the sexy woman he had married years ago. He had to admit it, he wanted his wife back. Walking to his car, he started it and drove off. His mind made up.

Lyric and Tyriq sat Indian style on the floor. She fed him and Tyriq loved it. After dinner, she served her favorite dessert—vanilla bean cheesecake. He moaned as he tasted it.

"I see dating you is going to be hazardous to my health." They both laughed at his comment.

"Does that mean you like the cheesecake?"

"Yes, and dinner was on point as well. I see why your bakery is getting the recognition it deserves. You are a beast in the kitchen."

Blushing, she leaned over and kissed his cheek. "Thank you. I appreciate your compliment."

"For you, anytime." He finished off the cake and patted his full stomach. Picking up her book again, he started reading. "You have a real talent for this. You should come down to the club and recite while I play. That would be hot."

"I will think about that. So what's your favorite so far?" she asked him, interested in what he was going to say. He flipped back through the pages and came across the one that he was looking for. Instead of telling her which one, he decided to recite it aloud.

Midnight Desire
Shivering, just in anticipation of the touch, I feel your hot breath on

my neck. As you stand behind me, I close my eyes wondering why you are torturing me this way.

I have to feel your hands on me. As if reading my mind, I feel you place your fingers on the top of my back and you go straight down, including the crack of my backside until you touch the tip of my hot spot. Instantly I open my legs slightly, wanting that feel. You say not yet, as you begin to kiss the trail your fingers just laid. I moan and try to arch my back. but you tell me be still as you continue the kisses. My legs tremble as I try to regain my composure.

What are you doing to me? I moan out loud. Not even really expecting a response, I bite my lower lip. I can feel my juices running down my legs, now. You bent me over and your face is in my hot spot, licking and teasing me and I scream, unable to hold in this passion. Your touch is so tender, like I'm being caressed by a feather. I want you so bad. I want, no, I need to feel your complete body on me.

I know this will be my undoing, loving you in my mind was never this good, I think. As the tears roll down my cheeks, you wipe them away with the base of your thumb. U slowly, slowly hit my spot over and over again, as I ride each wave until it stops.

I pull you away from me and I want you to feel what I feel as I trace your body with my tongue, not leaving anything untouched. Feeding off your moans, I want this to last as I open your soul with my heart. Everything seems to stand still as we both begin to ride the wave of ecstasy. Kissing you is like my wanton desire, tasting my juices off your tongue as I mix our desire together. As another wave hits our body we cling on for life. Can it always be this good, I ask. You respond of course, as we lay there spent.

"Wow, you make my writing sound like the hottest, sexiest thing out there," she told him. She tried to control the desire that was all over her. His voice was low and deep as he read the words and she sucked it all in.

"Trust me, you made it easy," he replied, smiling. She leaned over, kissed his cheek and then trailed kisses from his cheek to his neck and then back up to his lips. She licked his bottom lip and then forced her tongue in his mouth, sucking hard on his tongue as they kissed.

Tyriq pulled her closer to him as she began to undress him. They lay there exploring each other's body as he pulled her maxi dress down and began circling her nipples with his tongue. As Lyric felt her juices running down her leg, the more turned on she became from his touches. He pushed her lightly to the floor and got on top of her. Ready to enter her, he remembered he didn't have any condoms with him.

"I don't have any protection with me. I wasn't trying to go this route tonight," he said, a little breathless.

"It's okay. Check that tin over there." She pointed to an old cigarette tin. She always had toy parties and kept them there as a joke. Tonight they came in handy. Tyriq came back over to her and sat down with his back to the wall and motioned for her to join him. She came down on his shaft slowly, wrapping her legs around his back. She took control and began moving up and down as they began kissing again. The soft music in the background aided her movements as she grinded her pelvis on him. Tyriq wanted to help her, but she squeezed her walls on him and he laughed.

"Now you know that's my weakness," he whispered as she did it again. He tightened his grip on her waist. Lyric lifted her body some and turned in the opposite way. She slid on her stomach. The move caught Tyriq off guard. The movement caused a friction and feeling he had never experienced before. "Oh shit," he bellowed, thrusting into her. The room smelled of sweet sex as their movements matched each of the four songs that came on during their lovemaking. Their bodies were drenched in sweat. Lyric held on to the sides of Tyriq's ass as she felt her orgasm coming. He knew she was coming and thrust harder as he felt his shaft come in contact with her G-spot. He let it hum there while she squirmed. He thrust again and felt her come all over him. He followed her lead, spilling his seed into her.

They lay on the floor until they both drifted off. After a brief nap, Lyric got up and ran water into the Jacuzzi, adding jasmine and lavender to the water. She brought the wineglasses into the bathroom and lit candles. She heard him walking up behind her as he kissed her bare back. They got into the steaming hot water together. The music still played overhead.

"Hmmm, you know your brand of chocolate is going to make this man addicted."

"Is that so? That's the second time you mentioned that word 'addicted.' Must be something to it."

"Indeed, sweetness, indeed." He began to wash her body. He took the sponge and grazed her clit. She shook. He took his hand and caressed her clit with his finger, running it slowly back and forth over her enlarged nub. Lyric moaned, knowing even in the water she was wet. He inserted a finger inside her sweetness and began fingering her. He inserted another finger. The water sloshed around as she got more and more aroused with him playing in her hot spot.

He continued rubbing her clit, harder, and Lyric couldn't hold it anymore. As she came hard into his hand, her body rocked with erotic spasms. He kissed her wet body but didn't move his hands as he continued his sweet torture, causing her to cum three more times while they bathed.

They lay in the bed with Tyriq holding her hand to his mouth. He kissed her knuckles and then each finger. The man was driving her crazy. She needed to let him know she had the upper hand.

Reaching into the drawer by her bed, she pulled out some massage oil and told him to lie straight on his back. She propped some pillows behind him. Getting on her knees, she spoke softly. "Concentrate on what I am about to do…on the feeling. Clear your thoughts." She tied his hands to the bedpost. "Do you want to be blindfolded, or watch?"

"Watch?" he said, anticipating what was about to happen.

Lyric got ready to perform the Lingam massage. She worked his body slowly, gripping and releasing his shaft. She felt him about to come each time and she stopped. Tyriq's eyes were glazed with desire as he watched her movements. He paid attention to every movement that she did, just as she had instructed. Lyric rubbed more oil on her hands and gently blew on it. Instantly, Tyriq felt his skin get warm. The more she moved her hands up and down him, the more he felt like he was about to explode. She ran her hands down his thighs, cupping his balls, squeezing, and kneading him. He felt himself about to cum and he knew this time she was going to let him explode. She did a move that sent him over the edge. He couldn't even tell what it was, but the blood ran straight to his tip and he exploded, his semen flying up like an erupted volcano. His body shook like hers had in the bath. She didn't stop stroking him and within seconds, he exploded a second time, calling out her name. That had never happened before. Tyriq had been turned out. He closed his eyes and allowed the feeling to settle in. She untied his hands and laid her head on his chest. He wrapped his arms around her and they both fell into a deep sleep.

Over the next five weeks, they spent each night together. She had gone down to Club Intense and watched him play, and had even performed a writing piece. The crowd loved it. Soon after, a poetry night was introduced.

It had been a while since she had seen her fri[...] girls' night, but it felt different. It was the first [...] be seeing Tyriq. Lyric finally decided that sh[...] her friends about her and Tyriq.

"Girl, you have been so hard to get ahold of lately. The bakery [...] been slamming, I hear," Erin chimed in as they munched on spinach and artichoke dip.

"Yes, and the renovations will be complete in another month. We will be holding a grand reopening," she informed them. The ladies raised their glasses.

"To new and exciting things." They all clinked glasses. Donna stared at her. "We all noticed you are glowing tonight. Anything you want to share?"

Before Lyric could respond, the back door opened. They all turned around and saw Vince come into the room.

"I knocked and rang the bell; no one answered. I wanted to make sure you were okay." He looked in Lyric's direction as they all looked at him with shocked expressions.

"How did you get a key?"

"I don't have a key; you must have left it unlocked."

Sighing in relief, she did remember she had left it unlocked so that the ladies could come inside while she got dressed and finished preparing.

"So what do you want, Vince?" Erin asked him, her face looking disgusted.

"I came to talk to my wife if that's okay with you?" he said to no one in particular.

"Don't you mean EX-wife?" Donna corrected.

Vince never liked her, of all of Lyric's friends. She always had an attitude like she wore the pants in whatever relationship she was in.

"Donna, I wasn't talking to you?" He glared at her. Donna took a long sip of her drink.

Lyric, can I speak to you alone for a minute?"

Lyric didn't want to talk to him, but she knew if she didn't, he would ruin their evening.

She told her friends she would be back in a few minutes. She and Vince went into the den. "What do you want, Vince?"

"You kicked me out a few weeks ago so I never got a chance to talk to you."

"Okay, you have five minutes and the time is ticking."

"I want to take you on a date."

"Why!"

"Because…because we have unresolved issues. There was no closure," he lied quickly.

"Humph, I had all my closure when I caught you and Angela at that hotel. By the way, how is your girlfriend?" she asked, really not caring anyway. But yet she quickly regretted it when she heard his rebuttal.

"How is your boy toy?" he said loud enough for her friends to hear.

"I see you haven't grown up yet. Was that necessary?"

"Well, it seems you aren't hiding it, the way you two have been painting the town?" he blurted out. Lyric looked at him like he was crazy. Why did this fool care about who she was with, because she couldn't care less about him? Lyric took Vince by the hand and led him to the front door.

"I knew I should have made you leave when you walked in; it's time for you to go. We have nothing to discuss. And the answer to your date is *hell no*," she told him as she once again closed the door in his face. She ran her hand over her hair and stood there. Were people talking about them around town? Did she care? Lyric headed back into kitchen, and the ladies all stopped talking when she walked in.

"So I guess you all heard," she said to them, throwing her hands up in the air.

"Yes, we heard," Erin said.

"But the real question is why didn't you tell us? We are your home girls," Donna said.

"I was about to tell you all right before Vincent got here. Do you know he had the nerve to ask me on a date? That man is crazy. Talking about we need closure."

"Do you need closure?"

"No! Well, I don't think so."

"Maybe you need to think about it. There is nothing wrong with you getting closure. If Tyriq is who you want to be with, then you will be okay." Lyric didn't respond but just refilled their glasses.

"So how long have you and Tyriq been messing around?" Nicole asked.

"Since the night of my divorce party," she said low, because she knew what was about to come next, as all three women screamed.

"WHAT!" The women looked at her and all laughed. They suspected but could never prove she was seeing someone; they never would have thought it was Tyriq.

"Wow, is he good?" Erin asked.

"And then some," she said, laughing and blushing. She proceeded to tell her friends about the last two-and-a-half months.

"Well, I'll be damned. Stella done got her groove back!" Nicole said and they all laughed. Later that night, she let the ladies out and went to her room. Tyriq's band was performing out of town so she decided to focus on pampering herself. She had a hair appointment in the morning. The thought had crossed her mind to cut her hair short, but she was still conflicted. She would make up her mind before her appointment. As soon as she was getting in the shower, her cell phone rang.

"Hello?" Lyric said into the phone.

"Hey, Sweetness, did I wake you?"

"No, I was just about to jump in the shower. How was the show?"

"It was a good night, but I'm missing my baby. Did you have a good day?"

"Yes, it was ladies night, and then my ex showed up, unexpectedly tripping." She sat on the phone awaiting a response but heard nothing. She called out his name, "Tyriq? Are you still on the phone?"

After a few more minutes, Tyriq answered her. "Yea." She noticed that his tone had changed. "What did he want?" Tyriq didn't like her ex-husband dropping by.

"He claimed he was coming by to talk."

"Oh yea?"

"Tyriq, you don't have anything to worry about; I have no interest in talking to him. So please relax?"

"I know I have to trust you, but it just makes me uneasy to know he is coming around. I just got you comfortable in our relationship."

"I know, I know. I will take care of this. Don't worry," she told him. She heard him sigh into the phone. Trying to change the subject, she talked to him about the rest of his trip and when he would be back home. They talked for another half hour and then hung up. When she was in the shower, she thought about the conversation that she had just had with Tyriq; he was jealous. It kind of surprised her. She wasn't prepared for that reaction from him. She knew there were feelings between them both, but they never really talked about anything long term. For the moment, she was just taking it day by day.

Getting in bed from her shower, she noticed she had two messages. One was from Tyriq; it read, *I can't lose you; I am falling in love with you.* Shocked, she covered her mouth with her hand. She was afraid to look at the next one, as it was from Vince. His read in all caps. *I WANT MY WIFE BACK.* Looking at both messages again, Lyric began to tear up. Why was this happening? Was she being punked? Vince didn't want just her when they were married. What was he trying to prove now; was it because she was with Tyriq? And Tyriq, falling in love with her? She shouldn't have been surprised. She had noticed he had changed recently—being more attentive, wanting to spend as much time together as they could. She enjoyed the time spent with him, but she wasn't sure how she felt. Confused, she didn't sleep much. When she finally fell asleep, she was awakened by the sound of her doorbell ringing. Looking at the clock, it was just after eight a.m. Going to the door, she opened it and in walked Tyriq. "Tyriq, what are you doing here? What's wrong?" she asked him confused by his appearance.

"I...I couldn't sleep. I got up and just started driving and this is where I ended up. When you didn't respond to my text, I got worried. I have never felt this way about a woman before, let alone an older woman. I think about you all day; I want to be with you all the time. I just want to be able to show you how I feel. I love you, Lyric. From the first time I saw you at the breakfast house, I knew you would change my life," Tyriq told her. He felt like he was rambling so he just stood there, holding her hand and looking at her. It was the first time he'd noticed that she was crying.

"Why are you crying?" he asked her. He released her hand to get her some Kleenex from off the table. He ushered her to the couch so they could get out of the doorway. He sat in silence as she got herself together.

"I have never had someone express such words to me. I owe you an apology."

"An apology? For what?" he said, looking at her strangely.

"I never once thought that what we were sharing was more than a good time and good sex."

"But, I told you when we started back talking that I wanted more; you didn't think I meant that?"

"You have to understand something: my ex-husband was the first man I had ever been with, relationship wise and sexually. I am not proud of that, but I did learn a lot from him. He was very sexual and experimental. We tried everything from S&M, threesomes, foursomes, bondage, to role playing to sex clubs. But even in doing all that, I was never enough for him; he still needed more. That caused me to get depressed and I ate. Before you met me, I told you I lost weight, but I didn't tell you much. I lost almost a hundred pounds. I weighed over two hundred pounds. This body that I'm in is who I feel comfortable in, but it took me a long time to get there. The last year of my marriage, he was abusive."

"He hit you?" Tyriq interrupted, clearly mad.

"No he didn't hit me, but he took away my spirit. He took away the last of my self-esteem. And I let him because I wasn't happy with who I was inside and out." She watched him as he calmed down. She stopped and went into the kitchen to make coffee. He followed her and they fell into their normal kitchen routine with him taking the items out for breakfast. She continued to bare her soul to him. "It took for me to go see someone to get my self-worth back and she got me into a diet and exercise program. While I was seeing my therapist, Vince was seeing someone else. I suspected but couldn't prove it. Until one day he left his credit card at the hotel and they called the house. I asked some questions and found out they met there twice a week and the next time they did, I made sure I showed up. I had never felt so much hurt as I watched them together. I think what hurt the most was that she was young. Maybe your age or younger. I made sure they saw me and when he got home, all his things were packed. I had already changed the locks," she told him through tears and he stopped and held her.

She cried tears she didn't even know were still in her. For her this was her closure. She didn't need nor did she want to be with Vince; he truly was her past. Once she stopped crying, she excused herself to the bathroom. Looking at her reflection, she realized she was a different person than she was a year ago. Her life changed when she got that hotel call. Returning to the kitchen, Tyriq had finished making breakfast and was waiting on her to come back.

"Are you okay?" he asked, looking concerned. She sat across from him at the table and took his hand and squeezed. "Thank you for letting me talk. I needed that. I have deep feelings for you, but I can't say that I love you just yet and it would be unfair of me to even try and play on your feelings. I know how that feels and I would never do that to anyone."

"I appreciate your honesty. I am not going anywhere," he told her. They ate in silence. While she was cleaning the dishes, Tyriq came up behind her and opened her robe and he began kissing her neck and down her back. He turned her around and lifted her into his arms. They began kissing while he slowly moved them over to the nook counter. He sat her down and sucked her breasts, while Lyric leaned slightly back supporting herself with her arms. Tyriq went into the fridge and pulled out some honey, chocolate syrup and whip cream. He poured the honey on her breasts and went back to enjoying his feast. The sticky, sweet aroma filled the air as she watched him lick and eat all the honey off of her. It was such a turn-on to watch him. Next he took the whip cream and chocolate and told her to lie back. He wrote "I love you" from her navel to her hot spot and followed it with the syrup. He placed her open legs wider and bent them so she could see what he was doing, as he proceeded to once again finish his dessert. The syrup ran in between her legs and pooled under her ass. She shivered. Tyriq ate her pussy like it was the last treat he was going to have.

He ran his tongue over her clit and pressed his tongue down on it, He felt it expand in his mouth as he pulled on the nub. As he was licking the cream and syrup off of her, she felt him place two fingers in her hot spot. She moaned, as an orgasm hit her wave upon wave. Tyriq licked all the cream, honey and syrup from her, then he turned her on her stomach and entered her. Tyriq gripped her waist and pounded into her wetness. Lyric gripped the edge of the counter as he fucked her harder and harder.

The lovemaking this time was a pure raw need. It was more intense and much more different than any other time. It was like he wanted her to feel how he felt as he took her body. After what seemed like hours, they both came hard. Tired and drenched, they both were shaking from the way they'd just come together. After she found her voice, she looked at him as she kissed him. She kissed him slow, sucking his tongue lightly and making sure she explored his mouth completely. Tears ran down her cheeks as they kissed. He stopped the kiss and then kissed the tears from her face. "Was it me, or was this different?" she asked him, but not really expecting an answer.

"Yes it was." He kissed her again and then carried her into the bathroom where they shared a shower. She walked him to the door and stood there. Tyriq had a three-hour drive back to the hotel where he was staying. He would be home tomorrow. He'd asked her if she wanted to come, but she had declined. She needed to check on the construction of the addition as well as finish a huge order for a party tomorrow. They kissed and she watched as he got into his car and pulled out of her driveway. Closing the door, she leaned against it and sighed. Tyriq did things to her body that she never knew was possible. Vince taught her about sex. Tyriq taught and showed her intimacy and passion.

Sitting in her office later that day, she was pleased with the way the extension was going and that they were on schedule. She was doing her reopening on Tyriq's birthday next month. His band was performing and she had a surprise for him: a music executive from A & M Records was attending. She finished working on the invitations and then went out into the shop. There was an event that evening, so the store was crowded. She spent the next three hours helping out. As she was locking up, she heard a knock on the window. Vince was standing at the door. This was the last thing she needed. She started to ignore him, but she knew he wouldn't just go away. Opening the door for him, he walked in and sat down at one of the tables. She sat down and looked at him waiting for him to speak. He looked at her for a few minutes and then spoke.

"You know, I can't get out of my mind how beautiful you look now," he told her.

"Really, is that what you came all the way down here to tell me?" Getting up from her chair, Vince grabbed her by the arm.

"Lyric, please sit down." Rolling her eyes at him, she did what he asked.

"I came down here to see if you got my text; you didn't respond." She laughed and seriously thought this man was crazy.

"Were you really expecting a reply? What type of reaction were you expecting from me, telling me that you want me back? Do you think that I really give a flying fuck? You cheated on me, you told me that no man would want me outside of you; I listened to you, believed in you even when you called me names. There are some things I can never forget. You don't deserve me and I sure as hell don't want you. We are divorced for a reason," she told him through anger. She stood up, knocking the chair over, its loud sound making her jump.

"I need for you to leave now. You are a selfish bastard and I want you to leave me alone, please."

"I can't do that. I am sorry I hurt you. But you know what I want, I get. And I am going to get you back," he told her, looking over his shoulder as he walked out of the door. Lyric locked the door behind him. She picked up her phone and dialed.

"Hey, are you free? Can you meet me at Intense in thirty minutes?" she said to the caller. Locking up the rest of the shop, she walked over to her Benz and saw her favorite purple roses on her windshield. She was tempted to throw them away, but saw a young couple walking past and offered the roses to them. Getting in her car, she headed to Club Intense.

Sitting at the bar, Donald walked over and greeted her. "Hey, princess, what you drinking tonight?" he said as he hugged and kissed her.

"Give me my usual," she said to the bartender as Donald nodded and told the server. Her drinks were on the house. Nicole sat down next to her.

"I hope that applies to me as well," she said, nodding to the bartender.

"Of course, Nicole, of course," he said, winking at her and walked away.

"So I see you still banging Donald," Lyric said to her, smiling for the first time the whole evening.

"Yea, not as much as he would like, but he serves his purpose," she told her best friend, sipping her drink. "So what's up anyway?"

"Where do I begin?"

"The beginning is always good."

"First, Tyriq told me he is in love with me and Vince said he wants me back and won't stop until he has me back as his wife." Nicole choked on her drink.

"Excuse me?" she said, wiping her mouth and glaring at her friend.

"Yep and that's the short version," she said, shaking her head.

"So what are you going to do? I mean I know that Vince is a wrap, no matter what his cocky ass thinks. But what about Tyriq? Do you love him?" Nicole watched her friend's facial expression as she asked her the question. Lyric looked at her drink and swirled her finger in it. "I told him this morning that I didn't love him. I am so confused; Tyriq is something I've never had before. My experience with relationships are limited, you know that. But I have to take all this into account. I do have very strong feelings for him. But I am afraid of loving him. I am afraid of the way he makes me feel when I am with him." Wiping away her tears, she took a long swallow and motioned for a refill.

Nicole was the one who had sat with Lyric for days, when she'd discovered Vince had cheated on her. She'd witnessed the verbal abuse he had lashed at her. Nicole also noticed how Tyriq made her glow, how they interacted with one another and she was even envious. "Follow your heart. You are good with Tyriq. He brings out something I haven't seen in you with Vince." She wiped away her own tears. The two women hugged. Lyric was glad she'd called her. She always could make her see things she didn't see on her own. They spent the next hour drinking and talking.

Donald came over as they were leaving. He saw the condition the ladies were in and motioned for his driver to come over. He told him to take Lyric home and Nicole would be going to his place. He would have her car brought to her home in the morning. When the driver walked her to the door, there was a package at the door. He set it in the inside of her door and made sure she got inside okay. Locking the door behind him, Lyric lay on the couch; she couldn't make it up the stairs. Taking her phone out, she dialed Tyriq's number. When he didn't answer, she left him a voicemail. "I just called to say I think I love you too." Smiling, she ended the call.

Vince stood over Lyric as she slept. He knew she would be mad as hell, if she knew he'd had a key made. Leaving back out the way he'd come, he had hoped she would open the package, but it was worth the wait. Hearing his phone, he knew it was Angela texting him. At some time he would have to tell Lyric the truth about Angela. But not before he got her back.

The next morning, Tyriq used the spare key Lyric had given him and he entered through the kitchen. He didn't see her car out front but decided he would just surprise her whenever she got home. He'd listened to her message after his performance and he'd re-played it over and over. Just to hear her say she loved him made him want to shout it out. He was just about to head upstairs when he saw something out the side of his eye. Walking to the couch, he saw Lyric, fully dressed sleeping on the couch. He laughed, as he could still smell the liquor. Gently shaking her, he called out to her.

"Sweetness, sweetness, wake up." Lyric stirred and opened her eyes. She smiled when she saw him and tried to lift her head up but was greeted with the worst headache ever. Laughing, Tyriq went to make her a hangover tonic. He made her drink it as she balked at its taste, but shortly, her headache was gone.

"Tyriq, did you use the spare key to get in?" she asked him as she sat up completely on the couch, facing him.

"Yes, I hope you don't mind."

"No, in fact, you can keep it. It actually opens both doors. Nicole has my other key; I don't feel safe with it being out there. I need to talk to you about something."

"Okay, I am all ears, but what's that box right there?" he said, pointing to the box that she recalled seeing on the porch.

"I don't know. It was on the steps when I got home last night."

"Do you want to open it?"

"Why, is it from you?"

"No. But aren't you curious?"

"Not really, but come on, let's open it and see what it is," she told him, as he brought the medium-sized box over to the table and opened it. Lyric gasped at the contents. She pulled out her wedding dress; it was restored to its first beauty. She pulled it all the way out and a note dropped to the floor. Tyriq picked it up and read it aloud, *"I look forward to seeing you wear this again, on our wedding day and yes, there will be another wedding day soon."* Tyriq's face scowled and Lyric dropped the dress back into its box. Tyriq began to pace the floor.

Lyric could not believe the nerve of Vince. This was crazy. She walked over to Tyriq and stood in his pathway. He stopped and looked at her. His jawline was set. He was mad. "Tyriq, you know I had nothing to do with this, right. That is what I wanted to talk to you about. Vince has claimed he wants me back and is going to try and break us apart. Don't give him that satisfaction," Lyric told him as she made him look at her. "You and I are going to get through whatever he throws at us together, okay?" Tyriq nodded and he wanted to believe her. He needed to. He knew that if he lost her, he would fight to get her back. So he could just imagine what kind of fight Vince was going to do to get her back as his wife. Tyriq pulled her into his arms and held her tight. "I love you, Lyric. We will do this together."

"I love you too. Can we please go lay down? My head is starting to hurt again." He picked her up and carried her to the bed. They got undressed and held each other.

Over the next two weeks, Lyric and Tyriq worked together on getting the bakery expansion completed. She put him in charge of the entertainment and gave him reign on how he wanted it to be done. Vince called her or texted her daily. Lyric sent him the dress back and he was mad. He had texted her last night and told her that he would be there for her when she found out about the real Tyriq. She wondered what he meant and didn't even bother to ask Tyriq about the comment. Later that evening, Tyriq was performing at Club Intense and she and her best friends went for dinner and drinks. The place was packed. They were all talking when all of a sudden, Donna screamed and grabbed Nicole's hand.

"Oh my goodness, what is that on your finger?" she asked her . She made Nicole blush. They all looked at her, then waited for her to reply.

"Donald asked me to marry him and I said yes."

"When did all this happen, Nicole? We all just saw you two days ago at the shop and it wasn't there."

"Right!" the other two ladies said at once.

"He asked me a week ago. I didn't give him my answer until last night." Lyric looked at Nicole and wondered did she really love Donald. But her best friend looked happy, so maybe she did.

"Congratulations, this calls for a toast," Lyric said, motioning for the waitress. The women all toasted as Donald came over and joined them. She hugged him and then he whispered in her ear that there was a woman at the front asking for Tyriq. Since he was on stage, he came and got her. Lyric excused herself and walked to the door with Donald.

"Hi, I was told you were looking for Tyriq. Can I help you with something?" She looked at the pretty girl who looked like she was about seven months' pregnant.

"And who are you? His mother??" the girl asked her rudely, looking her up and down. "I came to talk to my baby daddy, Tyriq. Now are ya'll going to go get him or do I have to make a scene?" the girl said, looking directly at Lyric.

"What...What do you mean 'baby daddy'; are you saying the baby you're carrying is his?" Lyric asked the girl, wanting to make sure she heard her right.

"I guess you're getting deaf 'cause I know that's what I said." She pushed past Lyric in search of Tyriq who was now walking in their direction. Lyric turned around and watched the color drain from his face when he looked at the girl and her protruding stomach. Lyric felt sick.

"Robin, what are you doing here?" Tyriq asked her.

"So...so you know her? She said that baby she's carrying is yours. Is that true?" Tyriq looked from Robin to her. "Are you going to answer me?" Lyric asked him, raising her voice.

"Yeah, aren't you going to answer her, Ty?" Robin said, laughing. Tyriq reached out to touch Lyric's hand, but she moved out of his reach. The tears were rolling down her face and by this time, her friends were by her side, trying to see what was going on.

"Lyric, please let me explain. Robin is my ex. I didn't know she was pregnant, I swear." Lyric wiped her tears and slapped Tyriq. Turning to leave, she didn't look back when Tyriq called after her. He tried to go after her, but Donald stood in his way and shook his head no. Turning back around, Tyriq looked at Robin who was smiling the whole time. He grabbed her by the arm and led her to Donald's office.

"Why didn't you tell me you were pregnant and how do I even know if the baby is mine?"

"I can't believe you would even say that. Ty, we were together for two years."

"And yeah, you seem to be forgetting why we broke up. I caught you with my cousin, remember? That baby could be his, for all I know." Robin showed no emotion either way. Tyriq told her to go home and he would call her. He needed to be alone.

Outside Robin got into a tan Cadillac. "I saw Lyric and her friends leaving. She bought your act," Vince said to her.

"Yep, hook, line and sinker. And so did Tyriq; he is all confused. Now can I have my first half of my money, please?" Vince handed the girl five one hundred-dollar bills, as she knocked on her fake stomach and laughed. It would be the easiest grand she'd ever made.

Vince dropped her off and then headed to Lyric's house. He sat in his car and waited until her friends left. Knocking on the door, he waited.

"I guess you're here to gloat," she told him as she opened the door and walked away. She grabbed her glass and walked into the family room. She didn't want him to see her cry. She laid her head back on the couch pillow. Vince looked at her and saw how hurt she was. For a few minutes, he actually felt bad about what he was doing. He walked over to the couch and sat next to her.

"I told you he wasn't good enough for you." Lifting her head up, Lyric slapped him. "How dare you come here just to see me hurt. Why are you so bent on making my life a living hell? You don't want me back because you love me; you want me back because you can't have me. And your precious ego can't take that."

"Lyric, calm down so we can talk. I know you are upset. But what can that boy do for you, that me as a real man can't? You are wasting your time with him. Seriously, you can do better." Neither heard Tyriq when he came in.

"And I guess the better that she supposedly can do, is with you?" they heard him say as they both turned toward his voice.

"How did you get in here, breaking and entering? How, huh?" Vince said, walking to where Tyriq stood. He was now in his face.

"Nah, I didn't need to do that, my WOMAN gave me a key," he told him, showing him the key ring. Vince looked surprised as he glanced toward Lyric.

"Tyriq, what are you doing here? I need some time to think, please. Matter of fact. Why don't you both just leave?" she said to both men. Tyriq and Vince glared at one another, sizing the other up.

"Lyric, I will leave after I say what I came here to. I drove around after you left and I went to see my cousin. See, when Robin and I broke up, it was because I caught her with him. So I asked him about the baby she is carrying. Funny thing is this, my cousin said he was just with Robin the other day and she was nowhere near seven months' pregnant."

"What do you mean?" Lyric said, confused by what he'd said. She walked to where they stood.

"I have a picture of them together at a party the other day," he said, showing her the photo on his phone. "I asked him to take me over there. So my cousin and I went to her house and just that quick, she wasn't pregnant. After my cousin threatened to leave her alone, she told us everything, how you came looking for her and paid her to be a part of your scheme," he directed at Vince. "See, what you fail to realize is even though she cheated on me, she does have some feelings for my cousin. She ain't going to risk losing him for you."

Feeling like the situation was slipping from him, Vince chimed in. "This doesn't change anything; you're still got a lot to learn about Lyric. You can't handle a woman like her; you're under her caliber," he said to Tyriq. Lyric still hadn't said anything as she handed the phone back to Tyriq.

Tyriq lifted her face up to his. "You told me just two weeks ago that we had to fight him together. This is his way of breaking us down. Don't let him tear what we are building together. You gave him that control once before; don't give it back to him. I love you, Lyric, and you know I would never do anything to hurt you. You are what makes my life complete. If there is anyone that doesn't deserve you, it's him. Not me," Tyriq said, pleading to Lyric. She turned her back to both men, trying to understand what she'd just seen and heard.

Vince grabbed her by the arm. "Baby, you are not going to fall for that bull crap he is telling you. So what if I did hire that girl; I needed you to see you don't belong with him. I know I made mistakes in the past, but I know now that I can't live my life without you. Give us another chance."

"Get your hands off her."

"Or what! What you think you can do to me, young buck. I am only going to take so much of this from you. You don't know nothing about me," Vince said as he let go of Lyric and got into Tyriq's face. Lyric stepped between them trying to diffuse the scene.

"Vince, I told you we are over and who I choose to be with is none of your business."

"But!"

"No buts, stooping this low even for you is a stretch. It's time for you to go and don't come back here, ever!" she told him as she headed toward her front door. When she opened it, a very pregnant Angela was standing there. "Ang...Angela, what are you doing at my house?" she said, startled at her appearance.

"I was about to knock, but I heard the arguing in here. I guess I don't have to ask is Vincent here," the woman said as she lined her eyes with Vince. "You told me you were over her. Now I hear you want her back. I guess this is what I deserve for betraying Lyric, but I just can't believe you," Angela said through heavy sobs and tears, holding her stomach. Vince came rushing over to her.

"Angela, how did you know I was here?"

"I followed you to Intense and saw you with that pregnant girl and then followed you over here. I have been sitting in my car for the past hour trying to convince myself that you weren't cheating on me with Lyric," she said, as she winced with pain and Vince took her by the arm to steady her.

"Are you okay?" Lyric asked.

"I...I don't know. I have been having sharp pains for the last few hours."

"Vince, she needs to get to the hospital *now*," Lyric told Vince who was beginning to look panicked. They all heard her gasp as blood began to pool on the floor.

"Tyriq, call an ambulance!" she told him as Angela looked down at the blood. She grabbed her stomach and a look of pure fear came over her face and then she began to fall back as Vince caught her. Lyric ran to get a blanket and covered her and held Angela's hand until the ambulance got there.

In the hospital waiting room, Tyriq and Lyric sat close together and Vince sat on the opposite side of the room. He wasn't allowed to go back because Angela had to be taken into surgery. The baby was in distress. After about an hour, the doctor came out and called Vince's name. He stood up.

"You have a beautiful baby boy, but unfortunately, Angela didn't survive the birth. She went into shock and lost a lot of blood. We tried to stop the bleeding, but with the delivery complications, we could not save her. I am sorry," the doctor told him.

Vince stood there stunned as the doctor walked away. The nurse came up and told him he could see his son. Vince looked over at Lyric and Tyriq and felt this whole night was his karma. He couldn't raise that child; that baby deserved better than him.

"Do you want me to go back with you?" Lyric asked, when Vince still didn't move from the spot he was in. She saw the tears on his face.

"I'm sorry for trying to break you two up," he said, barely above a whisper. "I can't. I can't do this. I can't raise a child. I didn't even want the baby in the first place and now I have lost Angela. I can't do this," he said to them both. He started pacing and they could see he was hurt over Angela's death. Tyriq looked at Vince and then at Lyric. Taking her by the hand, they walked over to Vince.

"Man, that's your son in there. He needs you now that his mother is gone. You can do it," Tyriq told him. Vince looked at him as if his words were trying to register. He was hollow and that was how he felt. He shook his head.

"No, you two go see your new son. I will call my lawyer and have the papers drawn up. You two will make far better parents than I ever could," Vince said. They both looked at him shocked.

"Vince?" Lyric said, looking at him. She couldn't have just heard him. He was going to give them his and Angela's baby?

"You know I never wanted kids and I would rather know he is taken care of in a good home than have him going into the system. My mind is made up," he said, putting his hand up to end the conversation. He walked down the hall, after asking the nurse if he could see Angela's body. They watched him as he went into a room. The nurse came over to the couple.

"Ma'am, I was told by Mr. Washington that you were going to be the baby's legal parents?" she asked Lyric for clarity. She looked over at Tyriq who had tears in his eyes, as he nodded. Guess that made it official; she had never expected all this to happen. They followed the nurse to the baby nursery, and they both smiled at the beautiful baby boy they were shown, agreeing they would name him Trey.

Two years later...

"Are you ready?" Nicole asked Lyric as she looked at her in the mirror. "You are absolutely glowing," she told her best friend. Donna and Erin walked into the room.

Trey ran to her, screaming "Mommie," and she reached down and kissed him, careful not to mess up her makeup. Erin came over to her and she kissed two-month-old Tyriq Jr. on the cheek.

"Ladies, thank you for all the help for this day. I couldn't have done it without you all."

"Well, it's not every day our best friend marries a Grammy-winning R&B artist," Donna said and they all laughed.

At the grand reopening, the A&M rep loved Tyriq and signed him immediately. Their lives had taken off. Her friends had helped her with Trey after she'd told them all that had happened that night at her house and the hospital. She and Tyriq were even better together and she fell even more in love with him. He could have chosen to walk. Instead, he embraced having an instant family that neither one of them created. Tyriq showed her he was way more than his age and she was so glad when he stayed with her and became Trey's father. They never heard from Vince, he never came to see the baby and she didn't have a way to reach him but through the lawyer who made the adoption legal. He sent her money for his care, which they opened an account for and never touched.

Today she was marrying the man who'd changed her life at her own divorce party. Her life was complete and she couldn't be happier. "Places, everyone," her coordinator yelled as she broke into her thoughts, lightly wiping her eyes. Trey and Tyriq Jr. were taken out and she headed to get into place. She could see Tyriq standing at the altar. The ladies walked down the aisle. Nicole held TJ and Trey was the ring bearer. Nicole handed TJ to her mother when she reached the front. Now it was her cue and Tyriq's voice filled the church. He looked so fine, smiling as she walked toward him. He sang to his bride as she and her father walked down the aisle. She overheard someone in the audience ask how they met.

The woman told her, "Girl, can you believe it, at her own divorce party."

Intertwining old-school romance and erotica, Nicola Motley (Jada Pearl) is set to bring you a stand-out reading experience from the normal approach on contemporary fiction. Born and raised in Detroit, Michigan, Jada Pearl started writing when she was thirteen years old. She always had a strong passion for stories, so much so that she began working in the Detroit Public Library and soaked in all the books she read. Her love for writing was reinforced when she hosted a Romantic Readers of Michigan meeting. Being around other authors and learning how they developed their craft, she knew there was nothing more that she wanted to do.

When she isn't penning, Jada Pearl spends her time with family, friends, setting up workshops for the community to learn computer skills, and working as a Payroll Specialist. She currently resides in Southfield, MI.

CHAMPAGNE
Whores

N'TYSE

A RIDE ON THE CAROUSEL

I t had been a long and grueling day at the office. I wanted nothing more than to kick off my red, Valentino studded pumps, snatch off this tight-ass dress, and fuck his young naïve heart right out of his chest. In fact, that was exactly what I was going to do, especially after having to console my mourning pussy for the past six hours as he eye-fucked me from across the room. Oh yes, he was definitely going to pay for my sexual misery before we left this building tonight.

I casually glanced over my right shoulder again, and as I suspected, Sergio was staring right back at me with those maple-colored bedroom eyes and full luscious butter-fucking-finger-licking lips. Talk about a well-endowed sex god. Lord have mercy! I worshipped that pussy-splitting dick and floor-mopping tantalizing tongue of his. Too bad I could never admit that out loud. Especially not to him. As the youngsters say nowadays, his ass might start "feeling" himself, and I definitely couldn't have that. I learned from the last one that emotional attachments always threatened the flow of business, and God forbid it dare attempt to threaten my twenty-two-year marriage. My husband, Larry Howard, and I, didn't always see eye-to-eye. We went through the typical marital trials and tribulations, but he was the sweet love of my life. I wasn't going anywhere and neither was he. And while our unorthodox relationship permitted me to have my cake and eat it too, I would never allow my fetish and high sex drive to destroy what we've built.

It actually wasn't until my husband was diagnosed with prostate cancer that our sex life took a backseat. The only option was to have a radical *prostatectomy* performed to remove his prostate. The surgery was a success, but the side effects left us hopeless. He was no longer able to maintain an erection. It was a very stressful time for us and I felt completely helpless. Helpless and selfish, because the reality of it all was that I still had my needs. I loved sex more than I loved my next breath, so being deprived of the very thing that invigorated me, had me resenting Larry at times. It wasn't fair and I couldn't understand why it had to happen to us.

When Larry finally realized and came to grips with the fact that our sexless marriage was starting to have more of an impact on our relationship as a whole, we had a heart-to-heart and discussed how we both felt. We put it all out there. He admitted his darkest feelings and I slowly began to shed my emotions. I was worried he would hate me for feeling the way I did. Hate me for defending my sexual needs. He heard me out and immediately confessed he had been thinking about trying something a little different. I was usually the open-minded one, so it was damn shocking when he proposed the unthinkable. He suggested we try an open-marriage lifestyle, well, actually his words were "swing off the chandelier." Boy, did that conversation get hot real fast. He had my undivided attention at that point. He looked me dead in the eyes and said, "You can carry on a strictly sexual relationship with any man you want, whenever you want. There's only one condition. I don't ever want to hear about it." I bucked my eyes in shock and asked if he'd lost his mind. I mean seriously, I thought my husband was playing some kind of joke on me. All this was coming from a man who went to church every Sunday, who didn't use profanity, who turned the channel whenever a sex scene would play out in a movie, and who avoided public displays of affection; yet here he was talking about lending me out to another man. It just didn't make any sense.

Our conversation eventually led us to a place of understanding. I could tell he wasn't overly thrilled at the idea he had proposed, but that he was doing everything in his power to save our marriage and to keep me happy. I could only imagine how much of a mental struggle it was for him. It was obvious he had suggested something that went against everything he believed in, but it was seemingly the only solution to the emptiness we felt.

Being the doting wife I've always been for the past twenty-two years, not once had I taken my husband for granted or made him feel any less of a man because of his predicament. I cherished and respected our arrangement and I constantly reassured him that he could quiet his worries because I would never leave him. Who and what I did outside of our bedroom never left my lips, but at times, I felt I was in way too deep. Deeper than I would ever concede.

When I agreed to represent Mr. Sergio Champagne and his exquisite artwork eleven months ago, I immediately laid down the law of the land. I figured if Sergio could adhere to my program, he and the others I had recruited as my side lover long before him, would prove to be the perfect solution for other married couples who were in a similar situation as mine; and I was more than happy to facilitate the process, all for a hefty fee of course. I had been right on the money about everything. A discreet division of my art gallery, Generation Studios, was soon born, which I aptly called Next Generation. My husband didn't even know about it. Of course, he would have likely shut down the idea of creating such a place where people could go to hook up. I liked to think of it as my own private community. It was an elite, membership-only swingers club and escort agency that catered primarily to married couples over the age of forty. It served a greater purpose than just sex. We were resurrecting marriages.

Occasionally, I would get the single cougar applicant who was extremely interested in joining the club and taking part in our kinky festivities. I would only allow those women in by referral. At the end of the day, I saw no problem in extending my services and expanding my reach, after all, I did have the finest and biggest dick slangers in Texas under my tutelage. So it was really only a matter of time before they sought me out. As a sex agent with an astounding reputation, I acquired the best of the best. The even greater part about it was that I got to sample all of the inventory first.

Out of the eleven young studs I currently represented, Sergio was my youngest and highest-ranking dick distributor. I profited a great deal off his sexual instruments, which was even more of the reason why I had to keep our personal shit intact. I hated the clingy type and that had been a problem with two of my past play-mates. If they weren't pussy whipped, they were merely search-ing for that motherly figure to supply them with the attention they never received growing up. I had to quickly remind them that I was not trying to audition for Mommy's role. That was the only, and I do mean only drawback to fucking and representing men half my age.

Sergio seemed more secure with himself. He was a twenty-four-year-old, delicious, irresistible tall bottle of brandy standing right at six feet three. He had soft, cocoa berry skin, perfect white teeth, ripped six-pack, and hung just the way I liked them. He was a gladiator in the sheets and could murder a pussy. His long and infamous tongue, which I had nicknamed "Carousel," belonged in the book of Guinness World Records. Brother was so equipped and inimitably qualified, he deserved his own national spotlight. He was a pussy connoisseur. One time he sucked on my sweet succulent cunt for an entire two hours straight. My legs and ass were so numb afterward, I could barely stand up straight, let alone walk.

I shuddered at my latest memory. I wanted to feel his trigger-happy, ten-inch pole climbing my walls, again. The only thing standing between me sinking my razor-sharp cougar claws into the tender flesh on his back this very instant was M-O-N-E-Y, and the fact that Mr. Nip Tuck himself couldn't decide on which painting he wanted to surprise his wife with for their thirty-fifth wedding anniversary. Hell, if the doctor was the slightest bit privy to Mrs. Hollis's acquired taste and in tune with her sexual needs as I happened to be, he would have known that she wouldn't give a shit about that painting he'd been obsessing over for the past hour.

"Victoria, I believe this is the one. It speaks to me!" The doctor nodded his head at his own affirmation, never taking his eyes off the masterpiece. "Janice is going to love it!"

I mustered a smile. "I couldn't agree more." I signaled Sergio, whose pearly whites peeped through an intoxicating, half-moon smile. He winked. It was his painting that the doctor had just chosen. I shifted my attention back around to Dr. Hollis. "And while Sergio is taking care of that, I'll get you a receipt." I quickly processed his payment and made small talk while Sergio wrapped the painting in an elegant floral gift wrap and beautifully tied bow.

"I hope your wife will enjoy this piece as much as I did creating it," Sergio said.

"Oh wait, you're the artist?"

Sergio nodded proudly. "Yes, sir! The entire top row is all me," he informed, pointing at the other paintings that hung proudly in my gallery.

The doctor's eyes lit up. He looked back at me and again at Sergio. "This is magnificent artistry right here young man. It's an honor to meet you." He extended his hand and the two engaged in a handshake.

"The pleasure's all mine."

"It was great seeing you, doctor. Tell that beautiful wife of yours I said hello," I said, smiling.

"Will do." He leaned in and gave me a kiss on the cheek.

Sergio walked and talked the doctor all the way out of the door while I took a moment to check my latest text message. It was that nineteen-year-old daughter of mine, Geneva, asking if I could wire her $800. My eyes bucked wide. What on earth could you possibly need $800 for? Ask your father, I quickly replied. Not even a second later, my phone pinged. I refused to deal with that right now. I had more important business to tend to like trying to decide who I would get to cater our Next Generation event in two weeks.

Instead of reading Geneva's response, I dropped my phone inside my purse. I would deal with that later. I heard Sergio come back inside. I could hear him locking the doors behind him. We both knew what time it was.

Without further delay, I located the remote control and with a press of a button, dimmed the lights. I sauntered over to my mouthwatering young stud who looked like a million-dollar hunk of fudge standing there, dripping with a swagger out of this world. He smelled yummy and I wanted nothing more than to eat him alive. His long, thick, black dreads were neatly pulled back into a ponytail, exposing every feature of his face. His full cocoa lips were the gates to any heaven and no one knew it better than this quintessential cougar herself. My candy cane began to melt in response to his horny gaze, leaving a mounting sticky puddle between my thighs. I slid my manicured fingertips down the left side of his face and along his square jawline, before tracing the slight curve of his mouth. I pressed my deft lips against his, hoping to arouse a sleeping Carousel. To my delight and satisfaction, he responded instantly. Holding our kiss, I unzipped Sergio's pants and stuck my hand completely inside to free Willy. His breathing turned jagged, his head swung between his dancing shoulders, and his hands latched around my head.

"Time to give daddy that pussy." His otherwise deep voice fell to a whisper. He kissed the skin on my neck before sliding Carousel along the edge of my left ear.

"Oooooh, baby," I moaned, my pussy getting even wetter from the way his tongue roamed my earlobe. His deep and heavy breaths made my skin melt underneath him. So strong and pulsating. I could feel my nipples peering through my dress, beckoning his attention. My lips found him again. He drove his tongue further down my throat, igniting a whole new fire within my soul. I moaned seductively in his ear and stroked his dick to a glorious awakening.

Interrupting our oral love affair once again, I eyed him weakly. Had he truly known how much I cared for him, how much he meant to me…he would have stopped fucking me so good. He would have gotten comfortable. Complacent. Territorial. Hell, he would have started smelling his own shit. And as much as I would have loved to keep Sergio all to myself, I couldn't. This was more than just sex. This was business!

I turned around slowly and headed toward the stairs that led to the second level of the gallery. Sergio followed closely behind. With every step I climbed, the weaker my knees grew and the wetter my pussy got. Once I reached that final step, I immediately began to shed every article of clothing. I faced Sergio and slow-walked backward into the middle of the room. I lowered my naked body to the cold hardwood, unconcerned with getting a little dirty. It wasn't like it hadn't happened before. I watched him sip and drink every inch of my luscious curves with his eyes. As if he couldn't take another second of being teased, he quickly undressed. Before I could blink my eyes, his hands were all over my body.

"Bend that ass over!" he commanded.

I responded with a coquettish grin, then turned around on all fours and did exactly as told. I tooted my round brown derriere in the air and hung it there in one of my favorite selfie poses. I glanced over my right shoulder, back at him.

"What are you going to do to me this time?" I asked innocently.

He gripped a handful of my ass like he owned it.

"I'm gonna nail a poster of this big, black dick on your walls."

He roughly pulled me into his groin, and without mercy, plunged his love stick inside of me.

"Can daddy do that, baby? Can I hang a poster of my dick on your love walls?"

He slid a finger down the crack of my cheeks and kissed me where the sun doesn't shine. I squealed in pleasure with the palms of my hands and knees waxing the floor. I arched my back even deeper as he began to enter, giving my pussy the leverage it needed to comfortably assist him with his task.

"Oh yes….yessss," I panted as he slammed his pelvis against mine. "Nail that big dick to my walls!" I shouted as he held onto my nicely trimmed waistline and took deep and long thrusts inside of my wetness.

I couldn't get enough of my twenty-two-year-old stud, and from the way he pounded my pussy, he couldn't get enough of me. Like the remarkable art pieces in my gallery, I was his master-piece. I resembled sexiness in the rarest form and unlike most women my age, I didn't look a day over twenty-five. My five-foot-ten-inch frame, shapely curves, and smooth olive skin appeared airbrushed under the sunlight beaming through the stained-glass ceiling rotunda. My erotic slanted eyes had mood swings where they'd alternate from a sky blue to a misty gray, hypnotizing many. I was a beautiful goddess, but what men seemed to love about me most was that I was a bonafide freak! It was no wonder my husband couldn't keep up. With his sex drive declining and mine escalating over the years, it was only a matter of time before I started looking for sexual alternatives to satisfy my craving. Thank God he's been onboard with my bright ideas every step of the way.

I raised my head slightly and my wicked cries of passion filled the entire gallery. My wild copper-spiraled curls freely bounced as our bodies rocked simultaneously to the beat of our own drums. I had my lovely Portuguese mother and Jamaican father to thank for the untamable mane. But as Sergio's fingers maneuvered through my tresses, getting tangled as he pulled at my roots, I began to scream, "Harder! Fuck me harder got dammit! That's right. Own this good wet pussy!"

Sergio quickened his pace. One hundred-plus pairs of painted and photographic eyes watched us copulate on the floor like crazed animals. We were creating our own remix of Kama Sutra as he penetrated my deepest spots. The more I yelled for him to fuck me harder, the deeper and faster his thrusts propelled, appeasing my voracious libido.

I could feel the thunderous rains of euphoria preparing to wash over me, willing me to tap out as my elbows and knees grinded into the floor, producing an even greater level of pain. I retrained my concentration on how good Sergio felt moving freely inside of me and how rewarding of a climax it would be. My eyes drifted closed and I began to imagine my gallery being crowded with art lovers alike. Some paying thousands, even millions, to see me nude like this, posed in the doggie-style position while being stroked by Sergio's paintbrush.

I slowly began to work the music playing inside my head, into my hips as I cast spells on my imaginary spectators. As if on cue, Sergio reached his right hand around me to palm my breasts. His fingers passionately stroked my gumdrop-sized nipples as if he were plucking the strings on a guitar. Suddenly, I had a surge of energy rush between my legs.

"I'm about to come," I moaned in ecstasy. He slapped me on my ass. "Oooooh, yesss!" He did it again.

"Give all this good pussy to daddy!"

"Right there," I panted. I reached my right arm around his neck and he adjusted his position but moved faster and with a deeper dedication. "It feels so good! Soooo good! I'm about to…I'm about to…" The force of my orgasm was so strong I nearly pushed Sergio out of me as if he were no longer welcomed inside of my body. I shuddered from the quake of my own violent tsunami.

Ring! Ring! Ring!

"Don't stop!" I demanded, ignoring my husband's ringtone. I began riding him backward. "I'm taking all of this dick tonight! All of it!" I got worked up all over again. I began pulling at my own nipples and sucking the life out of Sergio with the squeeze of my tight cunt, all at the same time. It quickly brought me to another, and even more violent climax than the first. I eased off his locomotive and did an about-face. He lifted me onto his strong, broad shoulders, my legs wrapping loosely around his neck in the process. He licked and sucked my breasts some more before suspending me high in the air.

"Why waste your time riding a pony when you can ride this Carousel," he said.

I creamed instantly once his long, thick tongue graced my slippery lips. I had waited all day for this. All day to be sexually healed. All day to be fucked out of my mind. He'd toyed in my wetness long enough for me to drench his face with my liquid candy. It felt so good. So rewarding.

Ring! Ring! Ring!

This time it was Geneva calling. My heart raced, my pussy throbbed, and my head was spinning like a fucking merry-go-round. Carousel had that effect on women. I didn't want to stop. Couldn't stop. Didn't want this feeling to ever come to an end.

"Oooooh, yes!"

He lowered me onto his long, meaty shaft and enjoyed me from another angle. The deeper he drove that dick inside of me, the harder my pussy choked him out, urging him to surrender his own creamy nut.

"Oh, fuuuckkkk!" he groaned. "I'm cumming," he warned.

"Let it all go. Cum in this good pussy," I chanted.

I slipped my tongue between his lips and Carousel instantly wrapped around it.

"Ummmmmm!" Sergio bellowed, ejaculating inside of me. I didn't stop kissing him until I had squeezed out every last drop. He slowly made his exit and lowered me back to steady ground. I looked down at the Magnum condom he'd worn, filled to its max.

"You know I love you, right?" His horny smile was usually infectious.

"And you know I hate when you say ridiculous shit like that!" I rolled my eyes hard. So hard my false eyelashes nearly popped off. It wasn't a smiling matter, and the longer he wore that arrogant mask on his face, the more irritated I was by it. I loved Larry and there was no room to love another. Dick might've controlled my checkbook, but it sure as hell didn't control my heart.

"Loosen up, ma." He laughed, sliding his finger down the side of my face. I withdrew from his touch. "I know the deal. I was only kidding."

"Well, I'm not!" I shot seriously, cutting my eyes.

He slipped on his briefs and blue jeans while I dusted off my aching knees. All the tattoos wrapped around his neck, arms, and chest, made him even sexier. While I was obsessed with the sex we shared on a daily basis, there were rules to abide by, and the more time we spent together, the harder it was becoming for him to remember that we were simply business partners. I never longed for anything too serious with any of my lovers. In fact, I encouraged them all, especially Sergio, to "date" women their own age as well. I wanted my boys to explore life outside of the fantasy world I had created for them, but it was beginning to seem more easily said than done.

I walked over to retrieve my clothes. "Larry and Geneva have been calling. I need to return their calls."

"A'ight. I'll be down in a minute."

I quickly dressed and headed back downstairs. Before I could dial Larry's or Geneva's number, an incoming call soared through my business line.

"Generation Studios," I answered.

"Just the queen bee I've been dying to talk to all day! This is Michelle."

"Hello, darling! It's always a pleasure to hear from you." Michelle was a die-hard Republican and a shrewd businesswoman. Much like myself.

"Likewise. I'll be in town attending a business summit all week. If it's not too tardy of a request, I would love to review some of your amazing artwork Senator Rawlings has been raving about."

"Mrs. Brown, I have exactly what you need. The senator informed me of your arrival this morning. Don't worry. I already have you on the books."

"Awww...perfect!" she said relieved. "The tension in my neck is already starting to subside."

"Expect your package around ten o'clock tonight."

"May I ask who's delivering?"

I raised my head. Sergio was coming down the stairs. He licked his lips and flicked his tongue at me. "Carousel," I said into the phone.

"Carousel?"

"Yes. And I can assure you he'll live up to every letter in his name. Satisfaction guaranteed."

"Asking price?"

"Senator Rawlings said to tell you this one is on her."

"Aghhhh...mighty predictable, that one is. Well, I better take advantage," she guffawed. "Because around this time next week, the old hag is going to hate me once I announce that I'm running for her position."

I laughed her last comment off.

"Thanks again, Victoria. I'll have my assistant email you the address of the hotel I'll be staying at."

"Great! And if there's anything else I can do for you in the meantime, please let me know."

"You can tell all of your friends to vote for me in the upcoming election," she tittered.

"Done!"

Sergio grabbed my waist from behind and pulled me into his groin. He was hard as a rock, which was nothing new. Michelle said something else, but her words went in one ear and completely out the other. Before I knew it, before I could do what it was I'd come downstairs to do, my young lover hiked up my dress, bent me over, and wore this tight pussy out all over again.

EMIL

SWINGING COUGARS

I made my way to the third floor of the mansion. It was my first time attending a Next Generation swingers' festival since inception, and I couldn't wait to see what all the whispers amongst my two coworkers were about.

I looked down at my sex address, then up at the gold letters on every closed door in the elongated hall. I didn't know what to expect tonight, however, I was certain of two things. I was craving a man's touch, and it was time I released the sexual tension I'd been lugging around for the past several months. My pussy was so stressed out, even it had its fair share of gray hairs.

I hadn't made love to my husband, Melvin, in what felt like decades. My love nest was starting to collect dust and if I waited one more day, I probably wouldn't remember owning one. Melvin had given me every excuse in the book as to why he couldn't make love to me. First it was arthritis in his knees, then back spasms, and oh, my favorite line of all was, "I may need to see the doctor. I think my blood pressure medicine is affecting downstairs, again." So many dead-weight excuses about why he couldn't be intimate with me, forced me to finally pay more attention to what my woman's intuition had been trying to tell me all along.

I only hated that I had to find out the hard way about my husband's infidelities. It was the day I decided to leave work early. Business had been extremely slow at the travel agency. Instead of going to the food market like I normally did on Wednesdays after work, I drove straight home. I pulled into the garage and was surprised to find my husband's SUV already parked inside at a time that he should've been at work. I walked inside our house and instinctively followed the music that was coming from our bedroom. Every step I took brought me in closer range to the high-pitched voice calling out my husband's name over and over again. I pushed the door open and prayed that God wouldn't force me to witness the act with my own two eyes. A jolt of anger had me hurling the bedside lamp at her instead of racing for the 9mm we kept in the closet. I missed her by an inch and instead, hit him. My eyes scanned the room. I picked up one of my Louis Vuitton pumps and hit her smack in the head. All of the "I do's" went flying out the window as I rushed her like a crazed woman. I swung my arms wildly at the sleazy Nicki Minaj reject. Melvin hopped his ashy ass out of bed and pulled me off of her. She was screaming for dear life while I screamed and cursed. With Melvin's hold on me, she managed to skate past me and flee out of the front door, butt-ass naked.

"Please calm down, Emil!"

"You don't tell me to calm down! What the fuck was that woman doing in my house, in my bed, with my husband?"

"I can explain. Please," he kept begging.

My heart began to ache and tears filled my eyes. I couldn't believe he would do something like this to me, again. I began swinging on him again, all while tears streamed down my face.

"I'm sorry, baby," he kept saying. Then he said the most stupid thing men always seemed to say once they got caught in the act. "She didn't mean anything." Was that supposed to make me feel better? Less hurt? I didn't understand how her not meaning anything to him was supposed to lessen the blowback of his lying, cheating ass.

Reflecting back on that horrific day six weeks ago had my stomach doing somersaults. I doubted that I could ever forgive Melvin for the pain and heartache he caused, let alone trust him again. The vivid images constantly burned in my mind, making it impossible for me to be optimistic about our future. I had even gone on a wife strike. I stopped cooking his food, washing his clothes, and even speaking to him. It was like he no longer existed.

Desperate to get even, I did something I never thought I'd do. I joined Next Generation, a swingers club for women my age. While they encouraged couples to swing together, I was at it alone. I was open for any and everything, no strings attached. I wanted to indulge in all the freaky fun my heart could handle. Melvin had created a beast and he didn't even know it. I was going to show him that two could play his games. I had forgiven him the first time he'd cheated on me. It was five years after we married. The affair resulted in a child which he had kept hidden for two years. It was by accident that I even discovered the little bastard. Eventually, I took Melvin back. And like a damn fool, I allowed it to happen again. This time, right under my nose.

The Lafite Rothschild swimming through my system, cheered me on, encouraging the payback. I had given up so much for him, starting with children. And now with my fiftieth birthday around the corner, my dreams of ever having any children of my own was crushed. I was way too old and I'm sure all the stress over the years had only added to my inability to conceive. I was so broken inside and my husband didn't even realize the damage he had caused. Or maybe he did and just didn't care. Deep down inside, there might have been some love left for him, but on the surface, there was not. I hated his black ass and there was no sure way to get over what he'd done, other than to go all out and do it ten times better than he did, I reasoned, turning the key to my suite.

I nervously closed the door behind me and walked through the candlelit room and over to the king-sized bed. It was covered in red and pink rose petals. On top of the petals lay a black silk robe, open handcuffs, and matching lace blindfold. I picked up the gold piece of paper that had step-by-step instructions. I was excited to experience something new. Something passionate, yet forbidden.

After soaking in a nice warm bath and indulging in a glass of wine, I came to the conclusion that I needed this. My body needed this.

I walked back over to the bed to complete the next step. I was nude underneath the black robe that hung open, displaying all my womanly goods. On a typical day I was self-conscious about my body, worried that all of the weight I had gained over the years was the reason my marriage had failed. There were many nights that I blamed me, however, at this final hour, my succulent chocolate curves were beautiful.

I stared at the bed to shake the returning nerves. Deep down a battle had ensued between my morals and the sweet satisfaction of revenge. I took a deep breath and flirted with temptation. I picked up the black lace blindfold and placed it over my eyes, just as the note had said to do. I climbed on the bed and lay flat on my back with my head against the plush pillows. I placed only my left wrist into the handcuffs and locked it.

Settling into a welcoming state of mind, I relaxed my troubled spirit. Shortly after slipping into serenity, I heard the door creep open. With the blindfold covering my eyes, I couldn't see a thing. My senses alerted me that this man, this stranger, was eagerly ready to please me inside and out. I composed my apprehension, feeling like a virgin about to experience intimacy for the first time.

The belt on my robe slowly became undone. It intensified the heat rising from between my legs, causing the room to feel warmer than it actually was. My lover caressed my voluptuous breasts, hips and thighs, causing musical notes to escape my lips. Once his large manly hands parted my legs, my breathing became labored as I anxiously anticipated his next move. Before I knew it, his lips and tongue wrapped around each of my toes.

"Ummmm…" I was surrounded by darkness. Another sensual moan lifted off my throat and managed to squeeze through my lips. My panted breaths filled the otherwise quiet room as this unknown being grabbed me by both ankles and slid his erection between the soles of my size tens. He shifted the heel of my foot to the base of his dick and measured his heavyweight against it for accuracy. With minimal guidance, I enjoyably stroked him to a stiffer erection. The electricity moving through my body had me tingling in areas I never knew could be turned on.

Suddenly, a set of warm tongues snaked around my breasts. I started to remove the mask but was stopped. All three men took turns pleasing me with their mouths, each armed with a trick or two of his own. I allowed my body to lose control.

"Oh yes… Yes…" I hollered out.

"I came to execute this pussy tonight," one of them said. "So when I tell you to ride this carousel, I want you to ride this motherfucker hard and fast!"

My breathing quickened.

"Oh yes… I'll ride it… Hard… and fast," I told him, giving in to my weakest desires.

I let out a stricken gasp as one of my lovers' tongues swept over my clit, and another my nipples. My third lover parted my lips with his thumb and pushed his dick inside of my warm, wet mouth. I couldn't believe what was happening. He tasted sweet on my tongue, better than any cotton candy I'd ever had. As I rolled my lips back and forth, the wetter I grew and the closer I came to releasing the shackles my husband had on me. I wanted to be freed from the deception. Freed from the feeling of inadequacy. Freed from the mental anguish and all the stress he had stored in my heart. I wanted to be free as a bird.

My head bobbed faster on his length. His dick tasted so good on my tongue but felt even better gliding down my windpipe. I was exhaling and getting my groove back all in one night. I had never experienced an orgy, swinging, or even being with another man. This was all new for me and I was loving every second of it. As I managed to drown out all of my insecurities and worries, my lovers became the perfect distraction and center of my oasis.

I was on the verge of erupting when I felt that long, hard dick that I could have easily made a pig in a blanket out of, rise up inside of me.

"Oooohhh!" I greeted with a sensuous cry of satisfaction. He maneuvered through my tightness, his strokes starting out slow. As my waves began to rise, his pace accelerated. One of the faceless men placed his lips on top of mine. Our tongues intertwined while another suckled my breasts. I didn't know which direction to go or whom to turn to. All I knew was that I was going somewhere, and that the journey felt so damn good.

I came from the top of my toes to the bottom of my feet, over and over again. It was the best head-spinning, toe-curling, pussy-pounding sex I had ever had in my life. When I left the mansion, I knew right away I had found my new family, and as long as we had each other, I didn't have to continue to be a victim of a selfish, lying, cheating husband anymore. Now that I was finally free to do me and slowly waking up that side I had suppressed for so long, I was ready to wave my freak flag and take this pussy to an entirely new level.

NYMFOMANIA

When I walked through the wooden double doors of his condo, Sergio's eyeballs nearly popped out of their sockets. He looked even sexier than I remembered, especially with his long, black dreads hanging off his broad shoulders. He had this rugged sex appeal that the old-fashioned and conceited Jackie would not have ever bat an eyelash or soaked a cotton swab for. Now, this good old pussy would get all juiced up over a tall, chocolate, young man sporting tattoos and baggy jeans. The more swag, the more turned on I was by it.

I had developed an acquired taste for the roughneck brothas, especially the ones that had the right package, which is why Mr. Sergio Champagne caught my naked eye. I had met him a few months ago at our local gym. I was getting ready to freshen up after an exhausting workout and he was coming out of the men's locker room. Our shoulders collided and it forced us to stop and just admire one another. When I laid my eyes on him, something told me we would be fucking before the night was up, and boy, was I right. I invited him over to my place and after a delicious home-cooked meal, we got our freak on.

Unlike most women my age, when I hit the big 5-O, my libido shot through the fucking roof like a cannonball. Mere thoughts of having sex in all sorts of positions and unique places became a daily high for me. Temptation was an aphrodisiac. Any man I couldn't have, I wanted, and I would go out of my way just to get him. I could never get enough of playing out my sexual fantasies in my mind, which eventually drove me to experimenting with different sex toys, watching porn, and even reading the raunchiest of erotica I could get my hands on. Other than my raging hormones, I couldn't explain why all of a sudden I was so horny all the damn time, and why I couldn't stop playing in my pussy every night. I was too embarrassed to talk to my doctor about it and way too private to run my mouth to my holier-than-thou girlfriends. They wouldn't even begin to understand what a sistah was going through. And Lord knows, I didn't need their conceited, can't-do-no-wrong asses judging me. Not when they were all married and had immediate access to in-house dick. The struggle for a single black woman these days was real. All the good men were already snatched up, gay, or even worse—dead. It wasn't like I wasn't good enough. I was very attractive, had a banging body, made my own money and had my own house and car—a customized Jaguar XF with the Louis Vuitton interior at that. I didn't have to showboat, but my bank account spoke for itself.

I had all this going for me but I couldn't find a decent man who was compatible with me. It seemed like every time I thought I had a relationship spark, it would quickly fizzle. Mainly because he couldn't compete with my sexual appetite. I had even been told I was coming on too strong. "You're too aggressive," were his exact words. I mean, what the hell...I'm damned if I do, and damned if I don't. As the saying goes, a closed mouth don't get fed. And I'm here to tell you, this bitch couldn't stop eating!

In the back of my mind, I had always felt I had an addiction to sex but would never accept it. Nowadays, I admit it proudly...I'm a nymphomaniac. I would masturbate at least six times a day, seven days a week. It didn't matter where I was. Home, work, gym, grocery store, didn't matter. Hell, I've even masturbated in church. That's right. In church. Pastor Garvin had always been my secret crush. I went to church faithfully every Sunday to praise and worship, but I also went to see my man. I would often imagine us getting in a quickie after one of his sermons. I know I was wrong, but I had a serious addiction. Sex was my food, and I had to eat in order to stay alive. Well, at least that was my way of justifying my sexual activities before I Googled it. I was surprised to find that I was not alone. I had found my diagnosis. I was suffering from a hypersexual disorder. That was why I couldn't help myself. I had my preferences, but honestly, I would fuck anything as long as it was legal. I even kept my old beaus in heavy rotation and often propositioned them to a good old-fashioned booty call. I mean, who in the hell in their right mind would turn down a good lay!

When I decided to accept me for me, I released any inhibitions that might have been hiding inside. Although I was reveling in my liberating lifestyle, I tried to be considerate of others. I had even made a few vows of my own. One, I would never involve myself with a married man. Two, I would never be someone's side chick or whore. And three, I would never date a man younger than twenty-five. Sad to say, I broke every last one of those rules.

My caramel-brown skin glistened under the dim lighting that established the mood we were both in. The dress I wore hugged every single curve on my short frame, as well as it should have, given what I paid for it. Underneath the wig I wore, I was a natural girl. But tonight, this $400 extension flowed like Indian silk down the center of my back. The bulge in Sergio's pants saluted me from only a few feet away. It was no secret that he couldn't wait to tap this pussy again. He had admitted that much in a text.

But what was hard to figure out about this man was if he was boy-friend material. I wanted something steady. Ongoing. And even in the short amount of time we spent together, I saw this thing that we had going on, headed somewhere. I just didn't want to scare him away by asking too many questions too soon. He was young and probably not quite ready to commit. That I could understand. But I wanted him all to myself and the best way to make that happen was to cancel out my competition. I didn't even know if he was seeing someone serious, but I sure as hell was going to find out.

I struck a sexy pose, giving him an eyeful of opportunity before strutting in his direction. I was poetry in slow motion that even a blind man could see. I had the body and the brains, so there was no doubt in my mind that he would be open to giving us a try.

His Versace Medusa head cufflinks made a wavering reflection over my gray eyes as he grabbed my face softly by the chin and kissed my lips. He didn't have to say a word. His hard dick pressing up against me did all the talking. Translating his every thought and desire.

"Something smells so delicious," I said after unwrapping my tongue from around his. He dropped another kiss on my lips and grabbed a handful of my ass. He gave it a good squeeze.

"That's just a little something I threw together...but this right here is the main entrée," he said, pressing his erection against my stomach.

"And is that right?"

"You damn skippy."

I smiled, loving the verbal foreplay.

"So what do you say I help you out of this tight dress so you can give that kitty cat room to breathe?"

"What's the rush? We have all night. Besides, aren't you going to show me around your bachelor's pad?"

He pulled me closer into his embrace. My head fell back as he began to tongue my neck.

"You wanna see the pad? I'll show you the pad all right."

I held on tight as he swept me off my feet and carried me over to the kitchen island. The polished red marble was cold against my skin, but the steam rising from my pussy quickly provided a blanket of warmth. We fell into another intense kiss and soon his fingers began going for a stroll. He removed my shoes before caressing my legs and thighs. He slid my panties down my smooth-shaven legs and let them drop to the floor. Slowly my dress began to inch above my waist, exposing my hairless snatch. He quickly undressed while kissing me simultaneously. My pussy was on fire and I couldn't wait for him to extinguish the flames.

I raised my dress above my head and tossed it behind me. He hungrily latched onto my perky D cups and proceeded to polish my skin with his warm, wet tongue.

"That's a good boy," I said, echoing a moan.

His warm lips circled my swollen, chocolate nipples while his right hand slid up and down one of my outstretched legs. He lowered his face closer to my pussy and kissed the tip of my arousal before taking it all into his mouth. Once he was able to get a nice grip, he took my budding flower between both his lips and sucked it like a skinless peach. With no hands, only his tongue, he divided the pudgy lips of my opening and reintroduced himself. I nearly came all over the place the second his lips met mine. I grabbed the back of his head and outstretched my legs into a V-shape. Half my ass hung off the island top as he lapped up my dripping nectar.

"Oh, baby!" I rocked my lower half against his face as he devoured me right there in the kitchen. After icing his tongue with my sweet cum, I turned completely around, pulled myself to my knees, and allowed him the pleasure of tasting me from behind. He slapped me on the ass a couple of times before eating me whole.

"Oooohhh, Sergio!" I moaned. "Keep it right there. Oh yes. Just like that," I coaxed as he tongue-fucked me doggie-style. I embraced his creativity while screaming for more of where that came from. "Yesss..." I moaned into a hard labored climax.

I slowly turned my body around and faced my new young lover. I was panting, but I was in full throttle. I slid off the island and dropped to my knees. He was hooked like a Chiquita banana, ripe and ready. I drenched his dick with my saliva and then flicked my tongue across his tip. Soon after, all ten inches found room inside my mouth. I sucked his dick with wisdom and skill, patience and appreciation. I needed him to forget about the other woman in his life, if indeed he had one. It was turning me on watching his eyes roll to the back of his head as I sucked out his creamy sauce. It meant I must've been doing one helluva job. My lips continued to gyrate up and down his pole. Once my mouth was good and wet, I relaxed my jaws and took him on a joyride back down my throat.

"Suck it, Vickie," he said.

I stopped and allowed him to slip out of my mouth.

"Who in the hell is Vickie?" I shot, looking around.

"Damn, I'm sorry, baby. Charge it to my head and not my heart." He gave me those innocent puppy eyes and all was forgiven. It was an honest mistake.

"The name's Jackie," I said. "And after tonight, you'll be reciting it in your sleep."

"Like that, huh?"

"I can show you better than I can tell you, pretty boy."

I grabbed him by his dick and led him onto the balcony. He had an incredible view of the Dallas skyline, which would serve as the perfect backdrop for what all I had in mind. I walked over to the ledge and took a look down.

"You ain't thinking about jumping now, are you?"

The nice cool breeze fondled my nakedness. I walked over to him, placed my hands around his neck and whispered, "I want a standing ovation." He appeared lost by my last comment.

His eyebrows folded in. "A standing ovation?" he teetered. "What the hell is that?"

I smiled at the youngster and replied, "I want you to stand up in this pussy." He flashed a knowing smile and without saying another word, he picked me up. He positioned his hands underneath my cheeks and slowly eased me onto his shaft.

I slid my tongue over my teeth. I could still taste his precum. Sensual moans lifted off the back of my throat as I received his entire offering. It was pleasure and pain being delivered all at once as he climbed my mountaintop. My breasts became the center of his attention as he rested his head between them. After grinding inside of me and making me cum all over him, he took two steps forward. When I felt my back up against the cold, wooden ledge, I tilted my head and looked up into the pitch-black sky.

I had never made love outside and the rush it gave me had my insides twisting. I started to moan even louder, hoping his neighbors could hear us. He palmed my neck, slightly squeezing before aggressively pumping my oil well.

"Harder!" I coached along. "If you're gonna fuck me, at least make it memorable!" That must have hit a nerve because he slammed that dick inside of me like a bulldozer. Shortly after, like two ticking time bombs, we exploded over one another.

I came back to my feet and walked back inside to retrieve my clothes.

"Where you going?" he asked, breathing heavy.

"Home."

"Home?"

"I have church in the morning." He gave me a look. "What? Is that a problem for you?" I quickly dressed.

He stared at me dumbfounded. "I'm going to leave that one alone."

"Don't judge me," I shot on the defense.

He walked over to the couch and flopped down on it.

"So when will I see you again?" he asked.

I slipped on my shoes, grabbed my purse and smiled. "When I need another refill, trust me, you'll be the first to know." I blew him a kiss and walked right out the door.

By the time I got in my car and started the engine, I had a text message from an unknown number come through my phone. It read:

Welcome to the next generation. Access granted.

MOTEL LOVERS

There I lay completely naked and sprawled across a borrowed king-sized bed, ready to slay the first dick in sight. I was inside of a rather old, sooty motel room that resembled every inner-city motel dump where I had ever gotten my freak on. It was all we could really afford. Well, all my cheapskate *husband* was willing to pay for, because the truth was, my man had major bank. He was just cheap as hell when he didn't have to be. He was still rolling in dough from when his former wife died and also collecting retirement from his government job until the day he died. So by no means were we broke, but we acted broke.

My eyes scanned the room and all I could think about was how this motel could use a few upgrades. There was nothing exciting about it other than the pleasure I created right in this bed. We came here often, usually had the same room, but I think it was about time we changed the scenery. The décor was a tacky hellafied combination of mauve, green, and brown. The paint that attempted to cover the smoke-damaged walls was starting to chip, and the cheap floral wallpaper plastered around the border had begun to discolor and peel at the corners. Again, nothing glamorous. But what did I expect when we were only paying by the hour. Or shall I say by the nut.

A piquant aroma produced from hot and sweaty one-hour-long sex, my lover's masculine cologne, and my imitation Chanel fragrance, clung to the dingy and cheap recycled cotton sheets. The love funk temporarily disguised the old stuffy room odor, which resulted from musty carpeting, dirty draperies, and an old pissy, cum-stained mattress. It was horrible. Degrading. But I was horny, desperate, and while I had caviar taste, my sexual expenditures had to be consolidated and remunerated from a beer budget. It was a sacrifice I was willing to make in order to explore my lascivious spontaneities.

I relied on my young motel lovers the same way I relied on my heart to pump. I was infatuated with the very idea of sex and the illicit fantasies that crawled in and out of my dreams. Bottom line…I liked to fuck! I wasn't always this way. Being a chubby girl in high school and all of my adult life kept me in a closed box. I was too embarrassed about my weight to ever approach the opposite sex, and when I did work up the nerve, they would laugh at me. It was no wonder I walked around feeling insecure. But all that changed when I met David. I discovered what had always been a part of me. I was a straight-up freak with whorish tendencies.

While I was somewhat exhausted from my last motel lover, slash my sweet chocolate dip, my heated pussy on the other hand was steadily throbbing and tingling for more penetration, assuring me that we were nowhere near the finish line. See, I was used to getting my pussy pounded and my back blown out. That was as routine as washing my face and brushing my teeth. Hell, and since I'm really keeping it real, I'll admit that I was even used to a little backdoor action from time to time. Throw me some K-Y Jelly and I'd bend it over and let him knock it out the park, Barry Bonds style!

Now for the record, a true freak like me had no time restraints or sexual limitations when it came to getting her kitty waxed. That's why in my bedroom, anything goes. So one could understand why it was hard for my whining pussy to accept the sudden intermission. It couldn't care less about Lucky having to work late at McDonald's or the fact that he was borrowing his mom's car just to come tap this ass tonight. When he stepped onto my turf, he knew that he had a duty to uphold, a mission to accomplish, and a purpose to fulfill. So best believe, I had a good mind to fire his country-talking ass right after I got my nut, regardless of the fact that I knew he needed the extra money to put himself through school.

I slowly rolled over to my left side, slid out of the bed, and blindly slipped into my red heels. I felt beautiful and worth a million bucks sauntering around in the designer shoes that I had purchased the day before.

I balanced myself as I walked directly over to the air conditioner unit, my voluptuous, oily brown ass jiggling every step of the way. I gradually bent down, lifted the top, and cranked it up another notch.

"I hope Lucky doesn't show up late like he did last week," I said finally, breaking the awkward silence resting in the room, although it was something I had grown to expect after my therapy sessions. I began finger-combing my tousled fourteen-inch hair weave as I walked around the tiny space. "Hell, he's on *our* schedule," I hissed.

As I headed for the mirror and sink so that I could freshen my pussy and touch up my makeup before my next gigolo arrived, my husband, David, gently grabbed me by the elbow and pulled me into his warm embrace.

"You know how much I love you, right?" David stared dead into my eyes. A pleasant smile creased my lips. This was the part where I had to babysit his feelings and reassure him that I loved him just as much. Nothing had changed. My husband took extreme pleasure in watching me have sex with younger men, but he often felt frustrated about not being able to join us.

I licked my lips and sucked in a short breath of air before exhaling. "Baby, I know you love me," I replied, kissing him on those succulent black lips of his. I detached the arms of his wheelchair before wrapping my hands loosely around his neck and straddling him. For a fifty-seven-year-old handicapped man, David cleaned up nicely. He kept his salt-and-pepper hair cut low and facial hairs trimmed, and he always dressed to impress—of course with the help of his day nurse or myself. His dark aging skin was soft to the touch. He even worked out on a regular basis at the rehab center where I took him for his weekly fitness classes. Another thing I loved about the man was that he never judged me. He accepted me for who I was. Big girl and all. My confidence grew immensely once he became part of my life. He would always tell me how beautiful I was and how I had the best voice he'd ever heard. I didn't believe him right away, but when he said I would put Mariah Carey to shame, I knew this man had to know what he was talking about. He believed in me and my gifts. Had even offered to sponsor my first album, but I was already in my mid-forties; what did I look like trying to get in the music business now? I was eleven years younger than him with smooth blackberry skin, deep-set brown eyes, short black hair and a curvaceous, size-26 body. He knew as well as I did that he was getting the best of many worlds. Plus, I knew how to skin a dick with no hands—a double bonus!

My David was the smartest, charismatic man I had ever met in my entire life. He amazed me with his intellect, and the more I got to know him, the deeper I fell in love. We met at Benderfield's Rehabilitation and Retirement Home, my former place of employment and his residence at the time. It was a late November night. While I should have been working and at the aid of my other patients, I was too busy in David's room giving him the blowjob of his life. Needless to say, one of the nurses on my shift caught me red-handed with my mouth stuffed. She reported me to management and I was fired on the spot. I still don't know what came over me that night and why I felt so comfortable releasing my inner freak with David.

Before that day, I had never jeopardized my job, but it was something about him that made me feel so alive and free. Besides that, we were compatible and enjoyed each other's company. Being married for only nine months and eleven days, we still had a lot to learn about each other. We were still getting to know each other as well, and while I tried my best to look past his crippling multiple sclerosis, it was the main reason David agreed to a third party, or shall I say parties. For the past three months, seeing other men had become our Saturday night ritual. It was no different than us enjoying a flick together. He had his good days and his bad days, but lately there were more bad days. It was times he couldn't even get out of bed or walk. When I married him, I chose to accept him and his condition and he understood and accepted my insatiable appetite for sex. The greatest part of our marriage was that we loved each other enough to compromise.

David wanted to do whatever made me happy, but most importantly, he wanted to do whatever kept me satisfied in the intimacy department. There was no way sex could ruin our perfect marriage.

As our talented tongues began to salsa, I carefully unzipped his jeans. I could feel the excitement pressing up against my bare ass as it leaped from his briefs. I interrupted our little love dance long enough to make a saliva pool out of my right palm, allowing me to lubricate him the old-fashioned way.

Following my lead, David placed his large arthritic hands on my wide hips while his full-grown dick cried out to me. I cradled it and began stroking him up and down, occasionally running my thumb across the split of the head. Our lips reconnected as I allowed him the pleasure of having me all to himself—at least for that moment. My starving and impatient pussy began to melt as it beckoned for attention, turning up the heat between my already pasty thighs. I dragged my left hand from around his neck and escorted it to my botanical garden. It was so wet that I couldn't help but moan as I glided not one, but two fingers inside my warmth. I was working with limited space but multitasking with one hand around his dick, the other in my pussy, and my tongue down his throat.

"Damn, baby," David let out barely. Sweat permeated his forehead and I could feel his heart pumping through his chest.

"Ooooh, I'm so wet, daddy," I sang over and over in his ears. I pushed my fingers further inside my pussy, deepening my strokes, and pleasing myself in ways that my husband never could. While I had finger-fucking myself down to a science, I wanted this intimate moment with my man to last for as long as it possibly could. I eased my fingers out of my wetness and climbed on top of his dick. It eased inside of me effortlessly. I worked my hips in slow motion and gradually increased my rhythm. I drove my candy-coated fingers down the side of his face and over his lips. He pulled them into his mouth, one at a time, sucking off my sweet nectar. I proceeded to ride him like I would Lucky's dick later.

David worked up enough strength to assist me along the way and began massaging my left nipple as he nibbled on the right. He loved my chocolatey DDD delights just as much as the next man, and he showed his appreciation by spending quality time with each one. My head almost fell off my shoulders as I bounced up and down on his lap like a cowgirl in a Texas rodeo show.

"Shit!" I yelled, riding the hell out of him. His lips fell against mine and his tongue straddled me. "Fuck this pussy!" I yelled. "Make me cum, baby!"

"Give that nutty nut to me, sweet thang. Show papa what all you got."

"I'm about to cum!" I could feel my orgasm floating along the edge. David grabbed both of my ass cheeks as best he could and gave them a soft squeeze.

"This is my pussy right here!" he declared, spanking me a second time. "Tell me it's mine!" he fired back in his husky baritone voice. That shit turned me on like something never imagined.

With my lips curled and my face contorted, "It's all yours!" I managed, telling him whatever he needed to hear to help him rest better at night. Especially since it was obvious it wasn't all his. I rocked harder, faster. I bucked my hips wildly, throwing my pussy back and forth against him in heavy strokes. I was nearing my peak. "I'm cumming, baby!" I screamed just before my body began to tremble and my violent rains poured down on him like a tsunami.

"Arghhhhhhhh…" he groaned, cumming inside of me.

I bit down on his bottom lip and tried catching my breath. I kissed him and placed my hands on the sides of his face. "I love you, baby."

"And I will always love you," he said, kissing me.

"Let me get you cleaned up, baby," I said, easing off of him. I readjusted his legs and placed the chair arms back on.

After giving him a quick wash-up, I jumped in the shower and prepared for the rest of that night's events. No matter how much he enjoyed watching me be pleased by younger men, I knew it also hurt him to accept that he could never compete with men much younger, stronger and better performing than him. It had to do something to a man's ego. Had to.

Yet he pretended that all was okay and that he was enjoying *our* sex life just as much as I was. I often questioned if I was being selfish, wondering if I had a right to be doing this? Was I taking advantage of the fact that my husband was crippled? I tried not to answer that and instead focused on *my* needs, that unfortunately, my husband couldn't meet on his own.

As I stepped out of the shower, I heard a quiet knock at the door. Me and my dripping pussy were ready for another round.

I greeted Lucky butt-ass naked by the third knock. It was the moment I had been waiting for and I'm sure he could tell it by the seductive look I gave him. My eyes smiled as I traveled every inch of his tall, lean, muscular physique, while my pussy on the other hand did jumping jacks. That's how excited we were to see him. The man was cut like a loaf of bread and had smooth brown skin and long wavy hair that he kept slicked back into a ponytail. The new bling in his ear and on his wrist made me wonder if perhaps he'd gotten a pay raise at McDonald's.

"I hope you didn't start the party without me," Lucky said, grabbing his profile in a teasing manner.

"Of course we did." I chuckled. "But you're just in time for some cake." I took him by the hand and escorted him inside the room. He acknowledged my husband with a respectful head nod gesture and followed my lead. With the lights dimmed and my husband sitting front-row seat, the mood was set. I didn't like to waste time talking so when Lucky opened his mouth to speak again, I silenced him by placing my index finger over his lips. Hell, he knew the routine. It was time to fuck!

"Save your energy, baby, because you're gonna need it," I warned.

Lucky licked the anticipation from his full mahogany lips and began stripping out of his wife beater and gym shorts. His eyes never left my body and for good reason. I positioned myself on all fours and commenced to brush my hand over my juicy brown derrière. I allowed him to examine me from behind. To see this pussy, inhale this pussy, then taste this pussy! He planted sensual kisses across my cheeks before sliding his index finger against my arousal.

"Ummmm," I moaned.

"Get that pussy wet for a G like me," he ordered.

I wiggled my huge ass a little and let it bounce around like Jell-O.

"Hell yeah. That's what I'm talking about."

He lowered his face toward my ass and wrapped his lips around my chocolate cherry. Like a slithering snake, his wicked tongue began to baptize my clit, over and over again.

"Just like that," I moaned, staring up at my husband as Lucky served me up from behind. David's blank expression left me wondering what he might have been thinking, but his attention never wavered. We became one again and no one else was in that motel room but me and my loving husband. And in that brief, desperate moment, I imagined that it was *him* eating my pussy instead of Lucky.

I pictured David and I posed naked in the sixty-nine position on a bed of blooming lilies, bathing each other with our tongues under the golden morning sunlight as a jealous breeze swept over our naked intertwined bodies. I could almost feel the stiffness of his long unforgiving tongue stroking me like a long and thick hard dick, yet massaging me like a feather. I would scream to the top of my lungs for mercy, only to have my words translated into a welcoming of continuous oral punishment. Submerged in his good loving, I showered his face while in turn swallowing the velvety texture spilling into my mouth.

"Oh David," I began to utter as Lucky's tongue gave my pussy a severe lashing like never before. He didn't let up and of course I didn't want him to. I began jabbing at his face, taunting him in the process. "Is that all you can do? Whip it, damn it. Whip it!" I yelled, slapping my own ass as hard as I could.

"Oh, I'm about to whip this pussy real good. You can bet on that. Yeah, I'ma put something on ya that's gone have you telling all your little cougar friends."

I looked over my left shoulder to find Lucky suiting up. He was ready to give me what I had been fantasizing about all week—determined to put me out of my misery.

"You talking all that nonsense, I hope you can back it up."

He spread my ass cheeks apart to get a better view of my hairless middle. I was wet, ready, and prepared to be taken places that only he could take me. He entered me one inch at a time, taking me back down memory lane. My hot and syrupy pussy gripped him tighter than a glove as it began a beautiful serenade.

"Ooooooh fuck!" I cried out in the throes of our hot wicked passion. With every thrust, a feeling so great washed over me. This was what I wanted. What I needed.

"You better take this fat, long dick!" Lucky demanded as he banged on my walls.

I raised my head, barely, to find my husband watching carefully as if he were studying our moves.

"Is this what you wanted?" Lucky questioned repeatedly as he pounded against my lucky G-spot. A choppy moan escaped my quivering lips. I couldn't speak. Only bear the greatness of the pain.

We went for two hours straight. Hard, rough, pure fucking! Missionary, doggie style, cowgirl...you name it, we did it. I stopped counting my orgasms when I reached number four. Once we were done, I handed Lucky $200 and walked him to the door.

"Same time next week?" I asked, completely forgiving him for his tardiness earlier.

He gave me a sad face.

"Actually, tonight will have to be my last time with you guys. I found a new gig."

My heart nearly stopped. "Oh really? So you just gone…leave us hanging like that?" My eyes begged him to reconsider. We needed him. Desperately.

His eyes instantly lit up. "You know what…you guys just might want to join me."

I pursed my lips. "What are you talking about?" I placed a hand on my hip. I was starting to feel the burn from our workout.

He reached in his pocket and pulled out a gold business card.

"Contact this chic, Victoria. Tell her Lucky Charm referred you."

I looked at the card and scrunched my eyebrows. "Boy, does it look like I want to buy some damn artwork?" I tried to hand the card for Generation Studios back to him, but he refused it.

"Trust me, Shalise. This artwork right here," he said, pointing to his dick and the card simultaneously. "You'll definitely be willing to pay for."

"Oooohhh," I said, a wide smile sliding across my face. "I get it." I tucked in my bottom lip and fell into deep thought.

"Give her a ring first thing tomorrow."

"Sure thing," I said.

He gave me a quick goodbye peck on the lips.

"I'll be seeing you guys around soon."

"You sound so sure."

"Humph. Well, we *are* the next generation." He winked and walked off.

To be continued in *Next Generation*, the novel! Follow N'Tyse for more updates.

A Dallas, Texas native, N'Tyse currently juggles her writing career with being a full-time mother, wife, literary coach, and filmmaker. She is the erotic-romance author of Twisted Seduction, Twisted Vows of Seduction, Twisted Entrapment, Stud Princess, My Secrets Your Lies; *editor of*

Gutta Mamis, Cougar Cocktales, *and the executive producer/ director of the documentary film* Beneath My Skin *which was recently acquired by Maverick Entertainment Group. Her shorter-length works have appeared in* Kontrol Magazine, Zane Presents Purple Panties 2: Missionary No More, Z-Rated: Chocolate Flava 3 *and other publications. Her Twisted Topics can be found on her "Sex, Love, & Relationships" blog/forum. She is currently hard at work on the next production from N'Tyse Enterprises LLC.*

Go beyond the book and connect with the author today!
www.ntyse.com
www.facebook.com/author.ntyse
www.twitter.com/ntyse
Email: ntyse.amillionthoughts@yahoo.com

Watch this hot Twisted *trailer by scanning this code!*